What Readers Are Saying About Faith Under Pressure

Wow! That's all I can say! What an exciting first novel! I really enjoyed getting to know Katie, her family and all her friends! The book is really engaging, and I believe it will be a hit with teens and young adults alike!

- Jen

I can't wait to share this with others, especially some in my youth group.

- Caryn

If you love a good, clean Christian fiction with cute romance and real talk about anxiety and other problems we face, than you NEED to order Courtney M. Whitaker's new book.

- Julia

Readers will be inspired by Katie's efforts to make friends and resolve conflicts, and by her courageous decision to start a Christian club at school.

- Liz

Faith Under Pressure

By

Courtney M. Whitaker

Parable Press

Cover Design by Breogan Book Covers
Book Formatting by Derek Murphy @ Creative Indie
Author Photograph by Joanne Whitaker
Interior images by Canva
ISBN 979-8-9856871-0-1

First Edition: July 2022
Second Edition: August 2022

10 9 8 7 6 5 4 3 2 1

To *my family and friends, who have been there for me every step*

of the way.

To *my cat, Precious, my most faithful writing companion.*

To *Jesus, my Lord and Savior who deserves all praise, honor, and*

glory!

Courage is grace under pressure

— Ernest Hemingway

Chapter One

My life has always been filled with as many adventures as the stars. As much joy as the sand that covers the Laguna Beach. From the time I was a kid, I have always known exactly what to expect; and that is the unexpected. A life completely consumed by a radical faith in Jesus.

My parents are missionaries in Africa. They have been for my whole life. I was born literally in the middle of nowhere, a thousand miles away from any trace of normal. According to them, I was delivered by a midwife named Zawadi. I don't remember Zawadi, but apparently, she was one of the first faces I saw when I was born. This was back when my parents were new to the mission field and still, to be bluntly honest, new to being *parents*. When they were still trying to figure out what it looked like to raise two kids and follow the dream God had placed inside of them.

They met twenty years ago, back in the early 2000s, when they were students at West Lake University. My mom was an English major, planning to become a teacher after graduation. She came to Christ when she was still young, and she was one of the most faithful Christians anyone knew. She was the girl found at every VBS program and every youth group meeting during middle and high school. A couple of times, she was even asked to be a guest speaker at her youth group—a request that she gladly accepted.

My dad, on the other hand, was a new Christian when he started attending college. He wasn't raised Christian, but when a friend shared his faith with him toward the end of high school, he knew he was all in. That same year, he put in applications to every Christian university he could find, and when he got an acceptance letter back from West Lake, he knew that was where God was calling him.

The week that they met, they were both praying about where God wanted them after they graduated. My mom, about whether God was calling her to be a teacher, and my dad, about his own calling. The night they met in chapel, they had a guest speaker who shared about life on the mission field. They were both so moved by the message that they were seriously considering changing majors and moving to another country after graduation to work full-time growing God's kingdom.

They were married a little over a year later, and two years after that, they had my older brother, Jackson. He had the luxury of being born in a real hospital back in the States. But by the time I came along, my parents were already knee-deep in mission work. I was and always have been a missionary kid.

That is, until exactly one month ago, when everything changed.

»›‹«

*I*t all started on a normal Sunday morning. My family and I were at church, the same one we attended every week with the other missionaries and local tribes. I greeted my friends and then went to sit down with my parents. We had our time of worship, same as usual, and soon after that, our pastor went up and started preaching. I can still remember what he said, even though I didn't know how significant his words would be at the time.

"I believe that God is speaking to someone today! God is calling you out of your comfort zone! To take a risk and step out in faith for the cause of Christ. God is calling you to something greater than you could think or even imagine. As Christians, we do not always know what the future holds, but we know the one who holds it—in the very palm of His hands."

My parents exchanged glances, as if they knew something Jackson and I didn't. Later that night, I figured out that my suspicions were right.

"Katie, Jackson," my dad said over beans and rice (classic missionary meal). "Your mom and I have something we've been wanting to talk to you about." He exchanged another glance with my mom as I exchanged one with Jackson—trying to figure out what was going on. "You know that sermon at church today? What Pastor Kip said about God calling us?"

"Yeah." I nodded, taking a gulp of beans and rice. "It reminded me of you guys—how you moved out here to the mission field after college."

"Yes," he said, hesitating as my mom placed her hand over his. "But sometimes, our callings don't last forever. Sometimes God calls us to something new. Something different."

"What do you mean?" I asked, my eyebrows furrowing together as I tried to figure out what on earth he was trying to tell us. Judging by the look on Jackson's face, I could tell he was thinking the same thing.

"Well," he began, slowly, as if struggling to get the words out. "A couple of months ago, I started having these dreams about a church in California—where I was the pastor. And after some time, I told your mother, who, as it turns out, has been having the same dreams."

"Your dad and I spent a lot of time praying about it and a lot of time talking it over," Mom added, as I felt my mind begin to race in a million directions at once—trying my best to absorb what they were saying. "This wasn't a spur-of-the-moment decision by any means. But the more we prayed about it, the more we felt God was calling us there. And the sermon by Pastor Kip today only confirmed it."

"So," he continued, "in four weeks, we're going to be leaving Africa to move to Southern California, where we will be working with a local church."

With that, my brother and I fell silent as I picked at the food on my plate—no longer feeling the least bit hungry. Our parents wanted us to move? Away from everything we've ever known?

To *California?*

"We know this is all a bit sudden," he confessed, as he studied the nervous looks on our faces. "It's definitely a huge change, but we believe this is God's will for us. And if He's leading us there, there's a reason for it."

"But are you *sure* He's leading us there?" I protested. "I mean, maybe you're hearing Him wrong! We've lived here our whole lives—this is all Jackson and I have ever known!"

"We know," my mom said. "Trust me, your dad and I are nervous about this too. But we believe we're doing the right thing, and that this move will be the best thing for all of us."

"Anything else you'd like to say, Katie? Any questions you have—or concerns?"

I shook my head. "Not right now, but may I be excused? I'm not really hungry anymore."

"Sure, Katie." My mom nodded. "We'll save the leftovers in case you get hungry later."

"Thanks," I said as I got up from the table and retreated to my room. Our parents were moving us to California? Away from the mission field? Away from our friends? Away from everything we had ever known and loved? I had no idea what this would look like, but I knew one thing with absolute certainty.

Nothing would ever be the same again.

Chapter Two

*T*oday marks exactly one month from the day my parents made the decision that would change our lives forever. And the truth is, I don't feel any better about it now than I did before.

I shuffled through the list of songs on my playlist as I sat on the plane until finally, I landed on one of my favorites, "Forever Reign" by the Newsboys. It was an old song, but somehow it always managed to calm my nerves in times like these. Times when my world was spinning out of control, completely outside of my power to stop it.

"If this is your will God, then please show me," I silently prayed, "because right now, I feel lost."

"How are you doing, Katie?" I heard my mom ask from the seat beside me. I pulled out my earbuds and forced a smile.

"I'm okay. I'm just trying to trust God, that's all."

"He's got a plan for us, Katie." She squeezed my hand. "We've just got to trust Him."

"I know. That's what I'm trying to do—I mean, He's never failed us yet, right?"

"Right. You know, I have a feeling that God has a plan for you in all this too, Katie. Your dad and I aren't the only ones being called here."

"You really think so?" I asked, a mix of doubt and curiosity filling my voice.

She nodded, looking more at peace than I felt. "I *know* so. You shined too brightly back home for God not to use you here."

"Thanks, Mom," I said, suddenly feeling a little bit better.

"You're welcome, that's what moms are for. You know, I think our plane is about to land soon—shouldn't be more than another fifteen minutes or so until we're on the ground."

"Cool," I said, staring out the window and thinking about everything that was about to change. A new house. A new school. A new city.

"Just another adventure, right?"

"Yeah," I said. "Just another adventure."

*W*ithin a few minutes, we were on the ground, and I soon found that California looked nothing like the remote tribal areas of Africa.

"Watch your bags, Katie! You're going to break something!" Jackson said as we headed through the airport with our luggage, his voice suddenly more like a frustrated father than a barely-two-years-older-than-me brother.

"I'm not going to break anything!" I insisted, with an equal amount of frustration in my own voice. "I'm not even carrying anything that I could break!"

"Well, watch it, OK?"

"Katie, Jackson," our dad warned. "I know you're both stressed but snapping at each other isn't going to help."

"Sorry," I apologized, turning toward Jackson.

"Yeah, sorry," Jackson added. "It won't happen again."

"Good," he said, looking somewhat on edge himself as he led us through the crowded airport. "Because if we're going to do this, we have to be a team. A lot of things are changing right now, but there's one thing that doesn't have to. Do you know what that is?"

"My klutziness?" I asked weakly, even though I knew that wasn't the answer he was looking for.

He shook his head. "This family."

"Right, Dad." I forced a smile. "We'll try to do better."

"Absolutely," Jackson agreed.

"We're all a little tired," Mom said. "Tomorrow should be better—a fresh start for all of us. I think that's exactly what we need."

Jackson and I murmured a couple of 'yeahs' and 'uh-huhs' as we got in our rental car and headed to our new home.

"Is this it?" I asked as we approached a neighborhood with cream-colored houses, only separated by trees and a couple of shrubs. The houses were small where we lived in Kenya, making the houses here look ginormous. And on top of that, each one looked identical, as if straight off an assembly line—lacking the familiar, cozy nature of the houses back home.

He nodded. "This is it. We're officially home."

"Right," I said as my brother and I both stared at the house. "*Home.*"

"Do you like it?" Mom asked. "We found it a couple of months ago online. It's only a few miles away from the church where your dad will be pastoring."

"Yeah, it looks nice." Jackson shrugged. "Just . . . different than I was expecting. That's all."

I knew exactly what he meant, but I didn't say anything about the *Clone Wars* houses. There was no sense causing our parents more stress when this move was already hard enough on all of us as it was.

"Come on," Dad said as he got out of the car and started toward the house. "Let's see what it looks like inside. You kids will get to see your new rooms too!"

"Great," I said, grabbing my bags—which suddenly felt like they weighed about a hundred pounds—and following behind. "Can't wait."

With that, the four of us headed inside and looked around, and as we did, I felt my heart begin to sink. The inside of the house was completely empty. All that was there were the four walls, the floor, the ceiling, and the kitchen counters.

"So?" he said, clearly trying to sound more excited than he actually was. "What do you think?"

"It's . . . big," Jackson said bluntly, as the two of us glanced around the room with the same blank expression.

Just as blank as the walls in our house.

Mom chuckled. "It looks big now because we don't have our stuff inside. Tomorrow we'll go get some furniture. Once our stuff is in it, it'll feel like home in no time."

"Great," I said as I pushed a strand of mousy, brown hair behind my ear. "Can't wait."

"Yeah," Jackson said, sounding less than thrilled. "Hey, mind if we go out walking for a while—to get used to the neighborhood?"

Our parents exchanged nervous glances, but finally, my dad spoke up. "You two can go, but only if you stick together and stay close by. I don't want you kids getting lost."

"Great, we will! Thanks, Mom. Thanks, Dad!" I said as I headed for the door, eager to get out of this far-too-big house that we now called home.

"And keep your phones with you!" Mom added. "So we can call you if we need to get a hold of you!"

"We will!" my brother promised as the two of us headed out the door, relieved to finally be back outside.

One of the few places that still felt somewhat normal.

"So, the house," Jackson said with a slow grin as we walked. "Are you thinking what I'm thinking?"

"That it feels like a giant claustrophobic box that we're being forced to live in against our will?"

"Exactly."

"Yeah, sort of," I confessed. "But who knows? It could turn out to be better than we think."

"I sure hope so. So, where should we go first?"

I shrugged. "We can't go too far. Mom and Dad will worry. Maybe just keep walking this way?"

"Sounds good to me," he said as we wandered through the neighborhood, staring at houses that all looked eerily similar, until suddenly, we were overtaken by a rush of fur coming our way.

"Whoa, down boy!" Jackson said, holding up his hands in surrender as a small auburn-colored dog ran toward us, with a guy around our age following close behind.

"*Tolkien*! Down boy!" he shouted as the dog stopped in place. "Sorry about that. He's completely harmless, but he tends to do that sometimes. He has way too much energy for one dog."

"It's cool," my brother assured him. "No harm, no foul."

"Good," he said, breathing out a sigh of relief as he stood to his feet, after kneeling down to pet the dog. "Are you guys new around here? I don't think I've ever seen either of you before."

"Yeah, we just moved here today," I said, my eyes catching his, which I suddenly noticed were a bright shade of blue yet, somehow, warm and welcoming.

"Oh, okay, where are you from?" he asked, still holding onto his dog's leash as he did his best to get away. The dog, not the boy.

"Africa," I replied. "Kenya, to be exact."

"Africa? Wow, that's a new one."

"Our parents are missionaries. Or *were* missionaries until recently. It's uh, kind of a long story."

"Gotcha," he said, sticking out his hand for us to shake as my brother gave me a funny look. "Well, welcome to the neighborhood. My name's Atticus. You already met my dog."

"Katie," I said, introducing myself as I shook his hand, suddenly noticing that my palms felt sweatier than before. "And this is my brother, Jackson." I paused, thinking about our new neighbor's name. "*Atticus*. Like Atticus Finch, in that old book, *To Kill a Mockingbird*."

"You've read it?"

"Loved it. I read it last year for school. My parents both love it too—they assigned it, actually. We were homeschooled. All our lives, pretty much. Until recently. I mean, we haven't started school yet, but we're starting soon, with everyone else."

"That's cool. Sounds like your parents have good taste in books." He smiled, easing my nerves as I felt my shoulders start to drop. "What school will you guys be going to?"

"Winter Oaks High School," Jackson said. "The one right near the Target, off Emerson."

"No way, that's where I go. Maybe I'll see you around."

"Yeah, totally!" I nodded as I stood there awkwardly in place.

"Cool. Well, I'd better get going, but it was nice meeting you guys. Don't be strangers, okay?"

"We won't," I promised, as he waved and walked away.

"What were you doing?" Jackson asked once Atticus was out of earshot. "Telling that guy our whole life story?"

"What?" I asked as we headed back to our house. "He asked questions and I answered them. What's the problem?"

"The problem is, now he thinks we're homeschooled religious weirdos who don't know the first thing about American culture."

"He's *not* thinking that." I rolled my eyes—convinced that my brother had officially lost it. "We were homeschooled, and we are missionary kids. What's wrong with that? It's the truth. Besides, I know plenty about American culture. I have every Taylor Swift CD since her self-titled album back in 2006. And I've never once missed an episode of *This is Us.*"

"Yeah, I know that, and you know that. But he doesn't know that." He paused. "Just try not to put a target on our backs, okay?"

"Personally, I think you're being ridiculous. But if it worries you that much, I'll try to be more careful."

"Thanks. And one more thing, Katie."

"Yeah?"

"No one uses CDs anymore. Try not to mention them to anyone, alright? I don't want people to think we got held back about ten grades."

"I won't," I said, as a grin spread slowly across my lips.

My life and location may have changed in a matter of weeks, but I still had the same brother with his same weird sense of humor. And for that, I couldn't have been more thankful.

Chapter Three

See! I am doing a new thing!
- Isaiah 43:19

Over the course of that week, our house slowly started to feel like a home. Like my parents promised, we all went shopping for furniture the day after we moved. And as the week went on, I began to feel a little more acclimated to California living. That is, until Monday morning—when it was back to all-things-new.

"Katie," I heard a gentle voice whisper as I rolled over in my bed, forcing myself to open my eyes just enough to see my mom standing in the doorway. "You've got to get up. It's your first day of school."

"Do I have to?" I groaned, my new bed feeling way too comfy to even think about moving. "Can't I have just five more minutes?"

"I'm afraid not. You don't want to be late, do you?"

"Is that a rhetorical question?"

"Katie," she warned, not saying another word yet somehow managing to get her point across *very* clearly.

I sighed. "OK. I'm getting up."

"Good. Breakfast will be on the table when you come down. I made pancakes—your favorite. Try not to let them get cold."

"I won't," I said, sitting up in my bed—my ears perking up at the mention of pancakes.

I had already picked out my outfit last night after having way too hard a time trying to fall asleep (a common problem these days). I figured if I decided on my outfit the night before, it would save me the hassle of trying to find something to wear today. After going through a few dozen fashion magazines at the grocery store to avoid looking totally out of place, I finally landed on a forest green sweater, dark blue mom jeans, Ugg boots, a cross necklace, and a pair of dangly gold earrings.

After trying it all on, I decided that it made me look somewhat like a high schooler.

At least, I hoped it did.

"God, please help me through this day. And help me figure out my new life," I prayed as I brushed my teeth. I exhaled, feeling my heart speeding up to the pace of my new electric toothbrush, as a lump formed in the back of my throat.

I could do this, right? Teenagers do this every day without a problem. I was going to be fine.

After I finished getting ready, I hurried downstairs, hoping I could still get a pancake before Jackson ate them all.

"Good morning, Katie. You look nice," my dad said as he sat at the table, drinking his coffee and reading the newspaper.

"Thanks, Dad," I said as I shoveled a pancake onto my plate and poured myself a glass of juice.

"Ready for school?" my mom asked as she sat at the other end of the table, eating a pancake of her own in her usual robe and pajamas.

"Ready as I'll ever be. I've got my books, I've got my bag, and I've got some new pencils. So, I'm good to go, right?"

"Absolutely," Dad said. "How about you, Jackson? Are you ready for your first day of school?"

"Ready as I'll ever be," he said as he drank his own cup of coffee, sounding less than enthusiastic.

"You guys will be fine. Remember Romans 8:31? If God is for us?"

"Then who can be against us," I finished.

"Exactly. Why don't we all pray before you go? Start the day off right."

"Sounds good to me," I said as we all sat down and folded our hands at the table.

"Dear Lord," he began, "please lead us and guide us in this new season we're in. Help us to be lights in this new place and push back any darkness that comes our way. Help us to be more influential than we are influenced. And help us to remember that you are with us wherever we go. We ask all these things in the mighty and powerful name of your son, Jesus, amen!"

"Thanks, Dad," I said as I heard the school bus pull up in front of our house. "That's my ride."

"Alright, have a good day, Katie. You too, Jackson."

"Thanks, Dad."

"Bye, Mom, bye, Dad," Jackson added, in the midst of the shuffle.

With that, Jackson and I walked out to our bus and followed behind the stream of teenagers who boarded in one by one.

"This is it," I said, turning toward my brother as we followed behind a kid with spiky blue hair and a nose ring. "Are you ready?"

"I think so. Are you?"

"I think so," I said as I scanned the bus, trying to find a place to sit. I had seen enough movies to know some things about the cliques in high school—the nerds, the jocks, the goths. But as I looked around the bus, it became clear pretty fast that it was way more complicated than that.

Suddenly, across the way, I spotted a girl with a folded-up wheelchair beside her. I began to make my way toward her, taking a deep breath as I walked—praying I could make at least *one* new friend today.

"Hi," I said in my friendliest tone of voice. "Is anyone sitting here?"

She shook her head. "No, you can sit here."

"Cool. What are you reading?"

"*Allegiant.* It's part of the *Divergent* series."

"That's cool! I've heard of that one—I'll have to check it out sometime. Um, my name is Katie—what's yours?"

"Jenny."

"Nice to meet you, Jenny."

"Nice to meet you too. Are you new around here?"

"Yeah, how'd you guess?"

"Because most people already have friends on the bus." She paused. "I'm new too. I used to go to Roosevelt."

"Oh, that's around here, right?" I asked, even though, in all honesty, I had no idea.

"On the other side of town." She nodded. "How about you? Where'd you go?"

"Uh, I used to live in Africa," I said, my brother's words coming back to me. "So, nowhere around here."

"Really? Africa? That's so cool!"

"Thanks, we actually just got here a couple of days ago. Maybe you could show me around sometime. Give me a tour of the city?"

"Yeah, that'd be great! I'd love that!"

"Cool!" I smiled, feeling a little more at peace. After all, if I could make a new friend within my first couple minutes on the bus, then how bad could this new school be?

"So, what are you into? Any hobbies?"

"Well, I love reading. And I like playing sports sometimes."

"Really? What sports?"

"Well, I used to play basketball with my brother sometimes back home. And I like swimming and playing soccer. How about you? Do you play any . . ." I stopped dead in my tracks—as my eyes caught her wheelchair once again. "I'm *so* sorry! That was probably so insensitive. I didn't mean to—"

"No, it's OK." She laughed. "I actually like basketball too, and I play a mean game of table tennis. You'd be surprised how much you can do in one of these things."

"That's cool. Were you in an accident or . . .?"

She shook her head. "I have CMT—it's a muscular disease that you inherit at birth. I can stand and walk around sometimes, but my muscles aren't as strong as most people's, so I can't do it for very long. Which makes this thing—" she tapped her wheelchair, "come *very* much in handy."

"Well then, I guess I learned something new today." I smiled, relieved that she wasn't offended. "Within my first five minutes on the bus. That has to be a new record."

"For sure." She laughed as the bus came to a stop in front of the school. "Well, it was nice meeting you, Katie!"

"You too!"

With that, she waved goodbye and got off the bus (with some help from the driver) as I followed behind her.

To my surprise, Winter Oaks High School looked a lot like the high schools that you see in the movies, with students talking amongst themselves, opening their lockers, and heading to their classes. And after a lot of searching, I finally found my locker. *Locker B12.*

"Here we go," I muttered as I moved the combination around, trying to get it to work. "Come on, come on, you can do this . . ." I've heard that lockers are hard to open, but now I was seeing for myself that they really weren't kidding.

"Having trouble?" I heard a male voice say from the locker beside me.

"A little. This locker sort of has a mind of its own."

"Yeah, all lockers have their *codes*," he said, with a weird look on his face as he leaned up against his own locker. "So, what's your code?"

"Excuse me?" I asked, caught off guard.

"You heard me. What *interests* you?"

"I'm sorry, but I don't know what you're trying to say. I just—"

The guy started laughing, and at this point, I was convinced that he had lost it. "Come on, don't play games with me. You and I both know what you really want—"

"Kent," I heard a girl say from behind me. "How many times does this girl have to tell you? She's not interested. And if I were you, I'd do what's in your best interest and make like a tree and leave!"

"And who do you think you are to tell me what to do?"

Suddenly, the somewhat large boy and much more petite African American girl were face-to-face, looking as if they were about ready to get into a *legit* fight.

"I'm the girl who could make your life a living nightmare by reporting you to the principal for sexually harassing the girls of this school. So, if you know what's good for you, you'll scatter on to your little intermediate algebra class that you're taking for the *second* time in your high school career."

To my surprise, the guy listened, slinging his backpack over his shoulder, and hurrying off.

"Wow," I said. "That was pretty crazy."

"You just have to know how to handle them, that's all. Guys like Kent talk a big game, but they don't go much beyond the talk if you know what I'm sayin'. You just have to beat them at their own game."

"Well, whatever you did, thanks. From now on, I'm hiring you as my own personal bodyguard."

She laughed. "It's no problem. You new around here?"

"First day." I smiled. "You?"

"Lived here my whole life. Went to school with half these kids since kindergarten. Kent used to try to eat my paste, which explains a lot. He's not all there in the head, if you know what I mean." She paused. "Name's Tanisha. Yours?"

"Katie. I moved into town a couple of days ago."

"Oh really? Where are you from?"

"Africa," I explained. "Well, Kenya, to be exact."

"Well, isn't that ironic."

"Yeah, I guess it kind of is."

"So, do you like it here so far?"

"It seems pretty nice. I mean, the weather's great, and the scenery's pretty cool. Plus, all the beaches and stuff . . ."

Tanisha laughed as if I had said something funny. "Give it time. It'll grow on you. Before you know it, this place will start to feel like home."

"Thanks. I hope you're right."

"I know I am. So, do you still need help getting your locker open?"

"If you don't mind."

"Not at all. You just turn it like this, and then like this, and *voila*! You are in your locker!"

"Thanks. You make it look so easy."

"It is once you get the hang of it. So, who's your teacher for first period?"

"Mrs. Addams. Biology 2."

"No way—me too! We can be lab partners!"

"Yeah totally!" I exclaimed, feeling a little less nervous. After all, with Tanisha as my new friend, what could possibly go wrong?

Chapter Four

*T*hankfully, after we walked into class, things started to feel a little more normal. And as my teacher came in and introduced herself, I began to feel a little more at ease.

"Good morning class," she began as she walked up to the front of the classroom. "My name is Mrs. Addams, and I will be your teacher for Biology 2. In this class, we will be learning about cells, reproduction, and our natural origins. This is a high school class, so I expect you to pay close attention and take good notes. You will get out of this class exactly what you put into it. Now, any questions? Yes, Riley."

"Will we have to, like, *dissect frogs* in this class?" a thin, blond girl with heavy eye makeup asked, wrinkling her nose in pure disgust.

"Yes, Riley. Dissection will be a part of this class. And unless your family is morally opposed to the dissection of frogs, I expect everyone to participate. Any other questions?"

"Will there be any pop quizzes?"

"No, Eddie. We will not have any pop quizzes." She smiled, answering a boy in the back of the classroom as I heard a couple of sighs of relief on every side of me. "But our tests will have material from the lectures. So, I expect you to take good notes and study for your exams, which you will take at the end of each module. Any other questions?"

No one else said anything.

"Alright class, in that case, we will begin. Our first lecture will be on the origins of our earliest ancestors. Please turn to page four in your textbooks."

I flipped to the place in my textbook where my teacher instructed us to turn and got out my notebook and a fresh sheet of paper. My parents and I had talked about this before today, and I knew that some aspects of Biology would be taught from a different worldview than my own. But I knew what I believed, and I was prepared. I'd just learn the information for the test and move on. No big deal.

I jotted down my notes and did my best to stay focused. Even though I had never been in a real classroom before, it wasn't all that different from watching educational videos back home. The only difference was this was live, and there were other students around. Other than that, it was just another year and another class.

It continued that way all through my next four classes. Same lectures. Same procedures. Same number two pencils. That is, until I got to fourth period—*lunch*.

My eyes darted back and forth in semi-frantic search of a seat. But the harder I looked, the less sure I felt about where I should sit—and the more I felt like one tiny minnow in a gigantic sea of whales.

"Looking for someone?" I heard a familiar male voice say from behind me.

I felt my muscles start to tighten up, worried that it might be that weird guy coming back to bug me again. But when I turned around, I was relieved to find that it wasn't him. Instead, it was Atticus—the boy from across the street.

"Just a spare seat." I smiled, trying to look less lost and confused than I felt.

"Well then, I think I can help you with that. Come on, follow me."

"Oh, I don't know—I don't want to intrude."

"Don't worry, you're not intruding," he assured me, as he led me over to his table, which was filled with a mix of guys and girls. And another face that I already recognized.

"Tanisha!" I exclaimed, both relieved and surprised to see her here. "Hey! I didn't know you had this lunch period!"

"I sure do." She smiled. "And I see you've already met my brother."

"Your brother?" I asked as they both laughed.

"I was adopted," Tanisha explained. "In case you can't quite see the resemblance."

"People are always a little surprised when they find out." Atticus grinned. "Trust me, we're used to it."

"Now that you've met us, why don't we introduce you to the rest of the gang," Tanisha said, speaking up. "Katie, this is Nathan, Amber, Maya, and Kyle."

"Nice to meet you." I waved, which I soon realized probably looked completely dorky, but it was too late to take it back now. "How did you guys meet?"

"Just over the years, at different places." Nathan shrugged. "Tanisha's head of the drama department, and I work backstage on the props and the lighting."

"And Atticus and I sat next to each other in AP English last year," Maya added, playing with an ombre lock of hair.

"Tanisha and I go way back—" Amber piped in, "and we reconnected again in high school."

"And Atticus and I got stuck dissecting the same frog in Ms. Lindsley's biology class last year." Kyle grinned, adjusting his glasses. "Good times."

"And *that*, Katie—" Tanisha said, "is how our weird little misfit group came to be."

"So, Katie—" Kyle began, popping a french fry, "tell us about yourself. What's your story?"

"Well," I said, thinking back to my brother's words, even though I still thought he was being ridiculous. "My family moved here about a week ago from out of the country—"

"Out of the country?" Maya asked, sounding surprised.

"Where?" Kyle asked, just as intrigued.

"Um, Africa. My parents, uh, worked over there . . ."

"That's so cool!" Maya exclaimed. "What was it like?"

"It was pretty nice." I hesitated, unsure how much I should say. "I mean, it was all I ever knew."

With that, the six of us went on talking, and as we did, I noticed something that caught me by surprise. The more I talked to them, the more I realized that they were just like me, and Jackson, and the people that I knew back home.

The only real difference was that they lived here.

"So, Katie," Atticus said as the bell rang, signaling that our lunch period was over, "what's your next class?"

"U.S. History with Mr. Weaver."

"No way, same! Since you're going there and so am I, why don't we walk together? I mean, if you want to that is—"

"Sure! I mean, yeah! That sounds great. Let me just dump out my leftovers, and I'll be ready to go!"

"Cool," he said, as we walked to the trash can to throw away the remainders of our lunch and made our way to our next class, as a familiar nervous feeling started to form in the pit of my stomach.

"So, Katie," Atticus began, as his eyes locked into mine.

"Yeah?"

"Why didn't you tell them the truth? About where you came from?"

"It was my brother." I hesitated, a twinge of guilt flooding over me. "He doesn't want us to be stereotyped—you know, the homeschooled missionary kids. So, he told me not to say anything."

"Well, that's too bad," he said, looking down and then back toward me. "Because I, for one, thought it was one of the coolest things about you."

"That I was homeschooled?" I asked as he shook his head, pulling a cross necklace out from underneath the neck of his T-shirt. "You're a Christian?" I asked before he had a chance to reply.

"My whole life."

"What about your friends? Are they . . .?"

This time he shook his head and then stopped himself. "The truth? I don't know. I think Amber might have some kind of Christian background—she goes to church, at least. And I know Nathan used to go, but I don't think he has in years. The others?" He shrugged. "I have no idea."

"Well, do they know you are?" I asked, not wanting to pry, but at the same time, genuinely curious.

"It's never really come up, to be honest. I mean, we talk about other things—movies, classes, hobbies, books . . . stuff like that. But our beliefs—"

"Not so much," I said, finishing his sentence for him as he nodded. "Have you ever thought about bringing it up?"

"I've thought about it. But at the same time, I'm not exactly winning any popularity contests around here. And I don't want to lose the only friends I have. I wish it was different, but that's just kind of how it is around here . . . people talk about school, they talk about who's dating who this week or who was dating who last week, and they talk about the ever-putrid cafeteria food . . . but never the things that really matter."

"Is your faith something that really matters to you?"

"Yeah." He nodded. "It's the most important thing about me. It's how I make all my decisions . . . and make sense out of life."

"And do you think it would help them too?"

"Yeah," he said, his eyes darting to the ground and then back toward me. "I think it would. If they'd listen."

"Then I think you should tell them. I mean, if it's such a big part of who you are, why would you keep it a secret?"

"Why are you keeping it a secret?"

"I'm not," I said, feeling convicted. "Not anymore."

"Well then, maybe I'll try to be a little less secretive too."

"Cool," I said, my cheeks feeling warm as I stood there talking to him. "Well, I guess we'd better go find a seat. But we'll talk later?"

"Absolutely."

"Wait—" I said before we went in, the two of us still standing in the hallway.

"Yeah?"

"My dad is uh, going to start working at a church right around here," I said, fiddling with my necklace. "It's called Hope Life. And I'm going to start going to the youth group there too. If you're not busy Wednesday night, maybe you could come with me. Tanisha can come too if she wants."

"I'd love that." He smiled. "And I'll ask her about it when we get home. I'm sure she'd love to check it out."

"Great." I smiled, shoving my hands in my pockets. "Then, I guess I'll see you around."

"Absolutely," he promised, as we took our seats at opposite ends of the classroom—in the only chairs left.

I smiled to myself. I definitely wanted to see him around.

Even though we had only just met.

»→ ←«

*T*hat night after showering, I decided to try to relax and adjust to my new room in our no-longer-so-boxy house. And as I sat on my bed rewatching an old episode of *This Is Us*, I couldn't help but take in the new atmosphere that surrounded me. My walls were a dull shade of white and the floor was comprised solely of wooden boards and a throw rug, but the rest of the room looked surprisingly like me. My mom bought me a bright yellow bedspread—my favorite color, and off to the side, I had a dresser with pictures of my friends from Kenya scattered across it.

Over my bed, I had fairy lights and a couple of posters of some of my favorite Christian bands. I also had a new bookshelf with my books proudly displayed and a chest at the end of my bed. *The chest.*

I groaned as I thought about it, remembering how my mom told me to 'Get around to cleaning it before it turned into nothing more than a wooden trash can.' I figured it wouldn't hurt to do some cleaning while watching TV.

As the intro to the next show began, I knelt by my bed and began sorting through my things. Some bathing suits, scrapbooks, old letters, old blankets, pillows, etc., etc., etc.

I began taking stuff out and placing it down on the floor beside me until suddenly, I noticed something weird with one of the floorboards. It was loose.

I stared down at the rogue floorboard. Should I try to move it? Finally, after a moment of thinking, my curiosity got the best of me. And as I moved it, I couldn't help but gasp.

Underneath the floorboard was a small, dusty old book. I flipped to the first page, which was dated September 26th, 1995.

Dear Diary,

I'm scared. There. I said it. I'm scared. I'm in the place that I've always dreamt of being, the place I've always wanted to be, and yet, I'm terrified. It's my first week of school, and already, I miss everything about my hometown. I miss my old friends. I miss my church. I even miss my annoying little brother (shocking, I know). I know I'm blessed to be here, but everything about this place feels new and uncertain.

Take the dorms, for instance. Never in my life did I ever think I'd be rooming with three other girls, all packed like sardines into one tiny room. And trust me, it's not at all like the show Friends. One girl, who I'll just call M, is only here because her parents made her come. When the dorm advisors aren't looking, she's sneaking around with guys and partying like crazy. Another girl (D) wants nothing to do with me. And the last girl (C) seems nice enough, but she's beyond shy. I think she's spoken five words to me in the whole time I've spent rooming with her.

It's nights like these that I want nothing more than to be back in my room at home with my dog and a pint of Rocky Road ice cream.

Until Next Time,
H.D.

I stared down at the book, reading over the first section five or six times, feeling that if I pinched myself, I'd wake up.

Though the writer of the diary was in college, and I was in high school, and though the entry was written before I was even born, I could relate to nearly everything in this book.

It was like someone had taken every one of my feelings and penned them down over twenty years ago. But how did it get here, underneath the floorboard in my new bedroom? Who were all these people, and why were they only referred to in single letters? Where was this college—was it somewhere near here, or a million miles away? And who on earth was H.D.?

Chapter Five

For I am the Lord your God who takes hold of your right hand and says to you,

Do not fear; I will help you.

- Isaiah 41:13

The whole rest of the week, I couldn't stop thinking about the strange book that I found, and the mysterious person who wrote it. Ever since I found it, I started reading a couple of entries every day. And each entry seemed just as relatable as the one that came before it.

Dear Diary,

Day by day, this place is growing on me. The skies and the frames of the autumn leaves are beginning to feel a little more familiar. And the pillow on my bed is starting to feel a little more like home. The other day, I stumbled upon a small, cozy coffee shop. I've pretty much adopted it as my own special place. On top of that, we recently had a guest speaker come and talk to my school about purpose.

Ironically, purpose is the one thing that I seem to be lacking lately.

Back home, I knew my place; I knew where I belonged. But here, I feel lost. It's like everything that has for so long been a part of my identity has been swept out from under me, leaving me to try to find something solid to hold on to. Even praying feels harder these days, and I don't know why.

I guess I can only hope that somehow, someway, I'm going to learn something through this experience. And that there will be better days outside the university coffee shop ahead.

Until Next Time,

H.D.

"Katie!" I heard my dad call from downstairs. "Are you almost ready? Youth group starts at 6:30 and it's already 6:00!"

"Coming!" I shouted before closing the book in my lap.

There would be time to figure out more about H.D. and the mysterious diary later. Right now, I needed to focus on getting ready for my first night at Ignite, the student ministry at Hope Life Church.

The three of us piled into my dad's Toyota and headed out as I stared out the window on the way there. In the part of Africa that we lived in back home, there was hardly a need for cars. And when we did drive, the traffic was nothing like it was here.

"*Dad*, look out!" I screamed as a small, red sports car pulled out in front of us My dad slammed on the brakes before it could hit us.

"It's okay, Katie," he said, not taking his eyes off the road. "I saw him."

"The roads are *insane* here!" I exclaimed, holding on to my seat belt for dear life. "I am *so* not getting on any of these roads alone anytime soon!"

My dad laughed, somehow seeming unfazed by the fact that we literally almost just died. "Honestly, Katie, I forgot how congested the roads could be back in the States. But you'll get used to it. I'm sure in another couple of months, once your mom and I are more comfortable, you and Jackson will be ready to drive."

"I hope you're right," I said, staring out the window as a knot began to form in the pit of my stomach—suddenly wondering how teenagers do this every day without the slightest problem.

Thankfully, once we were off the highway, things were a little less scary. The traffic cleared up, and before we knew it, we were in front of our new church—right on the corner of a street called Wilmington Drive.

"You kids feel alright about going in by yourselves? I can walk you to the door if you'd like."

My brother shook his head. "We'll be fine, Dad. Thanks."

"Yeah, don't worry, Dad. We're good."

"Alright, well, you kids have your phones with you. Call me if you need anything."

"Thanks, Dad." I smiled. "But we'll be fine. Really."

"Alright. Have a good time—I'll be back to pick you up at 8:30."

With that, Jackson and I said goodbye and headed inside. And as I glanced around the building, I saw swarms of teenagers in groups talking and a couple of younger boys playing video games off to the side, with an old song by Lecrae thumping in the background.

"You okay?" my brother asked as I glanced around the room, trying to get my bearings.

"Yeah." I nodded. "Are you?"

My brother nodded as a tall, thin man walked up to us—who I vaguely remembered from church last week.

Pastor Sean, I think.

"Hey—Katie and Jackson, right?" he asked as he shook our hands. "Pastor Will's kids?"

"Yeah." I nodded. "That's us."

"Well, I'm glad you guys came. I think you're both really going to like it here. Sammy will help you get checked in, and we'll be starting service in about five minutes. If you have any questions, you can ask me or my wife or any of the leaders here."

"Great, thanks," I said as my brother and I walked over to the iPad stand, where an older girl with light blond hair stood, helping people enter their names into the system.

"Hey," she said as the two of us walked up to her. "Are you guys new here?"

Jackson nodded. "First time. Our dad's the new interim pastor—Pastor Will?"

"Oh, okay. That's right—I remember seeing you guys last Sunday. My name's Sammy. It's nice to meet you!"

"You too," I said, immediately liking this girl, even though I'd only known her for barely a minute.

"What are your names?" she asked as she entered our family's last name into the system.

"Katie. And this is my brother, Jackson."

"OK . . . Your name tags should be printing in just a couple of seconds!" she said as the two name tags flew out of a small printer off to the side. "*And . . .* you are good to go! Have a good night. And don't forget to pick up your VIP bags on the way out!"

"Thanks, Sammy!" I said as my brother and I grabbed our name tags and headed toward the front entrance. "Nice meeting you!"

"You too!" she said as we made our way into the sanctuary.

"Hey everyone," a guy with dark hair and torn-up jeans said as he approached one of the mics. "Welcome to Ignite! Are you all ready to worship Jesus?"

The crowd clapped and cheered as the band launched into their first song—a fast one, called "When We Pray" by Tauren Wells, followed by a couple of others until finally, they had us sit down for Pastor Sean's message.

"Hey," I heard a familiar voice whisper as I took a seat with my brother near the front. "Mind if we sit with you guys?" I turned around to see Atticus and Tanisha behind us.

"Sure!" I whispered as Atticus sat down on the side of my brother and Tanisha sat near me. "I didn't think you guys were coming!"

"Sorry," he apologized. "Traffic was horrible."

"Don't I know it?" I grinned, thinking back to the traffic that I was sure was going to kill us all.

"Be strong and courageous," Pastor Sean began as he opened his lesson with a verse I was familiar with. "Do not be afraid or terrified because of them, for the Lord your God goes with you; he will never leave you nor forsake you.

"Many of us here tonight are familiar with this verse," he said as he looked around the sanctuary. "Some of you may have learned it in an Awana or a children's church program. Some of you may have seen it on mugs or T-shirts at the local Christian bookstore or on somebody's Instagram. But what does it mean to be courageous? Could I have someone answer that question for me tonight?" One boy raised his hand as Pastor Sean motioned for him to speak.

"Not being afraid?" he suggested.

"That's a good answer, Demitri." Pastor Sean nodded. "But actually, the dictionary definition of courage is to do something in *spite* of fear. To refuse to let fear stop you from doing what you want to do or what you are called to do."

He paused, allowing time for his words to sink in. "Fear is something we all experience, whether it's a rational fear, like being afraid of earthquakes, or an irrational fear, like being afraid of spiders. That's my fear, and I ask that you please hold your judgment until the end of this message."

A couple of students laughed along with Pastor Sean as a verse appeared on the screen above. "We all deal with fear, and as your pastor, I'm not exempt from this struggle. But as Christians, we do not have to let fear control us because we serve a God who is greater than any tactic that the Enemy can use against us. Including fear.

"In fact, Ephesians 6:10-18 talks about how we can fight against fear, worry, and temptation when they come our way. If you have your Bibles with you, please turn to this passage with me."

Jackson and I pulled out our iPhones and tapped on the *Bible App*, where we turned to the passage that Pastor Sean had up on the screen.

"As Christians, we have an Enemy that is intent on our destruction. But we also serve a God who loves us too much to leave us stranded on our own. A God who wants to see us stand victorious over fear, worry, and temptation. Who has given us direct access to Himself through Christ's death and resurrection on the cross."

Pastor Sean continued talking about fear and how to overcome it, and at the end of the message, we closed with two slower songs—both songs that I recognized from our church back home. And after the worship team struck the last chord in an old song by Chris Tomlin, Pastor Sean walked back up on stage to close the service.

"Next week, we are going to be continuing our series on overcoming fear. We will also be talking about how to be bold for Christ at school and with our friends. This week, if you need prayer to overcome fear, or for anything else, there will be leaders up front who would be happy to pray with you."

As I stood there and watched other teenagers go up to ask for prayer, I felt a slow tug on my heart. Lately, I have been dealing with fear. With being in a new school . . . With being the only Christian at my school that I knew of other than my brother, Atticus, and Tanisha . . . With being in a new country—away from everything I've ever known and loved.

Slowly, I made my way up to the front.

"Hey," Sammy whispered, "are you okay?"

"My brother and I are completely new to this area," I began, as I felt myself struggling to hold back tears. "Our parents were missionaries before we moved here. Recently, we moved into a new house. I started going to a new school, and I've been feeling kind of lost. And this is the first place I've come since I got here where I haven't felt totally alone in my faith. So . . . could you please pray for me?"

"Absolutely." Sammy nodded as she placed her hand on my shoulder and started praying. "Dear Lord, I come to you in prayer for Katie. I thank you for her life and all that you're going to do in and through her. We know that you have incredible plans for Katie, bigger than she could even think or imagine.

"We come to you today to pray for your protection over her. That she would feel your presence as she leaves your house and goes into her week. We pray for boldness as she goes into her school and that she would be a vessel for you to use.

"We pray that you would help her to grow through this season and help her to remember that you are always with her. That you will never leave her or forsake her. Jesus, we pray all of these things in your holy and powerful name, amen."

"Amen," I whispered.

"You're going to be okay, Katie. God is with you, and I'm here if you ever need to talk."

"Thanks, Sammy," I said, this time, unable to hold back the tears as she leaned in to give me a hug and a tissue.

Sammy was right. God was with me.

I just needed to trust Him to keep leading me.

Every step of the way.

Chapter Six

Trust in the Lord with all your heart and lean not on your own understanding;

in all your ways submit to him, and he will make your paths straight.

- Proverbs 3:5-6

After Wednesday night, it was easier to go to school on Thursday and Friday, as I felt just a little bit more courageous than I did before. And before I knew it, it was Friday night, with the four of us gathered around the table for beans and rice. Just like old times.

"Katie, could you please pass the hot sauce?" my dad asked as we sat around the table, and I thought about H.D.'s diary, which I planned on reading after dinner.

"Huh?" I asked, snapping out of my thoughts. "Oh yeah, sure."

"Somebody's deep in thought," my mom noted as she scooped another serving of beans and rice onto her plate. "Something on your mind, Katie?"

I shook my head. "Just something I'm reading, that's all."

It wasn't a total lie. I was reading H.D.'s diary.

But it wasn't the whole truth either.

"Hey—Mom, Dad, I was thinking," Jackson said, changing the subject. "This guy Darrin is having a couple of people over to his house tomorrow night. Is it alright if I go?"

"Where does Darrin live?" Dad asked.

"Just a couple of blocks from here."

"Do you know him from church?"

"No, from school. He sits next to me in AP Bio."

"Are his parents going to be home?" Mom asked, a hint of concern in her voice.

"I don't know."

"Sorry, Jackson," Dad said, giving our mom a knowing look. One that said they were both in agreement on this one. "But if his parents aren't going to be home, the answer is going to have to be no. If we meet him, and we meet his parents, then we'll talk."

"Come on, Dad. I'm not a little kid anymore. I'm seventeen! I'll be a legal adult in less than a year."

"Sorry, Jackson," Mom said. "But the answer is still no. That's our final word."

"Fine," Jackson muttered under his breath.

"On a different note," my dad began, glancing over at me and then back toward Jackson, "I was talking with the staff today, and we're thinking about putting on a children's production for the Christmas Eve service. They're looking for some older students from Ignite to help direct if either of you are interested."

"I am," I said, perking up at the mention of a Christmas play, which was something that we used to do all the time back home. "I'd love to do it. Maybe I can get Tanisha and Atticus to help out too!"

"Great, the more the merrier. The committee will be meeting every Tuesday after school and Saturday evenings. Think you can handle that on top of your schoolwork? I don't want you falling behind because of this play."

"I won't, I promise. I'd love to do it! And I'll see if any of my friends are interested too."

"Wonderful," my mom said, pausing as if deep in thought. "Tanisha and Atticus. Why do those names sound so familiar?"

"They're our neighbors from across the street," I reminded her. "I met them the day we moved in. They came to church with me last Wednesday for youth group, remember?"

"Oh, that's right. That's wonderful, Katie. I'm so glad that you're making friends here so fast."

"Thanks, Mom. Me too."

"How about you, Jackson?" Dad asked as my brother fiddled with the food on his plate. "How'd you like to be a part of the Christmas production this year? You did a phenomenal job helping out last year, back in Kenya."

"I don't know," he said. "It's a little corny, don't you think? Same thing every year. I think I'll sit this one out."

"It's your call, Jackson. But I'd love for you to join in if you change your mind."

"May I be excused?" I asked, at this point, only half-listening. "I'm finished eating, and I'd like to get some reading in before bed."

"Sure, Katie." My mom nodded. "Why don't you go read outside and get some fresh air. It's not dark out yet, and the weather is beautiful tonight."

"Alright, I'll do that. Thanks!"

"You're welcome, Katie," my dad said, "and remember—"

"Get my schoolwork done before the weekend." I grinned, after finishing his sentence for him. "Don't worry, Dad. I will."

With that, I excused myself from the table and headed upstairs to get the diary to read on the rocking chair in front of my house. Suddenly, noticing a familiar face across the way.

"Hey, stranger," I said, after walking across the street, where a very deep-in-thought-Atticus sat on the steps of his house. "Whatcha doing?"

After a long pause, he looked up, caught off guard.

"Katie," he said, covering the mess of papers with his hands as he glanced up in my direction. "Hey, I was just working on something. It was, uh . . ."

"Homework?" I asked as he shook his head.

"Just this project. It's nothing really. It's just—"

Before he could finish, a sharp gust of wind picked up from a distance and knocked the papers out of his hands, scattering them across the lawn. And before he could protest, I grabbed a piece of paper and began reading.

"It was a day like any other," I began, reading the words that seemed to dance across the page in an almost poetic way. "Nicholas Harding was not expecting anything out of the ordinary. He had been down the same roads so many times before, yet those roads were the very roads that would lead him to his destiny. A destiny that he had not yet discovered." I glanced over to Atticus, who pretty much looked like he wanted to die right there. "Did you write this?"

"It's a little rough," he said, "but yeah. I guess you could say writing is sort of a hobby of mine. It lets me escape. Kind of like music or art is for some people, I guess."

"It's really good," I said, pausing as I processed the words I had just read. "Like, bookstore level good. Have you ever thought about publishing these?"

"I've played around with it. I mean, I'd love to be the next Mark Twain or James Patterson. But the truth is, I've never actually written anything long enough to publish. Between school and the rest of my life, I usually start something and then just sort of forget to finish."

"So, you think Mark Twain wrote *Tom Sawyer* in one sitting?" I teased.

"No, I guess not." He grinned. "I don't know. Maybe it's teenage insecurity or just general angst, but sometimes I wonder if I'm actually good enough to make it as a writer."

"Well, you already have one reader. And I'm pretty sure she thinks you could."

"Well, then. You'll have to introduce me to her sometime. I'd love to meet her."

"Maybe I will. You know—if she's not too busy."

"Of course. So, what are you doing out here? Besides interrupting a writer hard at work?"

"Soaking up the sun." I shrugged, wondering how much I should tell Atticus about the diary. A diary that suddenly seemed like too good of a secret to keep to myself. "And reading."

"Oh yeah, what are you reading? Anything I'd know?"

"Actually, probably not," I said, as he pretended to be surprised. "If I tell you something, do you promise to keep it just between the two of us?"

"Cross my heart," he said, making a crisscross motion across his chest.

"OK, well, when I was organizing my room a couple of weeks ago, I found something under my floorboard. A diary, by someone who goes by the initials H.D., who's managed to remain anonymous through pretty much every entry I've read so far."

"Sounds like an interesting person," he noted. "Is this H.D. a guy or a girl? Or is that a mystery too?"

"A girl. But that's about all I've managed to figure out so far." I paused. "You've lived in this neighborhood longer than I have. Is there anyone who lived in our house before us with those initials? Who could've written it?"

He shook his head. "Just an older man named Arthur, but he's lived alone for as long as I can remember, and he just moved into a nursing home. And he wasn't really the diary-keeping type. Did the author leave any clues? Like an object or a picture?"

I shook my head. "The only possible clue is a code written in the front of the book. 5-9-6. Maybe because that's the address of the house where she used to live—where we live now?"

"Huh, that is weird. Mind if I take a look for myself?"

"Be my guest," I said, handing him the diary. "I haven't gotten anywhere trying to figure it out myself."

Atticus thumbed through the pages, looking as if he had stumbled upon a long-lost treasure.

"Do you know who it could be?" I asked after a few moments of silence, partly out of curiosity and partly because I hate the sound of silence.

"No, but I do know someone who might."

"Really? Who?"

"Mr. Larson. He's the town librarian. He's lived here for years and knows more about the people who've lived in this area than anyone else I know. If we took it to him and asked a few questions, we might be able to find something out."

"Really? You want to help me find her?"

"Are you kidding? This is the kind of stuff a writer lives for. An old diary? Found under the floorboard of your house?" He shook his head. "You didn't actually think I was going to let you figure this out on your own, did you?"

"I guess I didn't think much about it at all." I smiled, suddenly feeling excitement bubbling up in my veins. "So, when do you want to get started?"

"How about Sunday? The library is right near your church. I know because I've spent over half my life there. We can head over there after service and see what we can find out."

"What if we don't find anything?" I asked, small doubts fighting their way to the surface of my mind.

"Then," he said with a grin, "we don't stop looking until we do."

Chapter Seven

*T*hat Sunday, Atticus remained true to his word. Right after third service, we headed over to the library to talk to Mr. Larson about H.D., hoping to find some answers to the millions of questions that we had about our mystery writer. And as we walked, I noticed that the sun was high in the sky as a slight California breeze blew through my long, reddish-brown hair.

"So, do you think we'll be able to find her?" I asked, my dark brown Ugg boots crunching against a cluster of autumn leaves as we made our way toward the large glass doors.

"H.D.?" he asked, as he walked in step beside me.

"No." I rolled my eyes. "The ice cream man. Of course, I mean H.D.!"

Atticus laughed. "I sure hope so. If anyone would know, it's Mr. Larson. I guess you could say he's sort of our own personal stage manager."

"Our stage manager?" I asked. I knew that teenagers in the U.S. had their own set of slang words, and that they changed rapidly, but that was a new one even for me.

"Yeah—you know, like in that old play, *Our Town*. The guy who knows all the people who live in the town and has like, crazy accurate information about everyone and everything."

"Oh," I said, still confused. "I've never read *Our Town*, so I guess I wouldn't know."

"You've never read *Our Town*?" Atticus asked, shock and disbelief ringing through his voice. "It's an American classic! Your iconic picture of all things American life. A homage to your ordinary, everyday citizens."

"Well, in case you forgot, my life hasn't exactly been what most people would consider ordinary. Or American."

"Valid point," he confessed as the two of us stood silent for a moment. "So, what was it like? Growing up as a missionary kid in Africa? Living out an adventure every day of your life?"

This time I laughed. "It wasn't always an adventure. We still had ordinary tasks, like schoolwork and chores. But it was pretty cool. I saw a lot of crazy things from a young age. People, from different tribes and cults getting saved. New Christians, abandoning their old lives to start churches or become pastors or missionaries themselves. I guess it probably sounds pretty crazy to a lot of people, but for me, it was normal. All I've ever known."

"Well, I think it's pretty cool," he said, deep in thought. "I guess life around here must look pretty boring. People going to school or work—doing the same thing, day in and day out . . ."

"Not really." I shook my head, looking down at my boots and then back toward him. "I mean, I thought so at first. And there are days when I still miss Kenya. But the more I look around, at school, and at places like this, the more I see that people are people everywhere. The same basic needs exist here that existed back home. You just have to know how to look close enough to see it.”

“You’re an interesting person, Katie. You know that?” he said as I felt my face flush bright red.

“Interesting good? Or interesting bad?”

“Interesting good. Definitely interesting good.”

“Well, thanks.” I smiled. “You’re pretty interesting yourself.”

This time, it was Atticus who looked red. “Come on, let’s go find our mystery writer.”

With that, the two of us walked into the cool, air-conditioned library, which felt nice on a warm, early fall day. And as we approached the front desk, we were immediately greeted by an older, graying librarian.

“Atticus,” a man who I assumed to be Mr. Larson said, as a smile spread across his face. “Good to see you! And who’s this lovely young lady?”

“This is Katie—” he said as I reached over the counter to shake his hand, “she’s new in town.”

“Nice to meet you, Katie.” Mr. Larson said with a firm handshake.

“You too, sir.”

“So, what brings you two here on a Sunday afternoon? Big research paper for school? Or just a trip to pick out some new books?”

“Actually, neither,” Atticus explained, as Mr. Larson raised his eyebrows. “You see, we found—actually, *Katie* found, this old diary written by some woman whose initials are H.D. and she lived at 596 Brookside Drive. We were wondering if you know who she might be. The diary entries were written sometime during the late 90s if that helps you any."

"Hmm . . . *H.D* . . . *H.D* . . . That's a tough one. Do you know anything else about the author of the diary? Maybe names of family members, or if she was ever married?"

I shook my head. "She doesn't give much information about anyone in her family. But I do know she was in college during the time of her entries. Does that help?"

He thought for a moment before speaking up. "You know, actually it does. There was a young woman who lived in this area in the 90s who went to school at USC, which is right around here. She stopped by all the time, and her name was Halle Dabre. She was a lovely young woman—probably in her forties by now. I haven't seen her in years, but she might still live around here."

"Can you tell us anything else about her?" I asked. "Where she lived, or where she might be now?"

"Sorry, kid. Librarians aren't allowed to disclose personal information. It's part of our policy. But you're welcome to look her up yourself. I'm sure you could find something on one of those social media websites you kids all use. Faceweb or Facebook, or whatever you young people call it."

"Facebook," I said. "Of course! That's a great idea! We'll look her up now. Thank you, sir!"

"Anytime. You're welcome to use one of our computers if you'd like. Just be sure to log off when you're done."

"Thank you. We will," I promised.

"Yeah, thank you, Mr. Larson," Atticus agreed. "We appreciate it."

Facebook. It was a perfect idea. My parents let me create an account a couple of years ago, even though I rarely used it. All I had to do was log in and look up Halle Dabre. The plan was foolproof. Well, almost.

"Great," I muttered as I went to log in to my account. "I can't remember my password."

"It's OK. We'll use mine," Atticus said as he logged in under his name. His profile popped up with an old picture and a quote that I recognized from *The Lord of the Rings.* He typed in the name Halle Dabre and narrowed the search to people within the area who went to the University of Southern California. And within just a couple of minutes, a profile popped up that was an exact match.

"Ha! We did it!" Atticus exclaimed, clicking on her picture.

"I can't believe we actually found her," I said, staring at the screen as we saw Halle appear before our very eyes. She was an older woman of either Italian or Hispanic origin, with olive skin and dark brown hair, standing next to a man close to her age.

For her quote, she simply had the old standby: Live, laugh, love. She also had a couple of pictures with a girl and boy close to my age, who I suspected to be her kids. And right alongside her other info, she listed California as her current address.

"Atticus, she still lives here!" I exclaimed, practically bursting with excitement. "Do you know what this means?"

"No, what does it mean?" He laughed.

"It *means* that we might actually be able to find her! And if we do, we could ask her if she really is the owner of the diary!"

"Do you think she still lives around here? I mean, California is a pretty big state. What if she moved further north?"

"There's only one way to find out—" I said, googling the name, "and it's called the miracle of modern technology."

"You do realize that you're shamelessly stalking this woman."

"Maybe," I confessed. "But if we don't look, we'll never know. Don't you want to find her?"

"Yeah, I guess," he said as I clicked a few more buttons. "I mean . . ."

"*There!*" I exclaimed, too excited about what I had just found to let him finish. "I found it! I can't believe I actually found it! It's 149 Willow Road. That's right near here! And it has her old address too. It's . . . Oh my gosh."

"What? What is it?" Atticus asked, jumping up to look at the computer.

"Atticus, she used to live on Brookside Drive. *596* Brookside Drive." I paused. "The same numbers that she wrote in the front of the diary—and the same house where I live now!"

Chapter Eight

The whole rest of the day, I felt adrenaline coursing through my veins, amazed that I may have just found our mystery writer. And as I boarded the bus on Monday morning, I knew that I had to tell someone about H.D.

"No way," Jenny said after I finished telling her the story. "She lives around here? Right across from your neighborhood?"

I nodded. "Just a couple of blocks from where I live now."

"That's so crazy!" She shook her head. "Who would've thought?"

"I know," I said, suddenly realizing that I had been taking up most of the conversation. "So, how have you been?" I asked, changing the subject and turning my attention back toward her. "Anything new or interesting?"

"Not really. Definitely not anything as interesting as your mystery writer. But they have sign-ups for after-school clubs today. I'm thinking about joining one. *Getting involved* and all that. That is, if I can find one that sounds interesting enough."

"That's so cool! Maybe I should join one too. I mean, it wouldn't hurt to get more involved. And besides, I've never actually been in an after-school club before."

"Ever?"

I shook my head. "There aren't really a lot of opportunities to join an after-school club as a missionary kid living in a remote part of Africa."

"True. Well, maybe we could sign up for a club together."

"Yeah, I'd love that! Where are the sign-up sheets usually at?"

"Right by the door. We can look when we go inside!" Jenny said as the bus driver helped her out, and she told him goodbye.

"OK, cool," I said as the two of us made our way through the doors of the school, where sure enough, there was a table with a list of sign-up sheets. "Wow, there are a lot of clubs here. The Foreign Language Club . . . the Future Democrats of America . . . the Young Scientists Club . . . Are there any clubs for, you know— all different kinds of people to hang out together?"

"There's the Chess Club," Jenny suggested, "and the Coding Club."

"Yeah, I'm terrible at chess," I said, as I glanced from the sign-up sheets back toward Jenny. "And I don't know how to code to save my life."

"Well, there's also the Drama Club. You don't even have to go on stage with that one. A lot of people just work on the props and lighting backstage."

"Hey, that's the club one of my friends runs," I said, thinking back to Tanisha. "And I'm pretty sure another one of my friends works on the props backstage."

"Do you want to try it?" Jenny asked, grabbing a pen and waiting for my response.

"I'll try it if you will," I said, signing my name—Katie Carter, toward the middle of the list, below some guy named Jacob Adams.

"Cool!" Jenny exclaimed. "I can't wait!"

"Same!" I chimed in as Tanisha walked over to greet us. "Hey, Tanisha! Guess who's joining the drama club?"

"Hmm, let me take a wild guess. You?"

"That's right! And so is my friend, Jenny. Have you guys met?"

"No, I don't think we have. My name's Tanisha."

"Jenny," she said, shaking her hand.

"Well, I'm glad you guys are going to be joining. Drama Club is pretty fun. I think you both will like it. Our first meeting is two weeks from now in the auditorium. We'll be starting at exactly 4:00, and snacks will be provided."

"Awesome, we'll be there!"

"Cool. I'd better get to class. I'll see you in Biology?"

"For sure!" I nodded.

"I'd better get going too," Jenny said as she looked down the hallway. "But I'll see you around?"

"Definitely. Bye, Jenny!" I said as I started in the direction of my first class. But as I began walking, I ran into something that made me stop dead in my tracks. Nathan—being pushed up against his locker by a much larger guy. The same guy who harassed me by the lockers on my first day here.

"Just give us your lunch money, and nobody will get hurt!" He held him in place by the front part of his shirt, looking angry and mean—as Nathan stood there, looking visibly afraid, surrounded by Kent and two other guys

"I told you, Kent, I don't have any lunch money! All I have is a chicken sandwich that my mom packed me this morning!"

"I know you have money," he said, his voice louder this time, more menacing, "so just give it to me, and we can all move on!"

"I already told you, I don't have any money with me!" he exclaimed, fear and frustration fighting for a place in his voice. Neither emotion seeming to win at that moment.

"Hey, leave him alone!" I said, my heart racing as I spoke. "He already told you he doesn't have any money. And even if he did, it wouldn't be yours to take."

"Oh yeah, and what if I don't?" This time, he walked up to me, looking about ready to transfer all his negative feelings toward Nathan onto me. I gulped. *God, help me.*

"Hey, leave her alone," one of his friends with a similar size and build said. "Even you're not a big enough jerk to beat up a girl."

"Did you say something?"

"I'm just saying, lay off, alright, man? Don't be like this."

Kent was silent, as if not knowing what to say until finally, he spoke up. "Alright. But only because I have to get to class. And *you!*" he shoved his finger in Nathan's chest. "I'll be talking to you later."

With that, they took off, leaving us alone in the hallway.

"Hey," I said, walking over toward Nathan, "are you alright?"

"Yeah—" he grunted, readjusting his backpack, "I will be."

"What's his problem? Why is he so mean?"

"Kent?" Nathan asked. "Kent's mean to everyone. He did that sort of thing to me practically every day last year. If it wasn't my lunch money, it was my height, my being in drama club, the fact that I take the bus to school." He shook his head. "You name it, he's tortured me and half the school for it."

"That's horrible. I mean, I've seen stuff like that in the movies, but I never thought anyone was actually cruel enough to act that way in real life."

"Welcome to high school," Nathan muttered, "where souls get crushed, and bodies get shoved into lockers. Honestly, if it weren't for Atticus and the rest of the gang, I'd probably fade into complete oblivion here."

"Well, now you have me too. Two is better than one, right?"

"Thanks," he said, a smile creeping across his lips.

"Anytime. I have to get to class, but I'll see you at lunch?"

"Definitely. Later, Katie!"

"Later!" I echoed, as I walked into my first class.

Thankfully, with Kent and his friends nowhere in sight.

*L*ater that night, I logged on to the old, clunky family computer to video chat with my friend Ellie back home. And as I typed in my code and password and pressed *join*, I soon saw my friend's face fill the screen.

"Katie!" she exclaimed, throwing her hands up in excitement. "Oh my gosh, it's been forever! How have you been? And how's California? I feel like we have so much to catch up on!"

"For sure!" I agreed, equally excited to see my old friend. "I've been good! California has been a bit of an adjustment, but it's been good too."

"That's awesome. What's your school like?"

"Pretty much just a regular school—I mean sort of like you would picture it being," I said, drinking a cup of green tea that I made for myself earlier, which always helps me relax. "We have tests, and homework—same as when I was homeschooled."

"What about the social scene? Is it like the movies?"

"Sort of." I hesitated, thinking about the situation with Nathan earlier today. "The good and bad stuff."

"Gotcha." She nodded. "Have you made any friends there?"

"A couple," I replied. "There's this girl, Tanisha, that I met who's pretty cool. She's in charge of the drama club, which I signed up for today. And there's this other girl that I met on the bus, Jenny. She's really nice too. And then there's Nathan, and this other guy, Atticus—he's Tanisha's brother, actually. They both live across the street."

"*Ooh*, a guy friend across the street. Sounds *very* movie-ish."

"It's not like that," I said, rolling my eyes. "Atticus and I are just friends."

"What's he like?"

"Sort of a bookworm. He wants to be an author someday. Deep . . . the intellectual type, I guess."

"He sounds nice. What does he look like?"

"Like a boy, I guess?" I hesitated, trying to think of how to describe him. "I mean, he's kind of tall, thin . . . blue eyes, brown hair . . . I guess he's sort of attractive. But nothing is going to happen between us. I mean, I don't see him that way."

"Right." She grinned. "Well, if you don't want him, maybe I could have him. There's no one cute over here."

"What about that guy you liked last year? Markus?"

"He's seeing someone else." She scrunched up her face. "*Lillian*, I think."

"I'm sorry. I know how much you liked him."

"It's OK. It doesn't matter anyway. I'm still not allowed to date 'til I'm sixteen."

"Yeah, same." I nodded, thinking back to my parents' no dating rule. A rule that was established a long time ago, back when we were still on the mission field. "So, how have things been back home? With all of our friends?"

"Pretty good. Tia just got glasses, and Kacey's teaching herself how to play guitar."

"Aww, that's cool." I smiled. "I wish I could play guitar."

"*Saaame!*" she exclaimed. "That would be so cool!"

We continued talking like that for a while before finally hanging up at 10:42. And even though I knew I'd be kicking myself for it tomorrow, I decided to read another entry in H.D.'s diary, curious to see what else she wrote before falling asleep. And as it turned out, the next entry didn't disappoint.

Dear Diary,

It's funny how much things can change, seemingly, in an instant. The other day, I talked to one of my old friends from high school and found out that she's engaged to a boy she started dating senior year. He seemed like a nice enough guy. Sort of a David Silver type. But it's crazy to think that someone my age is getting married.

Hearing her talk about that got me thinking about how fast things can change. How your life can look totally and completely different from one year to the next. And how one day, or a long stretch of time, can cause everything to be different. And it got me wondering—what will my life look like next year, or two years from now? Will I have finally figured out what I'm doing with my life? Will I have a boyfriend—or be married? Will I still be living in this dorm room or an apartment off-campus? And will I finally have this thing called adulthood figured out? I don't know, but it sure gives me a lot to think about.

Until Next Time,
H.D.

Chapter Nine

Jesus answered, "I am the way and the truth and the life. No one comes to the Father except through me.

- John 14:6

On Wednesday night, I had youth group, same as usual. Except tonight, Sammy came by my house to pick me up, since my parents had reservations at Rosalini's for their anniversary, and my brother was studying for a big test.

"All ready to go?" Sammy asked as she stood on my doorstep wearing an oversized USC sweatshirt and a pair of torn-up jeans.

"All ready!" I said, slinging my bag over my shoulder as I walked out the door.

"Great. Sorry my car is a little messy. College has a way of cluttering things up."

"It's OK—" I said, as she threw her bookbag into the back-seat, "my brother's the same way."

"Good to know." She grinned, pulling out of the driveway. "You OK with Crowder?"

"Love him," I said as she turned up the radio, which blared an old David Crowder song that I've known since I was a toddler.

"Sweet. You know, I actually saw him at a *Winter Jam* concert last year—along with Lecrae and the Newsboys. It was pretty lit."

"That sounds so cool!" I said, for a moment, wondering what it must've been like since I'd never actually been to a real concert before. "I've always wanted to go to *Winter Jam*, but I've never been able to."

"You should try to make it out when they come here again. It's a great experience, and Pastor Sean has taken the youth group a couple of times."

"Maybe I will—next time they're in town."

"You definitely should! Do you have a favorite band?"

"Probably Switchfoot. I've always loved their music, and my parents are huge fans. So, I've kind of grown up listening to them. How about you?" I asked. "Do you have a favorite band?"

"Probably Thousand Foot Krutch." She grinned. "They were pretty much my life support back in high school. I listened to their music all the time."

"That's cool. I'll have to look them up when I get home."

"For sure." She nodded, taking a sip of her Starbucks drink as we approached a stoplight. "They're really good." She paused. "So, how have you been doing with everything? You know, with the move and getting adjusted to California and all?"

"I've been doing okay." I hesitated, thinking back to my phone call with Ellie the other night. "I still miss Kenya, but I'm doing better. I'm finally starting to make friends here, so that's been nice."

"I'm glad. I know how hard it can be moving to a new city."

"Thanks," I said, pausing for a moment as I thought about what she said. "Did you live somewhere else before too?"

"Minnesota. I grew up there my whole life before my dad got transferred sophomore year. So, I guess even though it's not exactly the same, I could kind of relate to what you were saying about missing Africa. It's hard starting over in a new place like that."

"I had no idea. I guess I just kind of assumed that you lived here all your life. And that you've always gone to Hope Life."

"Not by a long shot." She laughed, shaking her head. "I wasn't even close to God until a couple of years ago. I mean, my parents believed, but I didn't start to make my faith my own until senior year, when my friend Logan invited me to this Christian club that he had after school, on campus."

"Really? I never would've guessed. I mean, you seem so strong in your faith now," I noted, my mind latching onto something she said. "That's interesting that your friend had a Christian club at a public high school. I didn't think you were allowed to do that. You know—with the separation of church and state and all."

"A lot of people don't," she said, "but it's actually fine as long as it's student-led. I mean, a teacher can't go in and just start sharing their faith in their classroom. But students can share their faith at school. Whether in the hallways or an afterschool club, like the one my friend ran."

"That's so cool," I said, the wheels in my mind turning in a million directions as she spoke. "So, how did he get this club started? Was it hard to do, or . . .?"

She shook her head. "Not any harder than any other club. I mean, you have to get it approved by the principal and find an adult faculty member to sponsor you. But other than that, it's pretty easy. Honestly, if it weren't for that club, I doubt I'd be where I am today."

"Wow," I said as she put her car into *park* in front of the church. "That's a really cool testimony."

A Christian after-school club. For some reason, that was something that had never even crossed my mind until now. But suddenly, it sounded like such a cool idea.

Could it really be that easy to start?

Unfortunately, I didn't have long to think about it, because a few minutes later I ran into Atticus and Tanisha, and soon after that, we started service. But as Pastor Sean preached that night, my mind immediately went back to that place.

"Hey everyone, welcome to Ignite," he said after the band played their last song—a fast one by Phil Wickham. "Tonight, we're going to be picking up where we left off last week, talking about fear and how to overcome it as Christians. But first, I would like to open with a Bible verse. So, if you have your Bible or your phone with you, please turn with me to Matthew 28:19-20, where Jesus is talking to His disciples right before He ascends to be with the Father. Are you all there?"

I heard a couple of 'yeahs' and 'uh-huhs', signaling that they were there.

"Great," he said as some of the leaders in the back put the verses up on the screen. "It says, 'Therefore go and make disciples of all nations, baptizing them in the name of the Father and of the Son and of the Holy Spirit, and teaching them to obey everything I have commanded you. And surely I am with you always, to the very end of the age.'

"In this passage, Jesus tells His disciples to go out into the world and make more disciples, through spreading the Good

News of the Gospel to every nation, tribe, and tongue. The same commission that we, as modern-day Christians, have today.

"Over the past couple of weeks, we have been talking about fear. And if we're honest, a lot of us struggle with fear when we're sharing our faith. Fear about how that person will react. Fear about how they'll receive it. Fear about how they might perceive *us*." He paused, giving his words a chance to sink in.

"I'm not saying this from a place of judgment because if I'm honest, I battle this same fear. But if you let it control you, this fear could be the very thing keeping that friend or that classmate from knowing the love and hope that comes from having a personal relationship with Jesus." He paused. "If you still have your Bible or your phone out, please turn with me to Matthew 10:28-33. 'Don't be afraid of those who want to kill your body; they cannot touch your soul. Fear only God, who can destroy both soul and body in hell. What is the price of two sparrows—one copper coin? But not a single sparrow can fall to the ground without your Father knowing it. And the very hairs on your head are all numbered.

"So don't be afraid; you are more valuable to God than a whole flock of sparrows. 'Everyone who acknowledges me publicly here on earth, I will also acknowledge before my Father in heaven. But everyone who denies me here on earth, I will also deny before my Father in heaven . . .' "

Pastor Sean continued talking about overcoming fear when sharing Jesus with our family and friends, closing with an old song by Everfound called "God of the Impossible", before walking back up on stage to give a few last words.

"Tonight, we talked a lot about sharing Jesus at your school and with your friends. But if you don't know Jesus, I would like to give you this time to make that personal decision for yourself. To accept the grace and love that Christ freely offers. If that's you tonight, please come to the front."

A couple of people came forward as the rest of us clapped.

"Now, if you're already a Christian, and you want to start stepping out in your faith to be bold for Christ, whatever that looks like for you, please come forward. There will be leaders at the altar ready to pray with you."

At that moment, I thought about my conversation with Sammy and everything that had happened over the past couple of weeks. With meeting Atticus' friends. With him telling me he didn't know what they believed. With seeing Nathan getting bullied by Kent the other day at school.

I walked up to Sammy, who was already standing at the front.

"Hey," she said as I went to go pray with her, "is everything okay?"

"It's kind of a long story." I hesitated, a million thoughts still running through my mind. "But there's something I think God is calling me to do . . ."

Chapter Ten

Do not be anxious about anything, but in every situation, by prayer and petition, with thanksgiving, present your requests to God.
- Philipians 4:6

*T*he next couple of days were a whirlwind for me. After Wednesday night, I went online and googled "How to start an after-school club in high school."

To my surprise, I found a lot more information than I expected, and the whole rest of the week I started making plans for the club—putting in my request to Principal Wembley and asking Atticus if he wanted to co-lead with me.

Now, the only thing left to do was wait and count down the seconds until Principal Wembley called back to give me an answer about whether or not I could host my club after school.

"Are you okay, Katie?" my mom asked as she set the table for dinner, anxiously awaiting Jackson's dinner guest. "You seem quiet."

"Yeah, I'm just thinking," I said as I stared at an old-fashioned clock on the wall as it ticked off the time.

One . . . two . . . three . . . One . . . two . . . three . . .

"About?" she asked gently, the way she always does when something is on my mind.

"The club I want to start. Whether or not it will happen. Whether or not Principal Wembley will say yes. Whether or not anyone will even show up if we do have it."

"Katie, what did I always use to tell you? When you'd get yourself worked up about something back home?"

"Give it to God?"

She nodded. "You can't keep worrying about this, Katie. If it's meant to happen, it will. And if not, then God has a better plan. You have to trust that He knows best."

"I know . . . It's just hard, because I *really* want to have this club. And I already told all my friends about it and Atticus—"

"I see," she said, a smile creeping across her lips.

"What? What is it?"

"Nothing. It's just this boy, Atticus. You've mentioned him an awful lot since we've moved here."

"Wait, what?" I exclaimed, shocked at what my mom was implying. "No! It's not like that. Atticus and I are just friends. That's all."

"OK," she said, checking the stove for dinner.

"Seriously, Mom. We're neighbors. I see him every day at school. He's one of the only close friends I've got here besides Tanisha, and she's his sister."

"OK," she said again, still looking as though she didn't believe me.

"I'm serious! It's nothing. It's just—"

Before I could finish my sentence, the doorbell rang, interrupting my perfectly well-thought-out response as to why I did *not* have a crush on Atticus Bentley.

But that would have to be a conversation for another time.

"Sydney," my mom said, opening the door for a tall, blond girl with a light California tan, a red sweater, and a pair of cutoff shorts. "It's so nice to finally meet you! I've heard so much about you."

"Nice to meet you too," she said, shifting in place as she played with a loose strand of hair. "Is Jackson here?"

"He's in his room getting ready. He should be down in a minute."

"Cool." She smiled as I studied her, trying to figure out if I'd seen her before. In a school of over four thousand people, the answer was a big fat *no*.

"Hi, I'm Katie," I said, sticking out my hand in hopes of making a good first impression. "Jackson's sister. Nice to meet you."

"You too," she said as I studied her once again.

Jackson has liked girls in the past. He even had a short relationship with a girl whose family worked with the mission back in Kenya. But Sydney seemed different than other girls that he's mentioned before. She seemed older somehow.

More sophisticated.

"Hey," Jackson said, nearly tripping on his way down the stairs, "Sydney—I didn't know you were here."

"She just got here," Mom said, studying the girl and then turning her attention back toward Jackson. "We've just been talking and waiting for you."

"Great. So, I guess you guys have met?"

"Yes, we have." She nodded, with something in her eyes that I couldn't quite read. "Dinner should be ready in a few minutes. Why don't you kids wash up?"

"OK, cool. Sounds great," my brother said, still out of breath.

Jackson, Sydney, and I went to go wash our hands and then walked back into the kitchen, where my parents were already waiting.

"You must be Sydney," my dad said, shaking the girl's hand as she walked into the room. "Jackson's friend."

"Yes, sir," she said with a quick nod.

"Nice to meet you. I'm Jackson's father. Do you like spaghetti?"

"I guess."

"Good. Well, you're in luck then, because my wife made a fresh pot with extra meatballs. And for dessert, we'll have our specialty. Apple pie—freshly baked."

"Cool. Sounds great," she said, taking a seat at the table next to Jackson.

"Great. Jackson? Would you like to say grace for us tonight?"

"Uh, sure. No problem," he said, looking caught off guard. "Um, Dear Lord, we thank you for this food. For family. And for every good thing. Amen."

"Great," my dad said with a quick smile. "Thank you, Jackson."

"No problem."

"So, Sydney," my mom began as she twirled a strand of pasta onto her fork. "What are you studying in school right now?"

"I don't know. The usual. Reading . . . math . . . science . . ."

"What's your favorite subject?"

"I don't know. Science, I guess?"

"That's awesome," Dad said. "So, how did you guys meet?"

"We have a class together," she said, glancing over toward Jackson and then, toward my dad. "Third-period Calculus."

"Well, that's nice," Mom noted. "Do you have any hobbies? Or after-school activities?"

"Just softball."

"Oh, that's wonderful. So, you're an athlete?"

"Mom," Jackson said, shooting her a look. "This isn't twenty questions, okay?"

This time, my dad shot Jackson a look. One that said, 'I'm not going to embarrass you, but please don't use that tone again.'

"So, Katie," Mom said after a long pause. "You've been quiet tonight. How are things going for you with school this year?"

"Pretty good," I said. "I have a big geometry test that I need to study for, but other than that, my teachers haven't been too bad. I'm sure it will get heavier as the year goes on, though."

"Well, I'm sure you'll be able to handle it just fine," Dad said, turning in my direction. "Just do your best. That's all you can do."

"Thanks, Dad. I will."

"So, Mr. Carter, you must know a lot about psychology," Sydney said, changing the subject as she wrapped a wad of spaghetti around her fork. "I find that fascinating. I'm thinking about going into that field myself."

"Really?" he asked. "That's wonderful. But why do you think I must know a lot about that?"

"Well, because Jackson told me you're a counselor. That you help people for a living. I find that totally commendable, person-ally. We need more good counselors in this city."

"Well, thank you, Sydney. Counseling is definitely part of what I do. But technically, I'm a pastor at Hope Life Church."

"Oh, a pastor," Sydney said, looking caught off guard as she glanced over at Jackson. "I had no idea. How . . . *interesting*."

"It can be." He smiled, clearly trying to hide the tension he was feeling. "Sometimes. But it's also very fulfilling."

"That's wonderful." She smiled, even though it seemed forced. "I've always believed that's how life is supposed to be lived. Find something that fulfills you and go after it."

My parents exchanged glances, and suddenly, I was the one feeling awkward. Why would my brother try to hide the fact that our dad is a pastor? And why would Sydney seem so uncomfortable with the fact that he is?

"So, I was talking to Tanisha the other day at school," I piped up, doing my best to change the subject and lift the awkward air that seemed to float like a rain cloud over the dinner table, "and she told me that they're doing *The Lion King* for the school play this year. I guess they're going to start working on the set next Friday. They're doing musical numbers for it and everything."

"That's wonderful," my mom said, looking relieved about the change of subjects. "I've always loved that movie."

"Me too," Sydney agreed, her shoulders looking noticeably less tense.

Thankfully, the conversation continued on a lighter note as the night went on. And about halfway through dinner, I heard the phone ring.

"Mom, Dad? Can I take it just this once? It might be Principal Wembley—calling about the Agape Club."

"The Agape Club?" Sydney asked, sounding confused. "What's that?"

"Just a club my sister wants to start. Nothing important," Jackson mumbled as he took another bite of his dinner.

"Jackson," Mom warned. "Yes, you can take the call, Katie."

"Sorry," he apologized under his breath as I pressed *accept* on my phone.

"Hello?" I said, as my heart pounded from the inside of my chest.

"Hello? Is this Katie Carter?" I heard a deep female voice say on the other end of the line.

"Yes, this is her." I nodded, even though she couldn't see me. "Is this Principal Wembley?"

"Yes, it is. I am calling about the club you wanted to start at Winter Oaks High School. A Christian club called the Agape Club?"

"Yes, that's the one."

"Wonderful. I called to inform you that your club has been approved for the fall semester. You will be starting this Thursday, along with the other clubs at Winter Oaks High School. And your English teacher, Mrs. Reams, has agreed to be your sponsor."

"Really?" I practically shouted into the phone—catching myself as I saw my family start to stare. "I can do it?"

"Yes, you can. And I expect you and Atticus to be in the Student Center this Thursday after school to start your first meeting."

"We'll be there! I promise! Thank you, Principal Wembley, thank you!"

"You're welcome. Have a nice weekend, Katie. Goodbye."

"You too! Bye, Principal Wembley!"

"So?" my mom asked as I hung up the phone. "What did she say?"

"She said yes!" I said, excitement ringing through my voice and a million thoughts racing through my mind. "She actually said yes!"

Chapter Eleven

For we are God's handiwork, created in Christ Jesus to do good works, which God prepared in advance for us to do.

- Ephesians 2:10

Over the course of that week, I did everything I could to prepare for the first meeting of the Agape Club. After buying some large sheets of paper, paint, stencils, and a variety of do-dads at the nearest Hobby Lobby, I had my friends over to help me decorate posters to advertise for the club.

And as I sat at the kitchen table with Tanisha, Jenny, Atticus, and Nathan, I couldn't have felt more ready.

"Could you pass me the glue?" Jenny asked as she worked on a bright purple poster with the word 'Agape' plastered boldly across the front.

"Sure," I said, handing her the glue stick as I worked on my own poster—an acrostic, with various crosses, hearts, and flowers scattered eclectically around the sides.

"Thanks, Katie," she said as she continued with her painting.

"This was such a cool idea you had—" Atticus noted, looking up from his sheet of construction paper, "making these posters and all. It will definitely grab people's attention."

"Definitely!" Tanisha agreed. "Although, I still think we should've gone with some sort of design software. These posters look pretty homemade."

"I don't know," Atticus said. "I kind of like it. It adds a personable touch."

"Personable." Tanisha grinned. "And just a little tacky."

"Just do your best." I laughed. "I'm sure they'll be fine."

"Hey, Nathan—are you still alive over there?" Atticus asked, changing the subject as he looked over at his friend. "You've been working on that poster for over an hour now."

"I'm good—just putting the finishing touches on it, that's all."

"Are you working on a poster or a Monet?" Tanisha asked with a slow grin.

"Hey, these aren't just posters—they're art. And if I'm going to put my name to this, I want it to be perfect."

"I'm sure it will be amazing," Atticus assured him, turning his attention toward me. "Nathan is sort of the artist of our group. He can draw anime sketches like nobody's business—he even won an art competition last year at school."

"That's so cool," I said, intrigued and for a moment, a little jealous—since I could barely draw believable stick figures. "I'd love to see your work sometime. I mean, if you don't mind showing it to me."

"Not at all." He shook his head. "Maybe I can bring my sketchbook to school sometime. Just as long as I can hide it from Kent and his friends. Avoid giving them something else to beat me up for."

"Are he and his friends still giving you a lot of trouble?" Tanisha asked, concern clear in her voice.

"A little." He nodded. "I'm trying to deal with them the best I can and not let them bother me."

"I'm really sorry," I said, thinking back to that day in the hallway when I caught Kent bullying him. "I wish there was something more I could do."

"It's OK. I try not to think about it when I don't have to." He paused, looking eager to change the subject. "On a more positive note, I think I'm finally finished with my poster. What do you think?" he asked, holding it up for us all to see.

To my surprise, the poster looked almost professional. It had a blackish blue background, and various colors flew out from every side. And the words 'Agape Club' sat promptly in the center.

"That looks amazing," I said. "I can't believe you painted that!"

"Thanks." He smiled, his voice modest, even though I could tell he was proud of his creation. "It took me a while, but it was worth it."

"Absolutely," Atticus agreed. "It looks great!"

"For sure." Tanisha nodded, quiet for a moment before turning toward me. "Hey, where did you get the name 'agape' from anyway? I mean, it's not exactly a word you hear every day."

"It's a Greek word that my parents taught me when I was living in Kenya," I explained. "It means unconditional love and acceptance. I guess I chose that name because at the end of the day, that's what we're all looking for, and that's what God offers through Jesus' death and resurrection. Love and acceptance."

"That's so cool!" Jenny exclaimed. "I love the meaning behind it."

"Thanks." I smiled, proud of myself for coming up with the name all on my own.

"Agape—" Atticus said, looking deep in thought, "I feel like I read about that a while back, in a C.S. Lewis book."

"The Four Loves?" I asked as he nodded.

"Yeah, that's the one! It was really good. I remember I loved the other book he wrote too—*Mere Christianity.*"

"You read that?"

"It's one of my favorites."

"Mine too!"

"Wait, C.S. Lewis," Nathan began, as if the name rang a bell. "Wasn't he the guy who wrote *Narnia?* That kid's book about the lion and the magical closet?"

"Yeah, that's the one." I nodded. "He wrote kind of an eclectic mix. Some fiction, like *The Chronicles of Narnia,* and some nonfiction, like *Mere Christianity* and *The Four Loves.*"

"That's cool. I remember watching that movie when I was a kid."

"I remember that!" I grinned. "That movie was practically my childhood."

"Same," he said, with a smile of his own.

"I love Lewis as much as the next person—" Tanisha said, speaking up, "but Atticus and I need to head back soon. My family is eating dinner at 6:00, and I don't want to be late."

"Yeah, Tanisha's right," Atticus said. "We'd better get going. But we'll see you tomorrow at school?"

"Absolutely." I nodded. "See you then."

"I'd better get going too," Jenny said, looking down at her phone. "My mom should be here any minute to pick me up."

"Same," Nathan added. "Can we help you clean up before we go?"

"No, it's OK. It's not that much to clean up. Thanks for all your help, though. I really appreciate it."

With that, we all said goodbye, and my friends headed out, leaving me to flip through about ten homemade posters. And after I stored them in a safe corner in my room upstairs, I pulled out H.D.'s diary to read another entry before dinner.

One that seemed totally relatable to me right now.

Dear Diary,

I'm finally starting to make friends on campus and figure out where I belong. The other day, I had a conversation with one of the girls in my English class, and as it turns out, we have a lot in common. We both like the same TV shows, we both eat the icing out of Oreo cookies first, and we both have a shared affinity for Sixpence None the Richer. Perhaps most importantly, we've both been feeling a little lost over the last couple of months as college freshmen away from home for the first time.

After I met her, she introduced me to some of her friends.

One who loves folk music and strikes me as the Bohemian type. Another, who talks at the rate that most people breathe. And another who I'm sure could make it as president someday. It's a unique little group. But in some weird way, it feels like home.

Until Next Time,
H.D.

Chapter Twelve

The week of the club I felt excitement rising in the depths of my soul, convinced that nothing in the world could stand between me and the start of my club; that everything was falling into place exactly as I had hoped. That is, until Thursday afternoon, when I saw something that caused me to stop dead in my tracks. The posters that my friends and I had worked so hard on were completely destroyed.

"What happened?" I gasped as I walked down the halls after my last class, pulling one of my posters off the wall in shock. To my horror, someone had scratched out every letter in the word *'Agape'* except for the *'A'* and written a much crueler, more obscene word in its place. And surrounding the word, they had drawn crude pictures and written out even meaner words and phrases.

Who would do something like this?

"Looks like someone defaced our posters," Atticus said, staring at the graffitied poster.

"Are they all like this?" I asked, picking up my pace as I walked, to my dismay, finding that every poster was worse than the last.

"Oh my gosh." I clasped my hand over my mouth as I took a seat on a nearby bench. "I think I'm going to be sick!"

"They're just posters," Atticus reminded me, trying to calm me down as I felt my heart beat against the wall of my chest. "They're not our club. This doesn't change anything."

"I don't think I can do this."

"Yes, you can. Don't let some idiot steal away everything you've worked so hard for."

"How am I supposed to run a club when I feel like this? Like my stomach's completely tied in knots?"

"You can do it. I know you can. And I'll be there to help you. Besides, we're not doing this alone, remember?"

I nodded, trying to pull myself together—wiping my eyes to avoid looking like a gigantic baby right there in the middle of school. I was *not* going to start crying right here in front of everyone. "You're right," I finally said, turning toward him. "Let's do this."

"That's the spirit. Do you have the notes for this week's lesson?"

"Yeah," I said as the two of us set up the tables and chairs. "In my backpack."

"Cool," he said, after a moment. "Do you want to pray before we start?"

"Yeah. But can you lead it? I'm still feeling a little shook."

"Sure," he agreed, as we sat down on two of the chairs after we had finished setting up. "Dear Lord, we come to you today in prayer over this club. We pray that hearts will be softened, and lives will be changed. We pray that you would push back the darkness and shine your light in this club today. God, we're just your vessels. We can't do this without you. And we ask that you meet us in this moment. We pray for all these things in the name of Jesus, amen."

"Amen," I echoed, feeling caught off guard as my eyes met his. "That was good. The prayer, I mean. It was powerful . . . and um, stuff."

"Thanks," he said as my mom's words came flooding back to me. *No, it was nothing.* I was just having a weird day, that's all. I didn't have a crush on Atticus, even if he did seem ten times more attractive right about then.

"So, are you ready?"

"I think so," I said after a moment of silence. "At least, I hope so." As if on cue, someone walked through the door. A girl who was about sixteen or seventeen, with a blue streak in her hair, a red and black shirt, and 90s-style Doc Martens.

"Hey," she said, glancing around the room. "This is the Agape Club, right?"

"Yes, this is it." I nodded. "I'm Katie, and this is my friend, Atticus. We're the leaders of this club."

"Nice to meet you."

"You too. What's your name?"

"Liv," she said. "Short for Olivia, but no one calls me that."

"Nice to meet you, Liv. You're actually the first one here, so we can just hang out until the rest of the group gets here."

"Cool."

"Do you live around here?" Atticus asked.

"Yeah. Right off Wilmington Drive."

"Oh, really?" I asked, the name ringing a bell. "My church is right off that street—Hope Life. Do you go there?"

"No, I don't go to church," she said, once again looking uncomfortable. "Or at least, I haven't in a while. I guess you could say that I'm searching."

"Well, this is a great place to find some answers," I said, as she smiled, seeming a little less nervous than before. And soon enough, various other students started streaming in, along with Mrs. Reams. First, mostly people we knew, and then a couple of new faces—some that I didn't even recognize.

"OK, everyone," I said, my heart racing as the gravity of the situation set in. "It's 3:30, and if everyone is here, we can get started. My name is Katie, this is my friend Atticus, and this—" I motioned to Mrs. Reams, who sat on the other side of me, "is Mrs. Reams, who has agreed to be the official sponsor for this club. Does anyone have any questions before we get started?"

Almost immediately, a spiky-haired boy raised his hand.

"Yes?" Atticus motioned for the boy to speak.

"You said on the flyers that this is a Christian club, right?"

"Yes, that's correct." I nodded, relieved that our first question was an easy one.

"What kind of Christian club is it? I mean, is it Baptist, Methodist, Presbyterian—"

"It's just Christian," I said, stopping him before he could continue. "We believe in Jesus and that he died and rose again to take our place. I'm sure we all come from a variety of different backgrounds," I added, my eyes darting around the room, "but in this club, we'll be focusing on the basics."

Thankfully, that answer seemed satisfying to spiky-haired boy.

"What if you don't believe in anything?" a girl dressed in all black asked, raising an eyebrow in my direction.

"Well, then you're still welcome here," Atticus said, not looking the least bit shaken. "Because all of us have been in that place at some point. And this is a safe space for everyone, regardless of their background or beliefs. Any other questions? OK, great. Katie, would you like to take it from here?"

"Um, sure. Before we get started, I was thinking we could go around the room and introduce ourselves. Is there anyone who would like to go first?"

To my surprise, Nathan was the first to raise his hand.

"Great, thanks Nathan." I smiled.

"OK, well, my name is Nathan—as you've probably already guessed. I'm fifteen and a sophomore. And in my spare time, I like drawing and reading comic books—*Marvel Comics* are my personal favorites."

"Great, thanks Nathan," I said, glancing around the room. "Who's next?"

With that, we continued down the line as people introduced themselves—some taking longer than others until finally, everyone had shared and gotten food from the snack table.

Meaning just one thing. It was time to begin.

"OK, everyone," I said, thinking about the material that Atticus and I had put together the other day and racking my brain to remember the points that I wanted to bring up in our meeting. "As you all already know, this is a Christian club, meaning that most of our discussions are going to be focused on the person of

Jesus. Most of you are probably already familiar with the concept of Jesus, but in this group, we're going to be learning about the character of Jesus. So, the first thing that I want to ask is, who do you think Jesus is?"

"A nice person," one guy suggested. "I mean, he always told people to do good stuff, right? Help the poor. That kind of thing."

"For sure." I nodded. "Does anyone else have anything they'd like to add?"

This time, an African American girl who looked close to my age raised her hand. "The Son of God," she said confidently. "He died to save us from our sins and from being in bondage to the Law."

"Absolutely." I smiled. "Keisha, right?"

"Yeah, Keisha."

"But wait—" the first guy interjected, "what do you mean, freedom from the law? I mean, God wants us to be law-abiding citizens, right? I doubt He'd be cool with people running around killing people and acting crazy."

"Actually, I think Keisha was referring to the Mosaic Law," Atticus said. "Back a long time ago, people had to follow a long list of rules to be right with God. The ones most of us are familiar with are the Ten Commandments, but there were actually 613 laws that they had to follow. But when Jesus came, things changed. It became about a relationship with Him, instead of just a long list of rules. Does that make sense?"

"I guess," Liv said. "But like, how do you have a relationship with Him? I mean, you can't see Him. Definitely can't touch Him. So how do you have a relationship with Him?"

"That's a good question," I said, thinking about her comment for a moment. "I asked my parents the same question a while back, and they told me that it's kind of like making a phone call. You can't see the person on the other line, and you can't touch them, but you know they're there—just as much as you are."

"You also get to know a person by learning more about them, right?" Atticus added. "I mean, the more I learn about Katie, the more I get to know her. And you can learn more about God by reading His words. That's why we have the Bible—so we can learn more about God."

"But wait—wasn't the Bible written like a long time ago?" a guy with a beanie cap, long hair, and hipster glasses asked. "How do we know that we have the real thing? That stuff didn't get lost in translation down the line?"

"That's a great question," I said, thinking back to something that I read in a devotional a couple of years ago. "Believe it or not, there's actually a lot of evidence that shows the Bible is still true to the original copy. You see, back when people wrote the earliest copies of the Bible, they had to copy it down letter by letter. If they made a mistake, they had to start over. And there are over five thousand copies of the New Testament in the original Greek, as well as a bunch of other translations in our language today. I believe that all these things show us that the Bible is trustworthy, even though it was written a long time ago. Does that answer your question?"

The hipster boy nodded, and from there, we moved on with the discussion, back to Jesus and his character. And after it was over, people lingered for a while until 4:30 hit, signaling that it was time to go home.

"I think it went pretty well for the first day," Atticus said as the two of us cleaned up, along with Tanisha and Mrs. Reams. "I mean, the discussion went well, and everyone seemed to have a good time."

"Yeah," I said as I stacked the chairs back in the corner where they belonged. "It's crazy." I paused as I replayed the events of the day in my mind. "There were a lot more people that were searching than I thought there'd be."

"Well, if you ask me, that's all the better," Mrs. Reams said as we headed out of the Student Center. "Those are the people who need this club the most."

"True. Thanks again for agreeing to sponsor the club. I really appreciate it."

"It's no problem, Katie. I'm happy to help. This school could use a little more light. And you two are the perfect people to run a club like this."

"Well, thank you. It's a lot harder than I thought it'd be."

"Yes." Mrs. Reams smiled. "But God will never give you more than you can handle. Maybe more than you could handle on your own, but never more than you could handle through Him."

"You're right." I nodded, her words reminding me of something my mom told me a while back when we were talking about something similar. "I'd better get going, but I'll see you next week. And I'll see you guys tomorrow?" I asked, turning toward my friends.

"Absolutely. See you then, Katie," Atticus said.

"Bye, Katie," Tanisha added as I made my way out to the parking lot, where my mom was sitting in her car, waiting for me.

"Hey," she said as I got into the car and buckled my seatbelt. "How'd it go?"

"Pretty good. We had a lot of people show up today. Some who had been Christians for a long time. And some who weren't sure what they believed at all. It's crazy." I paused as she pulled out of the parking lot. "There were some points when I felt like the least qualified person to lead this club."

"Well, if you ask me, that makes you the most qualified."

"Really? Why do you say that?"

"Because you're humble, and God can usually work the most when we feel the least qualified. But it gets easier, and you get stronger." She paused. "I have a feeling you and Atticus planted some seeds today."

"You think so?"

"Absolutely. Just keep being you and loving them like Jesus. When they see your actions, they'll be a whole lot more willing to listen to your words. As Pastor Kip would say—"

"Preach with your life?" I said, remembering his old favorite saying. "And love like Jesus?"

"Exactly!" She smiled.

"Thanks, Mom," I said, her words ringing over and over again in my mind the whole way home. *Preach with your life.*

I may still feel ill-equipped to lead this club, but I knew I could love like Jesus.

»→ ←«

*T*hat night, as I washed my hair and got ready for bed, I felt good about my day—even though it got off to a rocky start. But as I made my way downstairs to pour myself a glass of water, I heard something that caused me to stop dead in my tracks.

"Jackson," I heard my dad say. "There are some things your mom and I want to talk to you about."

"Um, sure. What is it?" he asked, sounding uncomfortable. Even though I knew it was wrong to eavesdrop, my curiosity got the best of me.

"Jackson, lately you haven't seemed like yourself, and we want to know what's going on with you. If something's bothering you, you can come to your mom and me. You know that, don't you?"

"Yeah, sure. Is that all?"

"Actually no, it isn't," Mom said, her voice sterner than usual. "The way you acted the other night when we had Sydney over was very disrespectful toward your father and me. Now, I understand that you want to impress this girl, but there's a way of doing that without being disrespectful. Do you understand?"

"Yes, Mom. I'm sorry."

"Jackson, it's not just that," Dad said, his voice sounding strained. "Lately, we've practically had to drag you to church and youth group. Back in Kenya, you were so on fire in your faith. But here, you seem completely apathetic toward everything that has to do with God. Your mom and I just want to know—is there a reason for that?"

To my surprise, Jackson didn't say anything.

"Jackson?" my mom asked, sounding worried.

"The truth? I guess lately I haven't quite been feeling the same way about my faith as I used to."

"Do you still believe in God?" Dad asked, trying to keep his voice steady and rational.

"I don't know. I mean, my whole life, I've been the missionary kid. But now, I'm seventeen . . . I'm getting ready to go to college soon. I guess I'm trying to figure out what I believe for myself."

"Is this about Sydney?" he asked, as I sensed a hint of anger in his voice, even though he never gets mad at anyone.

"No, it's not about Sydney," Jackson said, frustrated. "And since I know what you're going to ask next, no, we're not sleeping together."

"Are you thinking about sleeping together?"

"I guess it's crossed my mind," Jackson confessed after a long moment. "Would you guys be really disappointed in me if we did?"

"We'd be upset," Mom said. "Because we don't think it's the right thing for either of you. And we hope you make the right decision about this, but no matter what you do, your father and I will always love you."

"So, is that it?" Jackson asked, strangely callous. "Is that all you wanted to say?"

"Yes, son. That's it," Dad said as the conversation ended, with a million thoughts running through my mind. Jackson was questioning his faith? And he was thinking about sleeping with Sydney?

Suddenly, I thought back on the past couple of weeks, and how my brother has been acting at church and youth group, and his conversation with Mom and Dad at dinner—when he asked to go to that guy's house. Had my brother been struggling this whole time? And had I been too caught up in my own life to even notice? Just like this morning, I felt a sick feeling in the pit of my stomach. Except this time, it had nothing to do with the posters.

Chapter Thirteen

That Monday, as I helped Tanisha with the set for *The Lion King*, I felt totally distracted by the whole situation with my brother. I had noticed that something seemed off with him for a while, but I couldn't figure out what it was. But now that I knew, it seemed to be all I could think about.

"Katie?" Nathan said, snapping me out of my thoughts.

"*Huh?*"

"I was just asking if I could borrow the green paint."

"Oh, sure," I said, embarrassed for being so checked out. "Here's the paint."

"Thanks." He paused. "A little distracted today, huh?"

"A little," I confessed as I went back to painting my prop.

"Want to talk about it?"

"No, I'm fine. I just have a lot on my mind, that's all." I paused, determined to change the subject before Nathan could ask any more questions. "You're doing a great job on that. It looks exactly like one of the hyenas from the movie."

"Thanks." He smiled, pleased with his work.

"You're welcome. Where did you learn to paint like that?"

"Taught myself. Creative stuff has always come easy to me, I guess. It's a good outlet for dealing with stress."

"Yeah, if you're good at it. My art is mediocre at best."

"It just takes practice. Besides, you're good at other things. Like finding mystery diaries and running Christian clubs at high schools."

"Thanks." I laughed. "This is my first one, actually, but I'm glad you like it." I figured now would be as good a time as any to ask a question that I'd been wondering about but haven't had the guts to ask until now. "So, how long have you been a Christian? I mean, did you grow up that way or . . .?"

"It's complicated," he said, cutting me off before I could finish, something crossing his eyes that I didn't recognize.

"I'm sorry. I didn't mean to pry."

"No, it's fine." He paused, quiet for a moment as if debating whether to continue. "My parents were pretty hardcore Christians when I was younger. We went to church every Sunday and said grace every night before dinner. God was sort of my parents' 'thing', I guess—that and football. We always missed church for Super Bowl Sundays."

"So, your parents are sports fans?" I asked, getting the feeling that was important, even though I wasn't sure why.

He nodded. "I have two older brothers—Jake and Eddie. Jake's twenty-six and Eddie's twenty-two. Both of them were football players in high school. My dad was too when he was younger."

"And you?" I asked, even though I already knew the answer.

"Not so much." He grinned. "I still remember the look on his face when he found out I was pretty much horrid at all sports. At that point, I could have cured cancer or won the Nobel Peace Prize. Wouldn't matter if I couldn't throw a football."

"I'm really sorry," I said, suddenly, thinking about something else that he said. Something that didn't quite add up. "You said your parents used to be Christians. Are they still now?"

"The truth? I don't know. They got divorced two years ago, and ever since then, they hardly bring it up. Honestly, I rarely ever see my dad anymore. He's pretty much gone incognito since the divorce. But I guess that's just how things are sometimes." He shrugged, a noticeable pain in his eyes. "Nothing lasts forever, right?"

"I guess it all depends on how you look at things. I've always believed some things can last forever." I paused. "And just because your dad is like that doesn't mean God is."

"I hope you're right." He hesitated, thinking about his next words. "I guess that's part of what sparked my interest in your club—you know, trying to figure out who God is . . . That and the fact that you seem like a very different kind of Christian than the ones I've met in the past." He paused again. "I guess most of the time I'm not so sure who God is. He sort of just seems a million miles away."

"Tell you what," I said, sitting up straight as I put my brush back in the paint can. "Why don't you come to church with me on Sunday? See what it's like for yourself. If you don't like it, there's no pressure to come back."

"I don't know . . . I haven't gone to church in a really long time."

"Come on. We'll go together—it'll be fun. Just think of it as a new adventure."

"I'll give it one week. But that's all."

"Cool." I smiled.

From there, the two of us continued painting and talking about lighter topics, like school or Netflix or how we should design the set for the play. But at that moment, I felt a little better than before, certain that Nathan and I had just become closer friends. And with everything going on right now, good friends were exactly what I needed.

»→ ←«

"Are you *sure* your parents won't mind if I sit with you guys?" Nathan asked as the two of us walked through the doors of Hope Life Church. "I know church is usually kind of a family thing, and I don't want to intrude."

"Not at all," I assured him. "My dad was thrilled when I told him you were coming."

"OK . . . As long as you're sure."

With that, he took a seat next to me as the band went up on stage—launching into a well-known song by Cory Asbury. I clapped along to the old familiar tune as Nathan did his best to follow along.

I had told my dad a couple of days ago about Nathan's situation, and he promised to pray that God would reach him during service. And now, as I took a seat after the close of the last song, I couldn't help but pray for the same thing.

"Good morning, everyone." Dad smiled as he went up to the pulpit. "Before we get started, could we give it up for our first-time guests here with us today? If you're a first-time guest, let me just say that we love you, we welcome you, and we're glad that you're here. And if you have any questions, I'd be happy to meet with you in the lobby after service.

"We also have free coffee mugs for everyone who's here visiting, so be sure to pick one up on your way out. That being said, I want to talk about the focal point of our message today, which is the grace, love, and mercy of our God." He stopped for a moment in a dramatic pause, as he sometimes does during his sermons. "Jesus died for the world. He died for you, for your neighbor, for your friends, and yes—even for your boss who has you stay late working crazy hours.

"He gave his life so that we can have life. He exchanged His comfort for our freedom. He died for each one of us because this is the kind of radical love that our God has for each one of us. He has grace for us when we fall short. He has grace for *me* when I fall short.

"We live in a world that is starving for answers. That thinks hope is found in the next cause or a politician or smartphone. But none of those things, even if they're good, carry the one thing that our world is so desperately longing for. And that's *love*. The kind of love that doesn't come with a price tag. The kind of love that is one-hundred-percent free.

"As Christians, we know this kind of love, up close and personal. But so often, it's easy to lose track of it, and get so wrapped up in our responsibilities and schedules that we forget that we're called to look like love. The kind of love that can look at someone who hurt us and say, 'I forgive you.' That can look at our neighbor, who is so different from us, and remember that they bleed, hurt, and feel pain, just like we do. That can look at people who aren't always lovable and love them anyway. That is the way that Jesus loves, and the way that we're called to love—the way that *I'm* called to love."

"He's good," Nathan whispered, sounding surprised.

"I know," I whispered back, smiling as he continued with his message.

At the end of the message, my dad closed in prayer and asked the band to come up and play one more song. An old one called "Fierce" by Jesus Culture. And as I looked over at Nathan, I could've sworn that I saw him getting a little choked up.

"So," I asked, as the two of us headed into the lobby after church was dismissed, "what did you think?"

"It was good," he said, looking deep in thought. "It's weird. I've never heard anyone talk about God like that before. Well, outside of your club, that is." He paused. "Does your dad always talk about God like that?"

"Like what?"

"You know. A God who's loving and present, not distant and mad at the world."

"Yeah, my dad has always talked about God that way—for as long as I can remember. That's just who he believes He is. And that's who I believe He is too."

"My old church was so different than yours." He shook his head. "I guess it's just hard to wrap my head around, that's all."

"What was your old church like?"

"Cold. Sterile—like God's completely unreachable unless you do something wrong. Then He's just angry and full of wrath."

"Well, that's never how I've seen God," I said, thinking back on my own upbringing, which suddenly seemed so different than Nathan's. "You know, when I was little, there was this CD that my parents always used to play for me and my brother. And there was this one song that always played at the beginning of the tape. It went something like, "God's a big God . . . He's a big, big God . . . and He's watching over you. And there were dances and hand motions and everything."

"Sounds cheesy." He laughed.

"It *was*." I smiled. "But early on, that's how I started to see God. Like a parent or a friend."

"Right . . ." Nathan said, his tone changing, "God the *Father*."

I felt my stomach drop to the floor as I remembered everything Nathan had told me at school the other day. "Yeah, but God's a perfect Father. Which means He's way better than any earthly father could ever be."

He was silent, as if allowing my words a chance to sink in, when one of the college leaders from Ignite—Micah, came over to where we were sitting.

"Hey," Micah said, shoving his hands in his pockets. "Did you enjoy the service today?"

"Yeah." Nathan nodded. "It was really good."

"Was this your first time here? I don't think I've ever seen you around before."

"Yeah, first time. I came with her."

"That's awesome. My name's Micah," he said, shaking Nathan's hand to introduce himself.

"Nathan. Nice to meet you."

"You too. You know, we have a youth service here on Wednesday nights if you ever want to try it. Pastor Sean heads it up, and it's pretty fun. If you ever want to come, I'll hang with you. I know how awkward it can be going to a new place for the first time."

"Thanks," he said, seeming surprised by how nice Micah was.

"No problem. I'd better go find my family, but it was nice meeting you—and seeing you too, Katie."

"You too," Nathan replied.

"Later, Micah," I said as he walked away.

"Wow," Nathan said once Micah was out of earshot. "He seemed pretty nice."

"Most people here are," I said, suddenly realizing how different this must have seemed compared to his experience at Winter Oaks High School. "And Micah's cool. He's like everyone's big brother."

"It's crazy. I mean, people are so different here."

"People are people everywhere." I shrugged. "I mean, in a lot of ways, they aren't all that different from the people at our school. They still like a lot of the same movies and music and deal with stress the same as anyone else. But when people get to know Jesus, it changes them. If there's one thing I've learned growing up on the mission field, it's that."

"It sort of makes me want to get to know God a little better. I mean, I don't know if I'm ready to become religious or anything like that. But I'd definitely like to know more."

"Well, I'm here if you have any questions. No pressure, of course."

"Thanks. I'll keep that in mind." He smiled as my mom walked up to where we were sitting.

"Okay, guys, are you ready to head out?" she asked as Jackson followed behind her. "I promised Nathan's mom we'd have him back by noon."

"Yeah, we're ready," he said, turning toward my mom and then back toward me. "Thanks again for inviting me today, Katie. I really enjoyed it."

"Anytime," I said as we boarded into the car, suddenly feeling a buzz from the inside of my pocket. I smiled as I pulled my phone out and saw a text from my dad.

What did Nathan think???

I tapped back a response as I snapped in my seatbelt.

He really liked it.

I smiled and did my best to stifle a laugh as he replied, in all caps.

PRAISE JESUS!!

I followed with another text.

God is good.

This time I was sure that I cracked a smile as I saw his response, followed by several exclamation points.

Yes, He sure is!!!

Chapter Fourteen

That week, I walked into the Agape Club with newfound confidence. After all, if God could reach Nathan, who had so much baggage when it comes to God and church, I knew He could reach the other students in the club. I just had to trust what He was doing and trust Him to take the lead.

"Are you ready?" Atticus asked as the two of us walked to the Student Center after our last class to set up for this week's meeting.

"You know, I actually am. I feel good about this week."

"Really?" He sounded surprised. "What changed?"

"I guess you could say that I'm coming in with a fresh perspective." I adjusted the strap of my backpack as I thought once again about the events of this week. "I mean, God has brought us this far. He's not going to let us fail now, right?"

"You mean, what I've been telling you all along?"

"Have you?" I pretended to look surprised. "I haven't noticed."

"Come on," he said, ignoring my comment as the two of us walked into the room. "Let's get started."

With that, we set up the tables and pushed some old school supplies off to the side to make the room look nice and organized for the club. And once we were finished, it looked just about perfect.

"Hey," Liv said, slinging her backpack over her shoulder as she walked through the doors with two other students that I recognized, "are we early?"

"No, not at all." I shook my head. "You're right on time."

"Cool," she said, setting her backpack down by a nearby chair and plopping down on the couch. "How's your week going?"

"Good," Atticus said. "Busy with homework. But it's been good overall."

"Same." Cole groaned. "Our teachers are trying to *kill* us!"

"Who's trying to kill you?" Mrs. Reams asked as she walked into the Student Center. Cole stifled a laugh.

"No one, Mrs. Reams. We were just talking about school."

"Yeah, it's been a little heavy for us this week," I added.

"I see." She smiled as she laid out a tray of homemade fudge squares and snickerdoodles. "Is this everyone?"

"Not quite," I said, checking the clock. "We're still waiting on a couple more people."

"Well, I don't think you'll be waiting for long," Tanisha said as she made her way through the door, clearly out of breath. "I saw a bunch of people down the hallway, and it looked like they were all heading this way!"

"Wow, that's great," I said, glancing over to my friends as a bunch of students began flooding into the room. "Then I guess we're ready to get started."

"Okay, guys," Atticus said as everyone took a seat. "If everyone's here, we'll go ahead and get started. I'm happy to see most of you back here—and a couple of new faces. Today we're going to be talking about a lot of the same things we talked about last week. Who Jesus is and what it means to be a Christian. But before we start, does anyone have any prayer requests?"

To my surprise, the girl dressed in all black raised her hand.

"Yes?" I asked.

"Could you please pray for my family? My parents might be getting a divorce."

"Absolutely," I promised. "Anyone else?"

This time, a boy named Caleb raised his hand. "Could you please pray for my sister? She's had the flu for the last couple of weeks, and she's still not feeling so great."

"Definitely," I assured him, scanning the room. "Any other prayer requests? Okay then—we'll open in prayer and get started. Atticus, would you like to open for us?"

"Sure." He nodded as he prayed for the girl's family—whose name turned out to be Ky—and Caleb's sister.

And after he finished, I launched into this week's lesson.

"So, last week in this club, we talked about Jesus. His character, His life, and His ministry. But today, we're going to be focusing on what a Christian is—in other words, our response to His love for us. Does anyone have any thoughts on this? What it means to be a Christian. Yes, Liv?"

"Following God's words?" she suggested. "And doing what He says?"

"That's part of it. Anyone else? Nathan?" I asked, surprised to see him raise his hand.

"Loving God," he said, clearly still thinking about the message at church on Sunday, "and loving other people?"

"Excellent!" I smiled. "It actually talks about that right in Matthew—when Jesus was talking with His disciples. He told them, and us, to love the Lord your God with all your heart, soul, mind, and strength. And right after, He says to love your neighbor as yourself. Yes, Rita?"

"Hold up. You're saying that God wants us to love people, and that's great and all. But do Christians really love *all* people? I mean, I've met plenty of Christians who can be pretty mean. Especially toward people who don't live or believe like they do."

My heart sank as I thought about Rita's comment and then sped up as I realized that all eyes were on me.

"Some Christians can be like that," I said, thinking through my answer carefully. "But that's never how Jesus wanted his disciples to act toward unbelievers. In fact," I continued, thinking back to a passage I read this morning in the book of John, with the woman at the well, "Jesus was always the first to welcome the people that everyone else condemned. To reach out to the outcasts and the misfits in society. The same people that the Pharisees and the religious people rejected."

"So, you don't think Christians who act like that are a good representation of Jesus?" Liv asked, pulling her knees to her chest. "And how He would want them to treat people?"

"Definitely not. Jesus welcomed everybody and treated all people with dignity and respect. And He always left them better off than they were before. Yes, Daniel?"

"Well, it's a little off-topic. But I've been searching lately, and it's something I've been wondering about for a while."

"Go for it." I smiled.

"OK, well, most Christians that I've talked to seem to believe that God wants them to wait to have sex until they're married. Why is that—I mean, that God would ask people to do that when it seems so different than what the rest of the world does?"

"Can I take this one?" Atticus asked, turning toward me as I nodded. "God knows how we're wired as humans. He knows what's good for us, and He knows what will hurt us. And as a good God, He doesn't want us to do something that will hurt us or the person that we marry." He paused as Daniel nodded, looking interested in what Atticus was saying. "By choosing to wait, you're protecting your heart and saving something special for someone special. Someone who's committed to you and who will be there for the long haul. And who isn't just there for the physical stuff."

"So, you believe waiting to have sex is actually for our own good?" Daniel asked. "Not to punish us?"

"Absolutely. God's instructions are always to help us, never to hurt us. And every no that he gives us is a bigger yes to something else. Something better."

"Totally agree." I nodded.

The rest of the meeting flew by as we talked about what it means to be a Christian. And to my surprise, some of the students who were once so skeptical of God seemed just a little more interested in knowing Christ. By the time it was over, I couldn't have been more pleased with how it went.

"You two are doing a great job running this club," Mrs. Reams said after we closed, and everyone else had left, leaving the three of us to clean up after it was over. "I'm proud of what you guys are doing here."

"Thanks, Mrs. Reams," I said as I stacked a chair back in its rightful place. "I was a little nervous when it first started, but I'm happy with the way that it's going."

"That's understandable. But God is moving in this club, and you two are being faithful in stewarding it. I know that God is going to honor that and lead you as you lead others."

"Thank you," Atticus said. "We really appreciate your help. We couldn't have done this without you."

"Well, I'm happy to help however I can." She looked down to check her phone and see what time it was. "Hey, do you think you kids could take it from here? My daughter has a piano recital tonight, and I want to make sure I'm at her school in time to pick her up. And her school is on the other side of town."

"Absolutely." I nodded, looking around to see that there wasn't much left to put away. "Not a problem at all. Tell your daughter we wish her the best of luck."

"Yeah, absolutely. We can take it from here."

"Thank you. Have a good rest of your day."

"You too," I said as she walked through the door.

"Crazy day today, huh?" I finally said, breaking the awkward silence that sat between us.

"For sure—" he agreed, pushing one of the tables off to the side, "but you did a great job answering their questions today."

"Thanks, you did too."

"Thanks," he said, suddenly looking more nervous than he was just a minute ago. "Hey, Katie, there's this dance coming up next week, and I was thinking . . . would you like to go with me? As friends, of course," he added quickly. "Not like a real date."

"Yeah, sure!" I exclaimed. "I mean, yeah, sure. I'd love to go. That'd be fun. I've never actually been to a dance before. You know, uh, being homeschooled and all . . ."

"Cool. We can go together then."

"Great."

"Great. So, I'll see you tomorrow?"

"Yeah. See you then," I said as he walked away, my heart practically pounding out of my chest as I replayed the last couple of minutes over and over again in my mind.

What had I just done?

Chapter Fifteen

That weekend, I invited Tanisha and Jenny over to my house for a sleepover in hopes of getting the whole school dance thing out of my mind. The only problem was, that seemed to be all they wanted to talk about.

"I can't believe you and my brother are going out on a date!" Tanisha said as the three of us sat in my room, eating ice cream and watching *A Walk to Remember* for the billionth time. "My brother and my best friend—who would've thought?"

"It's not a date," I insisted as I ate another bite of my ice cream—mint with small pieces of chocolate scattered throughout. "We're just going as friends. He said so himself."

"Right," she said, rolling her eyes. "*Friends.*"

"What's so weird about going as friends?"

"Nothing. Except my brother clearly likes you as more than a friend."

"How do you know? Did he tell you?"

"Didn't have to. Anyone with *eyes* could tell."

"Do you like him?" Jenny asked, turning the question back toward me.

"I don't know. I mean, I like him as a friend. But between moving, and school, and church, and the club, I haven't had a lot of time to think about the whole *guy thing*—you know?" I paused, wanting nothing more than to change the subject and get the spotlight off Atticus and me. Not that there was an Atticus and me. "How about you? Is there anyone you like?"

"Well, there is this guy that I sort of like," Jenny confessed, her cheeks turning red. "But he already has a girlfriend."

"Really?" Tanisha asked. "Who?"

"Jackson," she said, sheepishly.

"Wait, *Jackson*?" I said. "As in, my *brother* Jackson?"

"That's the one."

"But he's my brother!" I exclaimed, suddenly realizing how ridiculous my reaction was, considering that Atticus was also Tanisha's brother.

"I know, but he's kind of cute—and he seems like a nice guy. But I would never do anything about it. I mean, with him dating Sydney and all." She paused. "Are you guys close?"

"Me and Sydney?" I asked as she shook her head.

"No silly!" She rolled her eyes. "You and *Jackson*! Your brother!"

"We were," I said, glancing over at Tanisha—who already knew the whole story. "Since we moved, I'm not so sure."

"He'll come around," Tanisha said, sounding more confident than I felt. "All siblings have their moments. Trust me, Atticus is cool and all, but he's not perfect."

"I know," I said, scooping out another spoonful of ice cream as the movie faded off into the old song by Switchfoot, my mind turning toward my relationship with Jackson. "I'm sure you're right. It's just weird. I mean, growing up, we hung out together all the time. We had the same group of friends and everything. Now, it's like we're practically strangers."

"Do you want to talk about it?" Jenny asked, leaning against one of the pillows on my bed. "I mean, I like Jackson, but you're my friend first. And if you need to talk, you can."

"Thanks, Jenny. But honestly, I'd rather not. It's been kind of a lot lately, and if it's okay with you guys, I'd rather just focus on having fun tonight—keep things light."

"Totally understand. So, have you picked out a dress for the dance?"

"Not yet." I shook my head. "I have one that I wore for Easter last year, but I don't think it would really fit. I mean, it still *fits*, but not for the occasion."

"What if we helped you pick something out?" Jenny suggested. "We could do it now if you want?"

"That would be great," I said, my voice a mix of gratitude and confusion. "Except I don't have my license. And I'm pretty sure my mom isn't going to want to drive us somewhere this late at night to pick out a dress."

"That's the miracle of modern technology," Jenny said, in a *'duh'* tone of voice, as if the solution was obvious. At least, to everyone except me. "We don't have to go anywhere—we can look online! You have a phone, right?"

"Yeah, right here," I said, grabbing it off my desk.

"Great," she said. I plopped down on my bed and gave her my phone as she went to www.forever21.com. "All you have to do is look through your options and order what you like. They'll deliver it right to your house."

"Don't tell me you've never shopped online before," Tanisha said, raising an eyebrow in my direction.

"I mean, I know about shopping online, but we didn't really use the internet all that much back home. We used it for school and things like that, but never for shopping."

"Well then, today's your lucky day." Jenny smiled. "Because any dress you could hope for is right within your reach. Your digital reach, that is."

"Nice," I said, scrolling through the list of dresses, in every size, shape, and color that you could imagine.

"Hey, how about that one?" Tanisha suggested, pointing to a long, purple dress covered in sequins.

"Hmm, it's pretty. But it's not really me."

"Ooh—what about that one?" Jenny asked, pointing to a black cocktail dress.

"No, it's a nice design . . . but it's a little short."

"But it's so pretty!"

"I know," I said, looking at the dress one more time. "But my parents would kill me if I left the house in that. Let's keep looking."

We went back and forth like that for a while, as we scrolled through various dresses until finally, we found something.

"Wait, stop!" Tanisha exclaimed, slamming her finger down on the screen, nearly knocking the phone out of my hand in the process.

"What? What is it?"

"That one! What do you think?"

I looked to where she was pointing, and to my surprise, it was a dress that I could actually see myself wearing. It was a royal blue knee-length dress with thick straps and light decoration. It was also right in the budget range that my parents gave me for the dance.

"It's perfect!" I said, amazed that we had finally found something. "That's the dress I want!"

"Well, it looks like our work here is done," Jenny said, fist-bumping Tanisha.

"Thanks, guys. I really appreciate your help."

"Anytime," Jenny said. "Hey, it's getting late. If it's alright with you, I think I'm going to crash."

"Yeah, I'm pretty tired too," Tanisha agreed. "Let's call it a night."

"Alright," I replied as we pulled out our sleeping bags. "Night, guys."

"Night, Katie," Tanisha said.

"Night," Jenny echoed, as I got into my sleeping bag and tried to fall asleep. Unfortunately, without much luck, as my mind reeled with a million thoughts about Atticus and the dance and my possible semi-crush.

I slipped out of my sleeping bag and pulled a flashlight and H.D.'s diary out of my drawer. Maybe a little light reading would help.

Dear Diary,

Last week over Thanksgiving break, I saw my best friend again for the first time in ages. And though we've known each other all our lives, it felt like I was talking to a stranger. She came over to my house, and we talked about college and all the new and exciting things that came with it. And during the conversation, she started telling me about this guy she's seeing, Brett. They've been going out for a couple of months now, and I guess it's pretty serious, which is great. I'm happy for her, but then she told me something that I never thought I'd hear her say. She and Brett have started sleeping together.

My best friend! The same girl that I grew up in church with. The same one who made a purity pledge with me at youth group and who was always on the same page as me when it came to guys and boundaries. But now? It's like all of that has changed, all because of some guy. And on top of that, she's started going to college parties. The kind with actual kegs and people hooking up. The sort of parties we've always promised we'd avoid. It's only been a couple of months, and I still feel like the same person I've always been. But hearing my best friend talk about her life now, I feel alone. And it's not just her. So many of my other friends are in the same place she is. Am I totally weird for keeping my convictions?

And is there anyone else who still is?

Until Next Time,

H.D.

"Who are you H.D.?" I whispered into the dark as I read the last sentence silently in my mind.

I stayed up a little while longer, reading and wondering about the girl behind the diary until finally, I felt my eyes start to droop, signaling that it was well past time for me to get some sleep. So, I closed the book and pushed it under my bed. There would be time to read more in the morning, but at that moment, sleep was the thing that won the battle for my attention.

And after a long and eventful week, I was more than OK with that.

Chapter Sixteen

. . . I am with you always, to the very end of the age.
- Matthew 28:20

*T*o my surprise, the day of the dance came quicker than I thought. And when it finally got here, I felt like I had a million butterflies fluttering around in the pit of my stomach. Each one felt more ferocious than the last. I took a deep breath, surveying my dress and my heels once more.

I had nothing to be nervous about, right? After all, Atticus and I were just going as friends. There was no reason for me to feel the way that I felt right now. *Was there?*

"Are you ready to go?" Mom asked, walking into my room as I stared at my reflection in the mirror, feeling like I was about to hurl.

"Ready as I'll ever be." I forced a smile and turned toward her. "Do I look okay?"

"You look beautiful. I think Atticus will think so too."

"Mom, we've been over this. I'm not interested. Not like that."

"I know." She smiled. "But you're always allowed to change your mind. You know, I remember my first dance in high school. I was nervous too."

"You went to dances in high school?" I asked, for some reason, surprised.

She laughed. "Not a lot, but a couple. My first one was in the ninth grade. There was this guy I liked, and I was worried the whole night about trying to impress him. When I got there, I was so nervous that I spent most of my time hanging out in a corner with my friends. Finally, I went to go get some punch, and I spilled it all over myself right in front of him."

"Then what happened?" I asked, taking a seat beside her on the edge of my bed, curious to hear how this punch story ended.

"He got me some napkins and asked me to dance. I was pretty embarrassed, but then I actually started having fun. Nothing ever went anywhere with him, but it was a good memory. And a good reminder to avoid punch when you're wearing a new dress."

"Thanks, Mom," I said, grateful for talks like these.

"That's what moms are for," she said as my dad walked into the doorway, knocking even though the door was wide open.

"Can I come in?" he asked, covering his eyes.

I rolled my eyes. "Yes, Dad. You can come in."

"We were just having some girl time," Mom said. "And talking about her dress for the dance."

"You like it?" I asked as I stood up to show it off.

"Absolutely. You look beautiful, Katie. Just like your mom."

"Thanks, Dad." I smiled as I heard the doorbell ring.

"That must be your male companion now," he teased as I jumped up to answer the door.

"*Dad,*" I said in my most exaggerated voice as I hurried to check the peephole and open the door.

"Hey, are you all ready to go?" I asked as he stood on my doorstep in a suit and tie, which was very much unlike his usual casual attire of shorts and a T-shirt.

"All ready," he said, looking even more nervous than I felt. "Whenever your brother is, since he's our ride." He paused. "You look incredible tonight. I mean, not that you usually look bad, it's just . . ."

"Atticus." I stopped him. "You're fine. And thank you. You look nice too."

"*Atticus*," my dad jumped in as he walked over to shake his hand. "Good to see you."

"You too, sir," he said, looking a couple of shades paler than usual.

"I hear you're going to the dance with my daughter?" he asked, clearly trying to sound tough, which on my dad, was almost laughable.

"Yes, sir. If you're okay with that, sir."

"You have my blessing. But remember, if you try anything, I will send people after you to kill you."

"I'll keep that in mind," he said as I laughed.

"Dad," I urged, giving him a look that said, 'Please, I'm begging you to stop.'

"OK, well, you guys have fun. And text me when you get there."

"We will," I promised. "That is, whenever Jackson is finished getting ready," I said, looking down at my phone, worried that we were going to be late.

"I'm here," Jackson said as he hurried down the stairs. "Sorry, I'm ready to go."

"Good," Mom said. "Have fun and drive careful. And don't come home too late."

"We won't," he promised as we headed out the door, and Atticus and I climbed into the backseat.

"Thanks again for driving us," Atticus said as we pulled out of the driveway, and he snapped in his seatbelt.

"Anytime," he said, at that moment, seeming more like the old Jackson. "We'll drive by Sydney's house to pick her up, and then we'll head to the dance."

"Cool." I smiled.

Before long we were there, and after Jackson walked up to the door and rang the doorbell, they both walked back to the car together.

"Hey, Sydney," I said as she opened the door to get in. "I love your dress."

"Thanks," she said, her voice void of emotion as she shot me a look that seemed to say, 'Why are you talking to me?'

With that, I was silent the rest of the way there, allowing myself to get lost in the radio music blaring from the car speakers until we arrived.

"Wow," I said as we got out of the car, and Jackson and Sydney went on ahead of us. "Talk about a big turnout."

"It's the first dance of the year." Atticus shrugged. "A lot of people usually come. It drops off toward the end of the year—until prom, anyway."

"It's funny," I said, raising my voice to be heard over the loud-speaker. "It kind of looks like something you'd see in one of those old teen movies."

"Well, they had to get it from somewhere, right?"

"Yeah, I guess."

"Hey, do you want to get some punch? Food? Anything?"

"It's OK," I said, thinking back to my mom's story. "I think I'd better avoid punch tonight."

"Katie!" Tanisha shouted, hurrying over with her new boyfriend, Mario, who drove her to the dance tonight. "What do you think? Do you like it so far?"

"It's . . . different," I said, trying my best to take in the atmosphere. "Definitely different."

"What? I don't get a hello?" Atticus asked, pretending to be hurt.

"You're my *brother*." Tanisha rolled her eyes. "I see you all the time. So, what do you say—want to join us on the dance floor?"

"Sure!" I replied, at that moment, more relieved than ever to have Tanisha at the dance with me. "I mean—if you want to?" I said, turning toward Atticus.

"Sounds good to me," he said as they played the first song I recognized that night. An old pop hit by Whitney Houston.

"This is pretty fun!" I said, the awkwardness that I was feeling before falling off and a flood of relief taking its place.

"Told you!" Tanisha grinned. "You know, for someone who's never been to a dance, you've got some pretty sweet moves!"

"You think so?"

"Yeah, girl, you're a natural!" Mario said. "Now, your friend here, I'm not so sure about."

"You know what they say." Atticus grinned, vainly attempting to keep up with the rhythm of the bass. "White boys can't dance."

This caused us all to laugh. And one by one, more of our friends started joining in, including Amber, Nathan, Kyle, Maya, and Jenny—wheelchair and all, until the fast songs came to a screeching halt. Replaced instead by a slow song by Jason Mraz.

"Hey, Katie," Atticus began, scratching the back of his neck as people started breaking off in twos. "Would you uh, like to dance?"

"Sure." I smiled. "I'd love to."

"Cool," he said as the two of us started slow dancing.

"You know, I really love this song. It's from one of my favorite shows, actually."

"Really? What a coincidence. It's from my favorite show too."

"You watch *This Is Us*?" I asked, surprise ringing through my voice.

"Are you kidding? I never miss it. Well, except for that one time my sister deleted my recording to make room for *The Terminator.*"

"No way—my brother did the same thing, except with *Shark Week*!" I exclaimed, causing him to laugh.

"Small world, huh?"

"For sure."

"You know, I'm really glad I met you this year. It's nice to meet someone who understands you. I mean, I guess what I'm trying to say is . . . I'm glad we became friends."

"Me too," I said, as I felt my stomach doing flipflops—at that moment, wanting nothing more than to be right where I was . . . dancing in time to the music with a friend who, for the first time, I was maybe starting to see as something more.

"Uh, Katie," Atticus began. "There's something that I, well, I don't quite know how to say this but . . ."

"Katie!" I heard another voice say—this one, coming from behind me, snapping me out of the moment. "There's something I've got to talk to you about."

"Huh? What is it?" I asked, turning around to see Nathan, who, for some reason, looked panicked.

"Well, it's your brother. I don't quite know how to tell you this but . . ."

"Wait, my brother?" I asked, cutting him off—feeling nervous, except this time, not from my feelings for Atticus. "What is it? Is he okay?"

"Your brother's drunk," Nathan said after a long pause. "I guess he was drinking with some guys in the back, and they got caught. They're sending him home now."

"Wait, *what?*" I asked, trying to wrap my head around what he was saying. "They can't send him home if he's drunk. He can't *drive!*"

"Well, that's part of the problem." He hesitated. "He thinks he can."

"We've got to go find him," Atticus said. "Where'd you see him last?"

"Heading outside. He's probably out there now."

"Come on," Atticus said as the three of us headed out the door. "Let's go check."

"Jackson!" I shouted as soon as I saw him. "Jackson, what the *heck* are you doing?"

"I'm going home," he said, his words slurring together. "This night has been horrible."

"Not without us, you're not! And not like this! I'm calling Mom and Dad. They'll come pick us up."

"Are you crazy? They'll never let me out of the house again!"

"Well, you can't drive like this—you'll kill yourself! Or someone else! And what about Sydney? Do you plan on just leaving her here? How do you think our parents would feel about that?"

"Sydney broke up with me, *okay?*" he shouted, at that moment, looking more defeated than I'd ever seen him before. "And *trust me*, I'm pretty sure she got a ride with someone else."

"Are you okay?" I asked this time quieter, looking him straight in the eyes.

He laughed, but it was a laugh that lacked any humor. "Do I *look* okay?"

"Katie, I'll stay here with Jackson," Atticus said. "Why don't you go call your parents?"

"OK," I said, feeling like I was about to start crying, even though I did my best to hold back the tears. "Thanks, Atticus."

I found my dad's number and pressed *call*, waiting only a few seconds before he answered.

"Hello—Katie? Is everything alright?"

"No," I said, shaking my head as I spoke, even though he couldn't see me. "No, it's not alright, Dad. Jackson's been drinking, and now he's drunk."

"What?" he exclaimed, clearly upset. "OK, Katie. Stay there and make sure he doesn't do anything stupid. Your mom and I will be down there soon."

"Okay. Thanks, Dad," I said, my hands shaking as I hung up the phone.

"Everything okay?" Atticus asked as I walked back over to where he and my brother were standing.

"Yeah, I just called my dad. He and my mom are going to be here soon."

"Are you okay?"

"I'll be fine." I smiled, even though it was entirely forced. "Thanks."

My parents came within a matter of minutes. And though they were quiet as they drove us home, they began talking as soon as we walked through the door.

"What were you thinking, Jackson?" Dad exclaimed, slamming the door behind him. "Getting *drunk*? Attempting to *drive* like that—when you could've hurt yourself? Or someone else? This isn't how we raised you!"

"I'm sorry!" Jackson exclaimed. "I was upset—this night hasn't exactly been the greatest for me either!"

"Why?" Mom exclaimed. "What could have possibly happened to make do something this stupid and selfish?"

"Sydney broke up with me, OK? *OK*? I got dumped by my girlfriend tonight—are you happy now? I'm sure this makes you *real* happy because this is what you wanted all along, isn't it? *Isn't it?*"

"Go to your room, Jackson," my dad said sternly, rubbing his temples. "We'll talk later when you're in your right state of mind."

"And Katie, why don't you go to your room too," my mom ordered.

"But I didn't do anything!"

"Katie," she warned, in a tone that said she wouldn't take no for an answer.

"Yes, Mom," I said as I made my way up to my room and shut my door—plopping down on my bed. What a mess. What had started out as my first dance and a fun time with my friends had turned into one of the worst nights ever. Never in my life had I seen my parents so angry or my brother spiraling so deeply out of control. At that moment, it felt like my family was completely falling apart.

"God, where are you?" I prayed. "What are you doing?"

"Do not be afraid . . . do not be discouraged . . ." I felt a voice say, from somewhere deep inside my soul—echoing an old familiar passage from Scripture. "I'll be with you wherever you go."

"God, I don't know what's going on," I prayed as I felt a tear escape out of the corner of my eye, "but I know that you're there. Please help my brother . . . God, please reach him . . . Please help him."

Suddenly, I felt peace deep within my soul. Somehow, someway, things would all work out, despite what I was seeing right now, because God was still with me. And that was one thing that would never change. No matter what.

»→ ←«

"Morning sleepyhead," I said as I walked into my brother's room to wake him up.

He groaned, clearly hungover. "What time is it?"

"8:55," I said, checking his clock and opening the blinds in his bedroom window. "Almost 9:00."

He groaned and rolled back over, grabbing a nearby pillow to cover his head.

"Oh no, you don't," I said, plopping down on his bed next to him. "What happened last night?"

"I don't want to talk about it."

"Jackson," I said, racking my brain for some way to get my brother to talk to me. "We've been brother and sister, and friends, too long for you to shut me out now. I mean, sure, we drive each other crazy sometimes, but you're still my brother. And I still care about you."

Jackson sighed. "Sydney broke up with me last night. She's the one who started drinking. I was sober. And at one point, she wanted us to go to her car. She wanted, uh, *things* to happen. And I thought I did too—but nothing did. I chickened out before anything went anywhere. After the whole thing happened, I was so humiliated that I ran into the guy's bathroom for a while to think. By the time I came out, Sydney was already dancing with—and kissing, some other guy. I tried talking to her, but she told me she didn't want to see me anymore. After that happened, I found the guys she got the beer from. I knew it was stupid, but the whole thing just hurt so much. But trust me." He shook his head. "I'm *never* doing that again."

"First off," I said, doing my best to process everything he had just said, "you're not a chicken for staying true to your convictions. If you ask me, that makes you pretty cool."

"Thanks, but that's the thing—" he said, sitting up on the edge of his bed, "I don't even know if they are my convictions anymore. I mean, our whole life, we've been taught these things about God and Christianity. But lately, I've been trying to figure out what I believe. Not you, not our parents, not anyone else, but what I believe, for myself. But even though I'm not sure what I believe, I still couldn't do it."

"Maybe that's because deep down, there's a part of you that still does."

"Maybe." He hesitated, for the first time, glancing over in my direction. "Why don't you seem surprised by any of this?"

"I kind of overheard you talking to Mom and Dad a couple of days ago," I confessed, as he cringed, reliving the moment. "I heard most of the conversation. And I guess if I'm completely honest, I had my suspicions before that."

"I just don't want to live with a borrowed faith. I don't want to accept everything our parents say as truth just because they're our parents. I want whatever I believe to be my own."

"And I don't think you should," I said. "Have a borrowed faith, I mean."

"But aren't you worried that I'll end up having no faith? That I'll wind up becoming an atheist or something?"

"No." I shook my head. "Because I guess I believe that in the end, truth will always lead you back to God."

He stared at me for a moment, looking some sort of cross between surprised and amused. "When did my kid sister get to be so smart?"

I shrugged. "Well, in case you haven't noticed, I'm not such a kid anymore. I'm growing up. And you are too."

"It's kind of scary," he confessed as I smiled.

"*Terrifying*," I agreed.

"Sometimes, I want nothing more than to go back to the way things were when we were two kids living over in Africa, somehow believing things would always be that way."

"Sometimes I want the same thing," I said as I thought back on our time there and the last couple of months. "But if things never changed, maybe we'd never grow."

"Maybe." He paused. "I guess it's all part of growing up."

"Yeah, but could you just promise me one thing?"

"Yeah?"

"Next time you go through some tremendously horrible growing-up experience, could you please just come to me, or Dad, or someone instead of getting drunk? It would be a whole lot easier on all of us."

"Promise," he said, a slow grin spreading across his face.

"Pinky promise?" I pleaded as he rolled his eyes.

"Yes, Katie. *Pinky promise.*"

"Good," I said, feeling just a little bit lighter than before.

Because at that moment, I had a feeling that things were finally starting to get back to normal between Jackson and me.

And for that, I was beyond thankful.

Chapter Seventeen

Peace I leave with you; my peace I give you. I do not give to you as the world gives.
Do not let your hearts be troubled and do not be afraid.

- John 14:27

The following week, things finally seemed to be getting back to normal. My parents had mostly forgotten about Jackson's mistake, and we were all getting along like we used to back home. And as I sat in the cafeteria at school on Friday, I had a little more peace. Which, after a particularly weird week, was exactly what I needed.

"What *is* this stuff?" Kyle asked, wrinkling up his nose and holding up his spoon for us all to see as something thick, wet, and pasty dripped down onto his plate.

"I think it's supposed to be tuna noodle casserole." Tanisha grinned. "But at this school, who knows?"

"Well, whatever it is, I'm not eating it. I'm pretty sure I'll puke if I try."

"Do you want some of my chips?" Jenny offered, holding up a small bag of Doritos.

"Do you mind?" he asked, a hint of desperation in his voice.

"Not at all. My mom packed me a sandwich today, so I'm free from the nightmare called cafeteria food."

"Thanks," he said, taking the chips and wolfing them down like he hadn't eaten in a month. "These things are amazing!" he said, between bites, holding up the bag to me as he chewed. "Want some?"

"No," I said, pretty much losing my appetite after seeing him chew with his mouth open. "I'm good. Thanks."

"No problem," he said as he continued inhaling the spicy corn chips.

"So, does anyone have any plans for the weekend?" Atticus asked, changing the subject and glancing around the table.

"Just homework," Nathan said, speaking up. "I've got a Geometry exam, and I've got to study if I want any hope of passing it."

"I've got to study too," Amber said, taking a sip of her Pepsi. "And work on an essay for English Comp on an influential figure in history."

"Any idea who you're going to pick?" Atticus asked as she shook her head.

"How about MLK?" Nathan suggested.

"Or William Shakespeare," Tanisha offered.

"I don't know, maybe. I'll figure it out. How about the rest of you? Any big plans this weekend?"

"I'm just going to visit my family," Maya said as she pushed her mac and cheese around on her plate. "My grandma lives in Colorado, and it's her birthday this weekend. We're planning on driving up to see her."

"That sounds nice," I said, suddenly realizing that it's been months since I'd visited my own family in Florida. "I don't really have anything going on this weekend. I have most of my home-work done already, and I'm planning on finishing the rest tonight."

"Same," Jenny said, taking a bite of her salad.

"That makes three of us," Tanisha added. "There is some-thing I've been wanting to try, though. Have you guys heard of that new karaoke club for teens down near the city? Burgers and Beats? They just opened a few weeks ago, and I've heard that it's a pretty lit place to hang out. They have burgers and fries and a stage if anyone wants to sing."

"I haven't heard of it, but maybe we could go together tomorrow night," Jenny suggested. "You know, the four of us. Make a night of it."

"I'd love to, but you'll have to count me out," Atticus said, popping a french fry. "I promised my parents I'd help them clean out the attic on Saturday, and that's going to be an all-day affair. Besides," he added, "I'm more of a writer than a singer."

"Then we'll make it a girl's night. What do you say, Katie?" Tanisha asked, excitement clear in her voice. "Are you in?"

"Yeah, totally! I'll have to ask my parents. But if they say yes, I'd love to go."

"Great," Jenny said as the bell rang, signaling that lunch period was officially over. "We'll all meet up then!"

"Sounds great," I said as we got up and threw the remainders of our lunch into the trash can.

I may have never been to a karaoke club, but if I could survive a high school dance, I was pretty sure I could survive anything.

>> <<

*A*s it turned out, my parents were totally cool with me going, even agreeing to let me carpool with Tanisha and Jenny.

And before I knew it, she was at my door to pick me up.

"Hey!" Jenny said as I swung the door open. "All ready to go?"

"All ready! Just let me get my phone, and I'll be right out."

With that, I ran inside to get my cell phone and say goodbye to my parents before hopping into the old, blue SUV with my friends—snapping my seatbelt firmly in place.

"Hey!" Tanisha said as I slid into the seat beside her. "Have you thought about what you're going to sing yet?"

"A little. I'm thinking something by Tori Kelly. I haven't picked out a song yet, though. How about you?"

"I'm going for a classic." Tanisha smiled. " "Single Ladies" by Beyoncé. I doubt I'll be able to do it justice, but it will be nice paying tribute to the *queen*!"

"Ooh, I love that one!" Jenny exclaimed. "I'm thinking about singing something by Ariana Grande, or maybe the Beatles!"

"Going old-school tonight." Tanisha grinned. "I like it."

"Thanks." Jenny's mom chuckled from the front seat of the car. "I feel very old right now."

"Sorry, Mrs. H."

"It's OK, Tanisha. You know, my mom saw them in concert years ago, before I was born."

"Seriously? No way!"

"Way." She nodded as she merged onto the interstate. "She told me about it when I was younger, and my friends were listening to the Beatles. Said it was a pretty *rad* experience."

"That's so cool!"

"For sure!" I agreed, even though I only knew maybe two songs by the Beatles.

With that, the three of us continued laughing and talking about everything from music to school until finally, we were there. And to my surprise, Burgers and Beats was a lot bigger than I expected.

Overall, it seemed like your average teen hangout. It had modern art hanging from every wall, and it smelled of burgers and body odor, reminding me a little of the type of place you would see on an old 90s show like *Saved by the Bell.*

"This place is so cool!" Jenny said as she wheeled into the restaurant, looking around. "Very retro."

"Totally," Tanisha agreed. "I figured you guys would like it."

"Where do you girls want to sit?" Jenny's mom asked as she examined the place.

"Over there!" Jenny said, pointing to an empty table. "Right by that old picture of Chicago!"

"Sounds good to me." Tanisha shrugged, turning toward Jenny and me as the four of us took our seats, and a young waiter walked over to take our order.

"Hello, ladies," he said in a thick British accent. "Can I get you any drinks to start out with today?"

"I'll just have a glass of water," I said as he scribbled down my order.

"Coke for me," Tanisha jumped in.

"Make mine a Sprite," Jenny added, looking more than a little interested in the blond British waiter. "Extra fizzy."

"OK, water, a Sprite, and a Coke for the young ladies. Anything for you, ma'am?"

"I'll have an iced tea," Mrs. Hoffman said as he jotted down her order.

"OK, ladies—your drinks will be right up!"

"Thank you, sir!" I called back as he turned and walked away.

"Sir?" Jenny exclaimed under her breath. "We're *young adults* now, Katie! And he couldn't have been more than a few years older than us!"

"Sorry," I apologized, instantly regretting my words. "I was just trying to be polite."

"Alright, ladies!" he said as he carried the tray over to our table. "Here are your beverages! Now, are you ready to order your dinner?"

"I am," Mrs. Hoffman said, looking at the menu and then back toward him. "I'll have the Caesar salad."

"One Caesar salad. How about the rest of you?"

"I'll have a burger, well done," Jenny said. "With a side of fries."

"I'll have the same," Tanisha added.

"OK, and how about you?" the waiter asked as I scanned the menu, suddenly feeling awkward and jittery, even though I wasn't sure why.

"Uh, I'll have a burger too," I said, trying to come across calmer than I felt since I was literally just ordering food. "And a side of fries."

"Well done?"

"Uh yeah. Sounds great."

"Wonderful," he said, tucking his pencil behind his ear. "Coming right up!"

"Hey, I have to run to the restroom real quick," Mrs. Hoffman said, once he was out of earshot. "Will you girls be alright here by yourselves?"

"We'll be fine, Mom," Jenny said confidently. "We're sophomores in high school! We can handle ourselves for a few minutes."

"Alright. I'll be right back."

With that, Mrs. Hoffman disappeared into the bathroom, as a girl close to our age went up on stage to perform a song by Paramore.

"I can't believe how cool this place is!" Jenny said, cutting into my thoughts, as she once again glanced around the restaurant. "The waiters aren't bad either." She grinned as Tanisha rolled her eyes.

"He's way too old for you, girl," Tanisha reminded her as she glanced at the waiter off to the side. "Besides, a guy like that probably has a girlfriend."

"You think so?" she asked, looking deflated.

"Positive. Besides, we didn't come here to waste our time looking for guys. We came for a girl's night! And I don't know about you, but I'm ready to get my karaoke game on!"

"Same," Jenny agreed, as out of the corner of my eye, I noticed a group of girls walking toward our table.

One, who looked strangely familiar.

"Sydney," I said, surprised. "I didn't expect to see you here."

"Yeah, same," she said as she leaned up against the empty chair. "Casey, right?"

"Katie," I corrected her.

"Right. Who are your friends here?"

"This is Tanisha," I said—turning toward my friend as she put her hand up in a waving motion, "and this is my friend, Jenny. We're in the drama club together at school."

"Did you get into an accident?" one of Sydney's friends asked, tilting her head to the side as she examined Jenny's wheelchair.

"No." She shook her head. "It's nothing like that. I have CMT, short for Charlotte Marie Tooth. I was born with it. I've had it for as long as I can remember."

"Oh, how unfortunate," Sydney said in a voice that sounded more patronizing than genuinely compassionate. "It must be awful, being crippled like that."

"Actually, it doesn't bother me."

"Well, that's good. So, I take it you girls are here to perform tonight? You know, since it is a karaoke club and all."

"Yeah, that's the plan," I said, feeling more than a little annoyed with Sydney for coming over to us after what she did to my brother. And for being so rude to Jenny. "I take it you're here for the same reason?"

She nodded. "I'm somewhat of a music connoisseur. I've been taking voice lessons since I was six. And I've performed on a few occasions, so this should be a breeze for me."

"Good for you," Tanisha said, an edge clear in her voice.

"I'm sure you know a lot about music too. You know, with music being so *rhythmic* and all." She smiled as I felt sure my jaw was going to hit the floor. Did Sydney really just say what I think she said?

"I know a thing or two," Tanisha said, looking about ready to lose it, even though she kept her voice calm and rational. "Of course, I wonder—how is it that *you* would know something like that? Since we've never actually talked before—have we?"

"Just a lucky guess, that's all." She shrugged, with an arrogant smirk. "I guess we'd better go get ready. May the best singer win." With that, she took off, her friends following behind.

"Wow, that girl was a grade-A—" Tanisha began, stopping herself before she could say what she was thinking, *"jerk*. Who does she think she is? Coming over and trying to get in our heads like that?"

"It's not you guys. It's me," I said, thinking back to what my brother told me last weekend, after the dance. "She and Jackson broke up, and I guess she's taking their breakup out on me."

"Well, she isn't very original." Jenny shook her head. "She had those cards right in her back pocket. If I had a dollar for every time someone has made some sort of comment like that, I'd be a billionaire."

"Yeah, and I should've seen that *rhythm* remark coming," Tanisha added. "To think, there are people in the world who are still that ignorant."

"I'm so sorry, guys," I said, feeling horrible, even though the whole thing was totally out of my hands. "I had no idea she'd be so mean."

"It's not your fault," Tanisha said, as Jenny's mom returned from the bathroom and the waiter came back with our food. "Trust me, Katie, we don't blame you."

"Well thanks," I said, thanking the waiter before turning back to my friends, "but I'm still sorry it happened."

With that, the three of us were silent as we ate. Until finally, we finished our burgers and picked out our numbers for karaoke.

And as luck would have it, I was scheduled to go first.

I took a deep breath as I went up on stage to sing "Hollow" by Tori Kelly, staring out into the crowd and then catching a glimpse of Sydney and her friends, who smirked and waved in my direction, as if waiting for me to fail.

You can do this, Katie . . . Deep breaths . . . You know this song like the back of your hand . . .

I began singing the opening lines as my heart *thudded* from the inside of my chest. At first, I tried to ignore it as I read off the lyrics on the screen . . . until suddenly I felt a tightness coming from the inside of my chest, fighting its way to the surface.

You're a loser . . . You can't do this . . . Nobody wants to hear you . . .

I felt my breathing start to shorten. And convinced that I was having a *legit* heart attack, I slammed the microphone back into its stand.

"Sorry, I can't do this," I said before running off to the bathroom to catch my breath.

"Katie!" Jenny exclaimed as she wheeled into the bathroom, Tanisha following behind her. "What happened out there?"

"I don't know," I said, feeling like I was gasping for air. "I felt my chest start to tighten and I . . . I . . . I, I can't breathe!"

"I'm going to get my mom—stay right here!" Jenny said as she and Tanisha hurried outside and, within seconds, came back with Mrs. Hoffman.

She grabbed me by the shoulders and turned me around to face her. "Katie," she said. "Listen closely. I want you to take some deep breaths."

"But I. Can't. Breathe," I gasped. "And I think. I'm having. A heart attack."

"Yes, you can. Now breathe in and breathe out."

I did as I was told, my breathing starting to go back to normal as the tightness in my chest loosened up.

"Is she going to be okay?" Jenny asked, sounding worried.

Mrs. Hoffman nodded, turning toward me. "Do you know what happened just now?"

"Yeah," I said, even though I wasn't sure.

"That was a panic attack. I used to get them all the time when I was younger. When that happens, you just need to take some deep breaths and talk yourself down."

"What causes them?" I asked, at first, thinking back to what I ate tonight, but then remembered what Mrs. Hoffman called it.

A panic attack.

That couldn't be caused by a burger and fries, could it?

"It's caused by severe anxiety," she explained. "They come when you're feeling nervous or afraid."

"I've never had anything like that happen to me before," I said, feeling guilty as I looked back to my friends and then to Mrs. Hoffman. "I'm really sorry that I ruined your night."

"You didn't ruin our night," Tanisha assured me.

"Yeah," Jenny agreed. "We're just glad you're okay."

"I'm feeling a little better if you guys want to go out and sing," I said, but Tanisha shook her head.

"It's been a long night. Why don't we head on home and come back when we have a better audience?"

"Yeah, on a night that Sydney isn't going to be here," Jenny added.

"Are you sure?" I asked as both of them nodded.

"Come on," Mrs. Hoffman said, "let's go."

With that, the three of us headed out, managing to dodge Sydney and the words that she would surely throw our way if she saw us. But the whole way home, I felt terrible. Our night was completely ruined.

And deep down, I knew it was all my fault.

Chapter Eighteen

I didn't say anything to my parents about the panic attack that I had on Saturday night. I figured since I got it under control, it was something that I could handle on my own. Besides, with my birthday a week away, I had plenty of things to keep my mind occupied. The one that consumed most of my thoughts was picking out my very first car.

Or, technically, the one Jackson and I would be sharing.

"What do you think of this one?" Dad asked as the four of us walked around the car dealership. "It's got a good engine, a steady transmission, and most importantly, it's never been in an accident."

"It's OK," I said, scrunching up my face.

"What's wrong with it?" Jackson asked. "It looks perfect to me."

"I'm just not big on the color." I paused, staring at the musty green car that, for some reason, reminded me of all things puke-and-illness. "I was thinking maybe something blue, or red, or purple . . ."

"You want a purple car?" Jackson asked in disbelief.

"Yeah, why not?"

"Why not?" he asked, as if he couldn't believe I was even asking that question. "Because! It'll look like the *Barney* mobile. We'd never live it down!"

"Well, at least it's original. I'd rather be original than look like every other boring car on the road."

"OK, you two." Dad held up his hand—motioning for us to stop fighting. "That'll be enough. Now, if we're going to get this car, you both have to agree on it. And your mom and I will have the final say. Do you understand?"

"Yes," I said.

"Yeah, sorry," Jackson added.

"It's OK," Mom said. "Let's keep looking. I'm sure we can find something you two can both agree on."

With that, we walked around the car dealership for over an hour, having some variation of that conversation about a billion times, before finally landing on something that caught our eye.

"Hey, how about this one?" I asked, motioning to a midsized blue car. "It looks safe, and it's in our price range."

"I like it," Jackson said, running his fingers over the body of the car. "It's classy, it's a good color, and it looks pretty stable."

"Your mom and I will need to check out the information on it. Make sure it's safe, and nothing's wrong with it. But from what I'm seeing, it looks like a good buy. And the size is perfect."

"Really?" I asked in disbelief.

"We're not making any promises," Mom reminded me. "But it's definitely a possibility."

"Can I help you with anything?" a salesman asked, walking up to us in a gray suit and slicked-back hair—which made him look like every used car salesman ever.

"Yes, actually." Dad nodded. "You see, we're looking to buy a car for our kids—Jackson and Katie, to share. They're both new drivers, and we're trying to find something that would be safe and affordable."

"Ah, well, you've come to the right place then, because this car would be the perfect fit for a family like yours. You see, the seats are like new, the car has great mileage, *and* its oil was changed every three-thousand miles. Plus, it's got a special compartment, where your kids can put their phones, so they'll be free of distractions while they drive . . ."

The man continued droning on about the car as my parents listened, asking him about a billion questions, until finally, my parents caved, agreeing to buy it. And, after another long, grueling hour, we drove home—with Dad in his car, and Mom, Jackson, and I in our brand-new car.

"This is incredible!" Jackson said as our mom turned up the volume to a song by Elevation Worship. "I promise I'll take good care of it."

"Me too," I added. "You know, after I pass my driver's test next week."

"Good," Mom said. "Now remember—"

"I know," Jackson said, stopping her before she could finish. "No one is allowed in the car unless we ask first."

"Exactly! And?"

"Be sure to fill up the gas tank before it gets too low."

"I've taught you well." She smiled as she turned the corner onto the next street. "Just be careful. And always be aware of your surroundings. I don't want you texting and driving or dazing out."

"We won't, I promise."

"Yeah, we'll be careful," I agreed. "Hey, do you think I could go for a walk when we get home? My homework is almost done. I just have a few assignments left, and they shouldn't take me too long to finish up."

"I suppose it would be okay—as long as you stay close by and promise to be home by 4:00, to finish your homework."

"I will," I promised, as my mom pulled in front of our house, and Jackson and I got out of the car.

"Hey, going for a walk?"

"Maybe." I turned around to see Atticus. "Why do ask?"

"I just thought you might want some company—unless you're more of a solo walker."

"Nah, I guess the company wouldn't hurt." I grinned, racking my brain for something clever to say. "If you're not too busy writing the next great American novel."

"I think the novel can wait."

"Great. So, have you been up to anything new and exciting lately?"

"Not unless you consider studying for my Geometry test and cleaning out my closet exciting." He grinned. "How about you? Anything new in the world of Katie Carter—former missionary?"

"Well, my sixteenth birthday is a week from today, so that's pretty exciting. And my parents took Jackson and I to the car dealership to pick out a car for the two of us to share."

"Nice. Do you feel ready to take the test?"

"If by ready, you mean have I practiced, yes. If by ready, you mean I'm not freaking out and having nightmares about this thing, then the answer is a big fat no."

"You'll be fine. Just stay calm and follow the instructions. And don't make any sudden moves unless your instructor tells you to."

"You really think it will be that easy?" I asked doubtfully.

"Considering ninety-nine percent of Americans have cars, I doubt it will be that hard."

"True," I said, praying he was right as we continued walking. "I'm sure I'll be fine."

"Definitely. So, have you thought any more about our club meeting this week? I've been trying to come up with something, but so far, it's completely blank."

"A little. I was thinking maybe we could do a series on thankfulness—with Thanksgiving a few weeks away and all."

"I like it. Do you know how you want to approach it?"

"Sort of. I was thinking maybe we could find a Bible story each week that relates to thankfulness and talk about it as a group. Like the leper, who came back and thanked Jesus for healing him. You know—talk about how it relates to us and what we can learn from it."

"Sounds great—we should do it," he said, quiet for a moment. "So, have you read any more of H.D.'s diary?"

I shook my head. "I've barely even had time to think about H.D. since we started the club. I've had so much going on with school, and church, and the club that I guess H.D. has kind of just slipped my mind."

"Well, we know where she lives. Do you want to go and visit her? See if she's home?"

"I can't. I'm supposed to be home in a half-hour to finish my homework. Besides—" I added, "my mom made me promise not to go too far. But we could go next Friday? After school?"

"I can't. I have a family dinner that night with my grandparents, and my parents would kill me if I missed it. It's their 50th anniversary, and we're all supposed to be going to some fancy restaurant to celebrate. We've been planning it for months."

"No problem," I said, doing my best to hide my disappointment. "I get it. I mean, family stuff is important."

"Yeah. But we'll plan a day soon. We just have to figure out a day that works for both of us."

"Right," I said, a slow grin passing my lips. "And coordinate with your busy writing schedule."

"Exactly." He laughed, with a glimmer in his clear blue eyes. "No promises though. The life of a writer never stops."

This time, I laughed as the two of us continued walking and talking, the minutes flying by as we made our way through the neighborhood. And after I got home, did my homework, and slipped into bed later that night, I decided to do some light reading. But as I plopped the small leather book down on my bed, I noticed something strange.

There was a pocket in the back.

And inside the pocket, there was a letter.

It was a little smudged, but I was still able to make out most of the words.

I am writing this letter to say the words that I fear I will never be able to say in person. The words that I want to say but that I'm too afraid to vocalize. From the moment I met you, I've had feelings for you. Feelings that I've kept hidden for fear of destroying our friendship. But as I'm sure you know, hidden feelings are just as real as the feelings we say aloud. And I can't let them hide in silence any longer.

You're different than any other guy that I've ever met. And that was what first drew me to you. Your joy, your enthusiasm, your passion for life. And most of all, your faith and your desire to live it out wholeheartedly. When I met you, I felt like I was getting to know someone I had somehow known all along. I don't know if you feel the same way. But I hope that somehow, someway, we'll always be in each other's lives, even if it's just as good friends.

Always sincerely,

H.D.

I read the letter about four or five times before finally putting it away. H.D. had feelings for someone? And she wrote a whole letter confessing them—without ever sending it?

I blinked, reading it once again to see if it really was what I thought it was or if I was just losing my mind. But when I closed my eyes and opened them again, the letter was still there, as plain as day—leaving me convinced of only one thing as I lay in bed that night.

My mystery writer had just gotten even more mysterious.

»→ ←«

*T*hat Monday, I knew I had to tell someone about the unusual letter that I had found in the diary. And as I sat in the cafeteria with my friends, I decided that I couldn't hold it back any longer.

"No way," Nathan said after I had finished telling them the story, not sparing a single detail. "Your diary girl wrote a letter to some guy and placed it in the back of the book? And she never sent it?"

"Yup." I nodded as I took a bite of my ham and cheese sandwich—careful to chew and swallow before answering. "I've never seen anything like it before. It was the weirdest thing!"

"No kidding," Atticus said. "I thought that kind of stuff only happened in movies."

"Same," Jenny agreed. "Do you know who she wrote it to?"

"No clue. The salutation was too smudged to read. I could make out most of the letter, but the opening was ruined."

"Has she mentioned this guy anywhere else?" Tanisha asked. "Maybe in another entry, later in the diary?"

"Not that I know of," I said, suddenly realizing how limited my knowledge of H.D.'s personal life really was. "But I haven't gotten too far. She might elaborate on it more in an entry I haven't read yet."

"Do you think she and this guy were close?" Amber asked, taking a bite of her salad.

"It seems like it. I mean, she said in the letter that she hoped the two of them would always be friends."

"It's so sad," Jenny said, swishing her spoon around in her soup. "Somewhere out there, there could be two people who were *destined* to be together but never ended up together. All because she never gave him that letter!"

"Jenny, come on. By now, I'm sure they're both happily married to other people," Tanisha noted. "This letter was written when the girl was in college. And they've both got to be in their forties by now. I'm sure whatever they had is long forgotten."

"But that's even sadder!" Jenny exclaimed. "It's like *Dear John*! I mean, come on, tell me that's not the stuff of tragedies!"

"I just wish she had given us more of a lead," Atticus said slowly. "If she had, maybe we'd be able to find both of them and get the whole story."

Before I had a chance to reply, the bell rang, cueing the eight of us to dump the rest of our food into the trash and head to our next class. That is, until something happened in the hallway that caused us to stop dead in our tracks.

"Hey," a loud voice boomed, as Kent appeared out of nowhere, shoving Nathan against the wall of lockers. "Look what I caught—a *shrimp*!"

"Hey, layoff, would you, man?" Kyle said, frustration clear in his voice. "No one thinks this is funny."

"Oh yeah? Well, I think it's pretty funny. Hey, Logan, catch a shrimp!"

"What's the matter? Too scared to fight?" Logan asked, grabbing him by the front of his shirt. "You know, I can't decide anymore—are you a chicken or a shrimp?"

"Maybe he's a chicken-shrimp!"

"I'm not chicken! Just let me go, OK?"

"Not until you prove to us that you're not a chicken," Logan said, slamming him against the locker on the other end of the hallway.

"Logan, you heard the boy!" Tanisha snapped. "Now, let him go already, would you?"

"Oh yeah, and who do you think you are? His bodyguard?"

"That's it!" Atticus exclaimed, suddenly sounding totally unlike his usual calm, sensitive self. "Either you let him go now or I'll fight you right here, right now. And my sister will get a good video of it to show Principal Wembley later. We'll see whose side she takes."

Kent's eyes darted from Atticus to Tanisha, who was already pulling out her phone—her thumb on the screen, ready to hit *record*.

"Fine," he said after a long moment. "But one of these days, you're not going to have your little buddies around to protect you. And you don't want to know what I'll do when that day comes."

"Are you okay?" Jenny asked as Kent walked away with his friends.

"Yeah, I'm fine. Let's just get going, alright?"

"Nathan, do you think maybe it's time to report those guys?" Atticus asked, concerned. "They're only getting worse. I mean, Kent threatened you today, and we all heard him. If you told Principal Wembley that, she'd take your side."

"What's the point?" Nathan asked, looking defeated. "They're still going to be going to school here, regardless of what I do. And one way or another, they're still going to try to make my life miserable. The way I see it, telling on them will just make things ten times worse."

We were all silent, at a loss for words or advice.

"Come on," he said. "I'll be fine. Let's just head to class, OK?"

We remained silent as we walked to our classes. But the whole way there, I felt my stomach tie itself into a billion knots as I replayed the situation over and over again in my mind. There had to be some way to help Nathan.

The only problem was, I didn't have a clue how.

Chapter Nineteen

Because of the Lord's great love we are not consumed, for his compassions never fail. They are new every morning; great is your faithfulness.
- Lamentations 3:22-23

The rest of the week went by quicker than I expected. Thankfully, without any more encounters with Kent and his gang, allowing me to put them out of my mind and focus on something a little more positive. Something that I've been planning for and preparing for over the last couple of months.

My sixteenth birthday.

"Katie, wake up," my mom said, as she sat on the edge of my bed, my eyes barely half-open as I examined my room and saw light flooding in through my bedroom window.

"Huh?" I muttered, as I forced myself to sit up. "Is it Monday already?"

"No silly, it's your birthday!"

I glanced at my calendar to see that it was Saturday the 15th. November 15th. The day of my sixteenth birthday.

"Happy Birthday, Katie," my dad said, walking up to my bed from behind her, carrying my favorite breakfast—chocolate chip pancakes.

"Thanks, guys." I smiled, taking a sip of orange juice, trying to urge my brain to catch up with the rest of my body. As a former homeschooler, I still wasn't used to early mornings.

"Ready to take your driver's test?" he asked, as it hit me like a ton of bricks. Today was my test at the DMV. The one that would determine my future as a licensed driver in America.

"Ready as I'll ever be." I smiled, even though I didn't feel ready at all.

"Cool, we'll head out at around twelve. And when we get back, we'll start getting ready for your party."

"Sounds great," I said as I got out of bed to brush my teeth. I totally forgot that my parents scheduled an appointment for me at the DMV today. As I thought about it, I felt a strange sense of nervousness and excitement bubbling up in my veins.

I was still a little apprehensive about driving by myself, but I was also eager to do it. After all, it was one of the biggest milestones of being a teenager, right? I was sure I could pass it. I just needed to stay focused and not let my emotions get in the way.

I was determined to try to look older today, so I brushed my hair, threw on some light lip-gloss, and wore a nice top and a pair of trendy jeans. Maybe if the people at the DMV thought I looked old enough to drive, they'd be convinced that I actually could drive. If nothing else, I at least looked decent enough not to cringe at my photo ID ten years from now.

"Katie! Are you ready to go?" Mom called from downstairs as I checked myself in the mirror one last time.

"All ready!" I called back as I hurried with my parents and brother out the door. My brother, not the least bit shy about making jokes the whole way there.

"After today, I'm going to have to text all of my friends," he said, taking a seat next to me as our dad climbed into the driver's seat.

"Why?"

"Because you're getting your license. I'm going to have to warn all of them to stay off the road."

"You're hilarious." I rolled my eyes. "Not!"

"I thought it was pretty funny."

"Jackson, don't antagonize your sister," Mom warned. "She's nervous enough as it is. Besides," she added, doubt clear in her voice, "I'm sure she'll do great."

"Yeah." I turned toward my brother. "Driving can't be too hard. You do it, don't you?"

"Alright, you two," Dad said in a voice that was calm, but firm. "Let's try to get along. It's Katie's birthday today."

"What? She's the one giving me a hard time!"

"Well, either way, I don't want to hear the two of you fighting. I want this to be a fun day. It's not every day someone in the Carter family gets their license."

"Right," Jackson said, this time more serious. "Sorry, Katie."

"It's OK," I said, even though I still felt irritated.

"So, Katie," Mom began, "remember, your hands should always be at—"

"Ten and two," I answered before she could finish her sentence.

"And you remember what to do when you want to get over or make a turn?" Dad added, as I suddenly felt like I was on a special driving episode of *Jeopardy!*

"Yes." I nodded. "You use your turn signal. And you always look before changing lanes."

"Excellent! Just remember that when you take your test today, and you'll be fine."

"Thanks, Dad." I took a deep breath as we parked in front of the Department of Motor Vehicles. *This is it.*

I sat down in the cold, clustered building and looked around at the cast of characters that surrounded me—still trying to figure out how I was old enough to be here.

"Number 147," I heard someone call over the loudspeaker.

"That's you," Jackson said, giving me a nudge.

"Right," I said as I followed behind my family.

"Are you here to get your license?" a lady with big, rimmed glasses asked, who seemed surprisingly friendly compared to some of the other people who worked there—who looked like they'd rather be trapped in a sewer somewhere.

"Yes, ma'am." I nodded, trying to sound more confident than I felt. Instead, my voice just went up around five pitches, making me sound like Minnie's cousin twice removed.

"Alright, what's your name?"

"Katie Carter," I said as she proceeded to ask me a string of questions before asking me to stand in front of a white piece of cardboard to take my picture.

"Alright, you're good to go! Good luck on your test!"

"Thank you," I replied as I walked outside, where I was met by an older, intimidating-looking man.

Apparently, I'm going to need it.

"All ready?" he asked, somehow reminding me more of a robot than an actual human being. I gulped as I felt my chest start to tighten, the way it did when I went to that karaoke place with Tanisha and Jenny.

"All ready."

"Good," he said as I buckled my seatbelt and turned on the ignition, slowly starting to drive around the property.

This isn't so bad . . . I've got this. I can totally . . .

"*Stop!*" he shouted as I slammed on the brakes, feeling panicked by the tone of his voice.

"Good," he said, making a note on his clipboard. "Go on."

From there, we went through several maneuvers, including a three-point turn that I practiced relentlessly with my mom in a Walmart parking lot. And before I knew it, the test was over.

"Did I pass?" I asked, putting the car into *park*.

"Hold on. You got seventeen points off. Your parking is sloppy, and your three-point turn could use some work . . ." he said, listing off all the things that I did wrong. Great. I failed. I didn't pass. Now I'm going to have to come back and take this test all over again, and I'm going to have to tell my family I didn't pass, and I'm probably the only sixteen-year-old on the planet who doesn't have a license and . . .

"Congratulations," he said. "You passed."

"I passed?" I asked, half-convinced that he had made some sort of mistake. "I actually passed?"

"Yes, you actually passed. If you want, you can go inside and tell your family the good news."

"Thank you, sir, thank you!" I exclaimed, practically flying out of the car. "I passed!" I shouted as soon as I saw Jackson and my parents.

"You passed?" my mom exclaimed, sounding almost as surprised as I felt. "That's awesome, honey! Congratulations!"

"Congratulations, Katie," Dad said, giving me a hug. "We're proud of you."

"Thanks, Dad. Thanks, Mom."

"Congratulations, Katie," Jackson chimed in. "I knew you could do it."

"Thanks, Jackson. I'm going to text my friends and tell them the good news."

I created a group chat with Tanisha, Atticus, Nathan, Jenny, and Ellie and sent them a text in all caps.

GUESS WHAT, GUYS? I PASSED!!!

>> <<

"Congratulations on passing your test!" Tanisha said later that night, at my party. "I knew you could do it!"

"Me too!" Jenny added. "Congratulations, Katie!"

"Thanks, guys." I hugged Tanisha and leaned down to hug Jenny. "Honestly, I'm just glad it's over. I had no idea how stressful it would be."

"Well, now that it's over, you can put it behind you," Tanisha said, in her usual ultra-chill tone of voice. "Now, you can just focus on your party. Atticus will be over soon. He's just picking up Nathan."

"No problem. We can have some girl time until they get here."

"Absolutely!" Jenny agreed. "Where should I put your present?"

"You didn't have to get me anything!" I exclaimed as she pulled a nicely wrapped present out from a bag on the side of her wheelchair. "I'm just glad you were able to come!"

"Don't be silly, it's your sixteenth birthday! Of course, I got you something!"

"Thanks, Jenny. Um, you can just put it on the table over there if you want?"

"Cool. I'll put my present over there too," Tanisha said as they placed their gifts down on the hard wooden surface. "So . . . how does it feel to be sixteen?"

"Pretty much the same as fifteen, to be honest," I said, scrunching up my face. "It doesn't feel that different. I always thought I'd feel older . . . but I kind of just feel like me."

"Yeah, that's how it was for me," Jenny agreed.

"Same," Tanisha chimed in. "People make a big deal out of it because you can drive. But it's just another year on the calendar. Nothing to make a big fuss about."

"Unless this is the year that you and Atticus finally end up together," Jenny teased—as my jaw hit the floor.

"*Jenny!*" I exclaimed in a hushed whisper. "Not so loud! My family is in the next room!"

"Sorry," she apologized as the doorbell rang. "That must be you-know-who now."

I rolled my eyes and hurried to get the door.

"Atticus, Nathan!" I said, trying to sound cool and casual, like we weren't just talking about him. "Good to see you! Come on in."

"Thanks, Katie. Happy Birthday," Atticus said as he and Nathan set their presents down on the table.

"Happy Birthday, Katie." Nathan smiled, looking much calmer today than he did last week.

"Thanks, guys," I said as one by one, guests started streaming in—while my brother connected my phone to the speakers to play the songs that I had arranged for my birthday. And after a couple of hours of hanging out and talking, it was time for cake and presents.

"Okay! The candles are on the cake," Mom said as she brought out the marble ice cream cake with sixteen candles on top. "Happy Birthday to you . . . Happy Birthday to you . . ." she began singing as the rest of my friends joined in, concluding with Kyle yelling for me to blow out the candles.

"What did you wish for?" Amber asked.

"I can't tell you. It might not come true."

"Fair enough."

"Can Katie open her presents while we eat?" Jenny asked. "I've been dying to give her mine!"

My dad laughed, exchanging glances with my mom.

"Sure," Mom replied, as Jenny rolled up to give me her present.

"I think you're going to like it," she said, as I opened the almost neurotically perfect gift—gasping when I saw what it was.

"A new phone case! With Proverbs 3:5-6 on it. I've been wanting one of these! Thanks, Jenny!"

"You're welcome. I remember you mentioned it to me at school."

"I did," I said, remembering how cracked my old phone case was from years of use and klutziness. "Thank you!"

"I call dibs on going next!" Tanisha said, grabbing her present and handing it to me. "This is for you, Katie. I hope you like it!"

"I'm sure I will," I said as I opened it. "Aww, a charm bracelet! And a new pair of earrings. Thanks, Tanisha—I love them!"

"You're welcome, girl. I thought you would!"

One by one, my friends took turns giving me their presents, until the only one left was Atticus. I unwrapped the shiny gold paper on his gift, and as I did, I couldn't believe what I saw. A leather-bound diary with my name on it. One that looked exactly like H.D.'s diary.

"I saw it online and thought you might like it," Atticus said, shoving his hands in his pockets. "I hope you do."

"I love it! Thanks, Atticus."

"You're welcome. Happy Birthday, Katie."

"Hey, Katie!" I heard someone else say, forcing me out of the moment. I looked over to see that it was Maya. "I have to get going—I have a piano recital tonight. But thanks again for inviting me. I had a lot of fun!"

"You're welcome. I'm glad you could come. I'll walk you out."

With that, my guests slowly started dropping off until Tanisha and Jenny were the only ones left. And before long, the three of us were sitting on my bed, watching an old Amanda Bynes movie—all in our pajamas for the sleepover.

"Hey, do you guys want to get some ice cream?" Tanisha asked about halfway through the movie as Jenny shot her a look like she was crazy.

"Are you kidding? I already feel like I'm going to be sick from all of the ice cream cake I ate earlier!"

"Well, don't get sick here," Tanisha said, scooting over, as Jenny *did* look slightly green. "That's just nasty!"

"I'm not going to get sick. Just don't say the 'F-word.' "

"Ice cream?" I asked, confused since it didn't start with an F.

"I think she means food," Tanisha said as Jenny hunched over.

"Don't say it!" she moaned.

"Are you going to be okay?" I asked, worried about my friend.

"Yeah, I just overdid it on the sweets, that's all. I'll be fine in the morning."

"You sure?"

"Positive. I think I'll just turn in a little early tonight if that's alright with you. I'm a little worn out from all the fun and festivities."

"No problem," I said. "I think I'll turn in early too. It's been a long day for me, with the DMV and the party and all. Between those two things, I'm pretty much beat."

"You guys are no fun," Tanisha said, even though I could tell she was only kidding.

"Sorry," Jenny apologized.

"It's OK. Honestly, you guys are probably right. I think we all could use some sleep. But could we wait until after the movie?"

"Sure," I said, turning toward Jenny. "I mean, if that's alright with you."

"Heck yeah." She grinned. "I want to see if this Sebastian girl ends up with Channing Tatum!"

"I'll give you the abridged version," Tanisha said, with a teasing glimmer in her eyes. "She does."

"Thanks for spoiler-alerting it for me!"

"It's not a spoiler alert if it's a rom-com. All rom-coms are the same. Girl likes guy. Guy loses girl. Guy gets her back again. The end. Roll the credits and cue the cheesy pop song."

"Quiet, guys, I want to see this!" I said as one of my favorite scenes came on. I may have seen this movie a million times, but it was still one of my favorites.

Finally, after the movie ended—the way Tanisha said it would—we turned out the lights. And after everyone was asleep, I pulled out my new diary. The one Atticus got me for my birthday. I still couldn't believe that he had found something that so closely resembled H.D.'s diary. And that he had gotten me something so nice. Part of me wanted to write in it, but the other part of me wanted to wait until I had something special to write about.

I stared at it for a while, running my fingers over the leather binding and flipping trough the crisp white pages before deciding that my first entry would be saved for another time.

At that moment, beyond thankful for the new diary.

And to have such great friends.

Chapter Twenty

Glory to God in the highest heaven,
and on earth peace to those on whom his favor rests.
- Luke 2:14

*I*n the weeks following my 16th birthday, our house was filled with the sights and smells of the season. The floor was covered in wrapping paper, bows, and tape, and the house was dressed in Christmas trees and decorations. And all through the house, you could hear joyful music playing from the radio, and smell the sweet aroma of freshly baked cookies. It was officially Christmas in the Carter house.

And I was so ready for it.

"Are you ready for the last meeting of the year?" Atticus asked as the two of us made our way through the halls of Winter Oaks High School.

"I think so," I said, readjusting my backpack as we walked. "We've been working all week on the lesson plan, and we've had a bunch more people coming to the meetings lately. I feel good about today."

"Me too," he agreed. "It's crazy how much this club has been blowing up lately."

"For sure." I nodded as the two of us walked into the old familiar Student Center, which was still just as messy and disorganized as ever. "Looks like we have some work to do."

We spent the next fifteen minutes tidying up and setting up chairs before people started heading into the room. And by the time we were finished, everyone had arrived.

"Alright, everyone," I said, taking a seat and glancing around the room. "If everyone's here, we can get started. As usual, we're going to open in prayer and then launch into the lesson. Yes, Nathan?"

"Can I open in prayer today?" He hesitated as he glanced around the room. "I know that usually you or Atticus do it, but I'd like to today if you guys don't mind."

"Not at all," I said, surprised to see Nathan, who's usually so quiet, volunteer to pray in public. "Go right ahead."

"Okay," he said, bowing his head and closing his eyes. "Dear God, we thank you for this day, for this club, and for the time that we have to study your Word. And we ask that you lead us through this study. We pray all these things in Jesus' name, amen."

"Amen." I echoed. "Thanks, Nathan."

"No problem." He smiled.

"Alright, since everyone is here, we're going to be taking a look at the Nativity story. Though it's a story that probably all of us are familiar with, I believe there's a lot we can learn from it. With Christmas right around the corner, I thought it would be the perfect story for us to close out with for the year. So, if you have your Bible with you, could you please turn with me to—"

Before I could finish, I heard someone walk up from behind me. And as my eyes landed on Nathan's face, I noticed that it was as white as snow. I turned around to see who was there. And as I did, I felt as though my stomach had climbed up into my throat.

"This is the Agape Club, right? The Christian club?"

"Uh, yeah. This is it," I said, doing my best to keep my composure.

Standing in the doorway was Ian Fairview. One of Kent's friends, who was there the day Kent tormented Nathan in the hallway. The same one who told him that even he wasn't a big enough jerk to beat up a girl. He wasn't as mean as Kent, but he was one of the biggest players in school, or so I've heard.

"Cool," he said, looking uncomfortable. "Can I come in?"

"Uh, yeah. Sure. Take a seat. We were just about to get started."

"Great," he said, taking a seat right between Tanisha and Cole.

"So, as I was saying, since we're in our last meeting of the year, and Christmas is just a few weeks away, we're going to be reading over the Nativity story today. Does anyone want to volunteer to read Luke chapter 2?"

No one said anything, so I scanned the room, looking for someone to call out. And almost instinctively, my eyes fell back on the unlikely candidate.

"Ian, do you want to read?"

"Me?" he asked, sounding surprised.

"Yeah, just this passage right here." I motioned to it so he could see which passage I was referring to.

"Uh, I'll pass," he said, folding his arms and shifting in his seat. "Sore throat. Don't want to strain it."

"Okay . . ." I said, not really believing him, but not wanting to waste any more time, I moved on. "Anyone else?"

"I'll read it," Liv said, raising her hand.

"Awesome, thanks Liv." I smiled.

Even though this was a Christian club, and Jesus would want me to welcome everyone, I couldn't help but feel a twinge of irritation with Ian for deciding to come to the Agape Club. After everything that he's put my friends through, did he really think I'd be okay with him showing up here today?

And why was someone like Ian coming to a Christian club anyway? When his behavior was literally the opposite of everything Jesus stood for?

Suddenly, out of nowhere, something hit me like a ton of bricks. A thought that I knew could only be from God.

Do not judge by what you see . . . the Lord looks at the heart.

I remembered reading those words in the Bible a long time ago, but what did they mean for this situation?

Liv must have finished reading because suddenly, all eyes were on me.

"Thanks, Liv," I said, trying to look like I had been paying attention and not totally spacing out. "In this passage, we see a lot that's familiar to most of us here today. Things that we read about at Christmas time growing up. But for the people living during this time, the events that happened were totally unexpected.

"You see, even though the Jewish people believed that God would send a messiah, and even though it was prophesied about in the Old Testament, most people believed that Jesus would come as a king or a ruler rather than a baby. They couldn't see that the savior of the world might be born in a place as humble and lowly as a manger. Yes, Cole?"

"Why did He do that? Come as a baby, rather than a fully-grown man? I mean, if I were God, I think I'd bypass the infant stage and go straight to adulthood."

"That's a good question," Atticus said, jumping in. "The truth is, I don't think that's something we'll ever know for sure until we get to Heaven. But if I had to guess, I'd say to shake up our expectations. I think sometimes we all have a limited idea of who God is and what He can do. It would seem to me, at least, that God was trying to get their attention by coming in an unexpected way."

"I have a question," Jenny said, raising her hand. "I mean, if there were all these writings and prophecies about Jesus coming, why is it that so many people still didn't believe? Shouldn't they have known better?"

"That's something I've wondered about too," I said. "But sometimes, when God moves in a new way, we don't always know to look. Kind of going off what Atticus said, sometimes our perceptions can drown out the truth of what's really there. Anyone else?" Since no one had any other questions, I continued with the lesson, forgetting that Ian was there, until I saw him slip out after it was over.

"I can't believe Ian had the nerve to show up here today," Tanisha said, once she was sure he was out of earshot. "I mean, after everything he and his friends have put us through, did he really think he could just waltz in here like that, expecting us to be okay with it?"

"I know," Jenny agreed, equal frustration in her voice. "I couldn't *believe* he came today!"

"Well, technically, he has just as much right to be here as we do," Nathan reminded her. "Besides, if he's searching, I sure don't want to be the one to stand in his way."

"You mean you were really okay with him coming?" Atticus asked, surprised.

Nathan nodded. "I guess too much has been going right for me to let Ian bother me today." He smiled as the four of us stared at him, partly in shock and partly in awe. "I've been doing a lot of soul searching this semester. And after a lot of reading and studying the Bible on my own, I've decided that I want to start following Jesus. Whatever it looks like, whatever it means, I'm all in."

"Nathan!" I exclaimed, surprise and amazement ringing through my voice. "That's amazing—I'm so happy for you!"

"Thanks," he said, a newfound peace shining in his eyes that wasn't there a week ago. "And you know, I've been thinking. I want to get baptized by your dad, at Hope Life Church, since that's kind of where my journey began. I mean, if that's alright with you."

"That would be more than alright. We're doing baptisms in January if you want to do it then?"

"I'd like that. And, I'd like to have all of you there with me. If you wouldn't mind staying after service to watch."

"Absolutely," Atticus promised. "We wouldn't miss it for the world."

"Agreed," Tanisha said. "We'll be there, cheering you on."

"For sure," Jenny added.

"Thanks. I'd better get going, but I'll see you tomorrow?"

"See you then," I called back as he made his way out the door.

"Later, Nathan," Atticus said, as we each followed his lead, suddenly convinced that nothing could put a damper on my day.

Not even someone as horrible as Ian Fairview.

»→ ←«

Over the next couple of weeks, my attention switched from the Agape Club and Nathan to Christmas.

And before I knew it, it was Christmas Eve.

"Katie, are you almost ready?" Dad called from the bottom of the staircase. "We're supposed to be at church in twenty minutes!"

"Coming!" I shouted, shoving on my last boot as I hurried downstairs—pure adrenaline coursing through my veins.

"You look nice," Mom said as I got to the bottom of the staircase, careful not to twist my ankle on the way down.

"Thanks, Mom. So do you."

"Thanks, Katie." She smiled as my dad hurried into the living room, adjusting his tie and looking just short of having a nervous breakdown—since he's never preached for a Christmas Eve service before, and the church would be more crowded than usual.

"Alright, if everyone's ready, we can get going."

"I'm ready," Jackson said.

"Me too," I added, shifting in my boots.

"Great." He smiled. "Then let's get this show on the road!"

With that, the four of us climbed into the family car and drove to church, watching the houses pass us by as we drove. Each one dressed in lights and decorations for Christmas.

"We've got to turn this one up!" Dad exclaimed, adjusting the volume on the radio. "Come on guys—there's a *woooorrlld* outside your *winnndoow!*"

"Dad," my brother groaned, sliding down in his seat. "Don't you think we're a little old for this?"

"You're never too old for Christmas, Jackson. Come on, sing with me," he urged as Jackson reluctantly joined in on the old 80s song. "You too, Katie!" Though I had to agree that this was the epitome of Christmas-family-corniness, I joined in. And before we knew it, we were all lost in the music and laughter—until finally, we arrived at Hope Life Church.

"Good luck on your sermon, Dad. You're going to kill it!" I said, fist-bumping my dad as we walked into the sanctuary.

"Thanks, Katie. Only with God's help." He smiled, as my mom, Jackson, and I found three seats near the front next to Atticus, Tanisha, and their parents.

"Katie, I love your outfit!" Tanisha exclaimed, hugging me before we sat down. "You look so festive!"

I laughed. "Thanks, Tanisha. You look great too!"

"Thanks, girl." She smiled, her silver earrings dangling as she spoke.

"Merry Christmas, Katie," Atticus said as the worship band went up on stage. "You look nice tonight."

"Thanks, you do too," I said, pretty sure that my face was as red as my sweater. But thankfully, I didn't have much time to think about it because before we knew it, it was time for the Christmas Eve service to begin.

"Merry Christmas, Hope Life Church!" Sammy exclaimed, grabbing one of the microphones from the stand as they dimmed the lights. "We have a very special service planned tonight, but before we get started, we're going to have a time of worship. And I want to invite you to worship God in whatever way feels most natural to you. Raise your hands, clap to the beat, bow your head, or just reflect on this moment. There's no wrong way to worship our Savior. That being said, I am so glad you all came out here tonight, and I hope you enjoy our Christmas Eve service!"

I smiled, clapping along as the church broke into applause, soon transitioning from the time of worship to the message.

"And so," my dad said, as he closed his message, "I want to leave you with one last thought. One that you can carry beyond this holiday season. What does hope mean to you? Does it mean a stable salary? A new house? A new boat? Or does it mean something more—something that can't be wrapped in a box or purchased with money? I believe that hope has a name. And His name is Jesus. Let's pray." With that, we bowed our heads and closed our eyes. "Dear Lord, we thank you for your precious gift of love this holiday season. We thank you for who you are, for your presence, and for your goodness. And we thank you that because of you, we can find life—true life that is better than anything this world has to offer. We pray these things in the name of your son, Jesus. Amen."

"Amen," a couple of people echoed from the audience.

"Before we dismiss, we have one last surprise for you. If you would stay seated for a few minutes longer, we have a wonderful performance put together by Ms. Charlette and the children of Hope Life Church. They've been working hard on this performance for the last couple of months, and I have a feeling they won't disappoint. Please welcome Ms. Charlette and her children to the stage for a classic live Nativity performance!"

I smiled and clapped along with the rest of the church as the kids walked up to the altar.

"Greetings, you who are highly favored! The Lord is with you!" a redheaded boy named Mikey exclaimed, causing a very small Mary to jump back in fear. "Do not be afraid, Mary. You have found favor with God! You will conceive and give birth to a son, and you are to call him Jesus! He will be called the Son of the Most High!"

The kids continued through the rest of the performance with only a few minor errors, until finally, the service was over—leaving us to go home and celebrate Christmas Eve together, the same way that we always do. We all opened one present and then watched *Miracle on 34th Street* before heading to our rooms to fall asleep. Only as I lay there that night, I couldn't help but toss and turn—my mind seeming to race with a million thoughts all at once. And as I got up to use the bathroom at around midnight, I heard footsteps walking around downstairs.

I was old enough to know it wasn't Santa, but curious as to who it was, I walked downstairs to see what was going on.

"Jackson?" I asked as I saw my brother sitting on the couch with a glass of milk and a plate of cookies, staring at the tree. "What are you doing up?"

"Same thing you're doing. Mostly just thinking. About what Christmas used to be like when we were kids. Everything seemed so big back then."

"I know," I said, grabbing my own plate of cookies and milk—since I had a feeling that I wasn't going to be getting much sleep tonight anyway. "It's crazy how much we've grown since then."

"I know," he agreed. "It's crazy. This will probably be my last Christmas living at home . . . since I'm going away to college next year."

"But you'll still come home to visit, right?" I asked, worried. Jackson and I have been getting along better lately, like we used back on the mission field, and the thought of never seeing him caused my stomach turn into knots.

"Of course." He nodded. "I'm going to try to stay close by too. I want to be able to visit often."

"Have you started thinking about colleges? Which one you might want to go to?"

"Well, I've thought about Berkley. But I doubt I'll be able to get in, with it being in the Ivies and all. I've also thought about UCLA . . . or Pepperdine."

"Wait, Pepperdine?" I asked, surprised. "That's a Christian school, right?"

He nodded. "That's another thing I've been thinking about lately. A couple of days ago, I rededicated my life to Christ. I haven't told Mom and Dad yet. I'll tell them tomorrow, but I wanted you to be the first to know."

"Jackson!" I exclaimed. "That's awesome! What made you decide to do that?"

"A couple of things. I've been talking with Pastor Sean lately and doing a lot of studying on my own about my questions and some of the doubts I've been having, and I guess you can say that I've made my faith my own. You were right, Katie . . . if you look for answers, you'll find them."

"I'm so happy for you, Jackson. Seriously, that's amazing. So, are you thinking about becoming a pastor, like Dad?"

"I don't know . . ." He hesitated. "I don't know if I can really see myself doing that. But maybe something in Law or Medicine. And a Christian university would give me a solid foundation for either of those fields. I mean, we need Christians in every field, right?"

"Absolutely." I nodded, taking another bite of my cookie. "Like Mom and Dad always say—ministry is something you live, not something you do."

"Exactly." He nodded. "Honestly, I think you'll be the one to carry on the Carter family ministry torch. I mean, just look at what you've done with the Agape Club. You've managed to attract people who at one point, never would've thought about stepping foot in a church or a youth group. That's not easy to do."

"You think so?" I hesitated. "I mean, I'd love to work in ministry someday . . . but I guess I've never really known if I was good enough. Or if God was calling me."

"Well, if you ask me, I definitely think you're called," Jackson said, taking a gulp of milk. "And based on what you've done with your club, I think you're more than capable of handling whatever ministry God leads you to."

"Thanks, Jackson. That means a lot."

"No problem," he said, as the two of us sat there in silence, eating our cookies and staring at the tree, which was colored with a hundred twinkling lights.

"I guess I should try to get some sleep," I said after a long moment. "Christmas is only a couple of hours away, and I don't want to be a total grinch in the morning." I grinned.

"I should head up too. See you in the morning?"

"See you in the morning. Night, Jackson."

"Night, Katie," he said as we headed to our rooms, a smile creeping onto my lips as I pulled the covers to my chest and stared at the ceiling.

Thankful to God for answering not just one, but two prayers.

Chapter Twenty-One

. . . God demonstrates his own love for us in this: While we were still sinners,

Christ died for us.

- Romans 5:8

$\mathcal{A}$ couple weeks later, the day finally came for Nathan to get baptized. And just like we promised, we were all there to support him.

"So, after we finish service, what happens exactly?" Nathan asked as the five of us walked through the large glass doors. "I mean, is there anything else I should know?"

I shook my head. "My dad will explain it in the class after service. He's going to ask you a couple of questions, and then he'll dunk you in the water and bring you back up, and it will all be finished. It's really simple—I promise."

"I hope you're right," he said as we took our seats.

"You'll be fine," Atticus assured him. "And besides, we'll all be right up front, cheering you on."

"Thanks. I'm really glad you guys came out today. You know, to support me."

"Aw, it's no problem, Nate," Tanisha said. "We're glad we could come."

"Have you heard anything from your dad?" Jenny asked, voicing the question we were all thinking about, but no one dared to ask. "Is he coming today to watch you get baptized?"

Nathan shook his head as a dark shadow crossed his face. "Nothing. I . . . don't think he's coming."

"I'm really sorry, Nathan," I said, sympathy coloring my voice. "I know how much you wanted him to be here."

"It's OK. It's not about him today, anyway. It's about Jesus. And celebrating my decision with the people closest to me? That's already way more than I could ask for."

Before we had the chance to say anything else, the worship team went up to play the opening notes of their first song, launching us into service. The message today was focused around staying close to God in the new year and letting Him lead you in your decisions. I jotted down notes in the new notebook that I got for Christmas, and before I knew it, the service was over.

"And so—" my dad said an hour later, "as we enter into a new year, let us also step into everything God has for us, as we strive to grow closer to Him. That being said, we are having baptisms after service. Feel free to stay and watch if you would like to be there to celebrate with us. If you are one of the people getting baptized today, please head on back to the green room. I'll be there shortly to discuss the details of this event with you."

"That means you, man," Atticus whispered to Nathan as he jumped up to go find the room.

"I can't believe his dad didn't show today," Tanisha said, shaking her head, once Nathan was out of earshot. "What kind of parent doesn't show up for their own kid's baptism?"

"To be honest, I'm surprised Nathan invited him at all," Atticus said. "His relationship with him has been rocky for as long as I can remember. He's barely even talked to him since his parents split up."

"Well, he seems to be handling it well," I noted. "Especially under the circumstances."

Within a couple of minutes, my dad's class came back for baptisms and each person was baptized, one by one, until finally, it was Nathan's turn.

"Nathan," my dad began as he climbed into the tub and stood beside him. "Do you believe that God exists in the form of the Trinity—through the Father, the Son, and the Holy Spirit, that He came down to earth through the person of Jesus Christ to atone for your sins, and that the Holy Spirit came to live and dwell inside of you upon accepting Jesus as your Lord and Savior?"

"Yes, sir!" Nathan answered confidently.

"And Nathan, do you wish to make this good confession, both here today and with the rest of your life, that Jesus is Lord?"

"You bet I do!" he exclaimed as my dad dunked him in the water, suddenly hearing a distinct male voice from among the crowd.

"That's my son!"

My head snapped around to see an older, gruff looking man who looked a little bit like Nathan.

Wait a minute. Was that Nathan's father?

"Is that who I think it is?" Tanisha whispered to me as Nathan came up from the water, dripping wet and staring in shock at the man, as if at a total loss for words.

"I think so," I whispered back, still studying the man. He had the same eyes as Nathan, and a similar face shape. And both of them had dark hair, except Nathan's was less gray.

"I can't believe he came," Atticus said, his voice filled with awe and disbelief.

"Me neither," Jenny added, as Nathan made his way out of the water toward his mom and who I assumed to be his dad. The three of them talked for a couple of minutes before Nathan made his way back to us.

"Congratulations, Nathan!" I exclaimed, hurrying over to hug him even though he was still wet. "How do you feel?"

"Amazing," he said, grinning from ear to ear. "Really good."

"Was that your dad out there?" Atticus asked, not wasting any time. "The guy who you were talking to just now?"

Nathan nodded. "That was him."

"So?" Tanisha asked, as if unable to contain her curiosity any longer. "How did it feel seeing him again?"

"Good," Nathan said, silent for a moment. "I'm not going to lie, it was a little weird, but it was good. He apologized for not being around more—you know, since the divorce. He also said that he wanted to take me out to lunch—once I'm dried off and in different clothes."

"That's great." Atticus smiled. "Sounds like he's turning over a new leaf."

"I think he is. I mean—it'll take time. But he wants to work on being a part of my life again. And seeing how Jesus has forgiven me has made me want to work on forgiving him."

"That's awesome." Jenny smiled. "I'm proud of you, Nate."

"Thanks. I should probably get going before the Sunday afternoon traffic kicks in."

"Alright, Nathan," Atticus said. "Have a good lunch!"

"See you tomorrow," I added.

"Thanks. See you tomorrow," he said as he walked off, and I headed home with my family—the details of the day playing over and over again in my mind. How Nathan, who was once so cynical, had decided to get baptized. How his dad showed up after being absent for so many years. How my brother was finally walking with God again. Life couldn't have been any better than it was at that moment.

"Hey—Mom, Dad—is it alright if I go for a walk around the neighborhood?" I asked as the four of us pulled into the driveway. "I'll be back before dinner."

"Is all of your homework done?" my dad asked, raising an eyebrow as he stared into the rearview mirror.

I nodded. "I finished early this week."

"Then I don't see why not. Just stay close by and keep your phone with you in case we need to get a hold of you."

"I will," I promised as I climbed out of the car. "Thanks, Mom. Thanks, Dad."

With that, I set out. And as I walked, I stayed in my thoughts, letting them wander until I hit the end of my neighborhood. Suddenly, remembering that H.D. lived just a few blocks away.

I stopped, hit by a wave of hesitation. After all, I told my parents that I would stay close by. And I knew that Atticus wanted to be there when I met H.D. But on the other hand, the odds of that happening anytime soon with his busy schedule and mine seemed unlikely. Besides, the woman in the picture looked harmless enough.

So, without thinking, and against my better judgment, I made my way toward the neighborhood, checking my phone to find the number of her house. 149 Willow Road.

Should I knock or ring the doorbell?

After debating those two options in my mind, I decided on the doorbell—praying with everything in me that she was home.

"Hello?" the tall, brunette woman said as she opened the door, staring curiously at the teenage girl on the other side. "Are you selling something?"

I shook my head. "I was just wondering, uh . . . Well, it's kind of a long story, but I found this diary under a floorboard in my bedroom, and I was wondering—"

"Aunt Halle?" I heard a male voice say from behind her. "Who are you talking to—*Katie*?"

"*Ian*? What are you doing here?"

"This is my aunt's house. What are you doing here?"

"I uh, just came because I think I have something that belongs to Hal—I mean, your aunt. I wanted to see if it was hers."

"Well, would you like to come in?" Halle asked, holding the door for me. "I made fresh cookies if you want some."

"Um, I'm good. Thanks," I said, keeping in mind that Halle was still technically a stranger, even though I kind of knew her nephew. "I can only stay for a few minutes."

"I totally understand," she said as I heard a noise. "That's my phone. I'd better take this, but as soon as I get off, I promise you can show me what you found."

"No problem," I said as Halle disappeared into the other room, leaving me alone with Ian Fairview.

AKA, one of my least favorite people.

"So," I began, attempting to make conversation, "what have you been up to?"

"Homework," he said, shifting nervously in place. "For Mr. Lancaster's class."

My eyes darted over to where his homework sat on the round wooden table, and I nearly gasped as my eyes fell on one of my old favorite books. *The Giver*, by Lois Lowry.

"I love this book!" I exclaimed, as I went to go pick it up—for a moment, forgetting that I was talking to Ian—chief jock and bully-sidekick. "I read it two years ago, back when I was living in Africa. What's your favorite part so far?"

"Uh, you know I really can't say. I mean, the whole thing is just so deep . . . and stuff."

"Come on. There must be one part that stands out to you."

"I guess it's when the guy . . . gets the gift?" he said as I eyed him curiously. "I mean, no. The part where he gives the gift. It's better to give than to receive, right?"

"Ian," I said slowly. "I really like page ninety-two. Would you mind reading it out loud to me?"

"Why can't you read it yourself?" he asked, sounding defensive. "I mean, the book is right there . . . Why do you want me to read it?"

"Oh my gosh . . . You can't read, can you?"

"What are you talking about?" he scoffed. "Of course, I can read! I just . . ."

"*Ian*," I said, stopping him.

"If you tell anyone, I'll deny everything." He sighed. "I can read enough to get by, but it's really hard for me. I was diagnosed with dyslexia when I was eight, and I've always had this thing with mixing up words . . . reversing letters . . . That sort of thing. That's why the whole football thing's such a big deal to me. If I don't get a scholarship, I don't stand a chance of getting into college."

"And that's why you put up with your friends' behavior," I said, more as a statement than a question. "Because you feel like you have to be on the team to get into college. And you don't want the people you're around so much making fun of you too."

"I know it sounds stupid, but I always felt like football was my only ticket to some kind of future. And I thought the only way to be accepted by the team was to keep my mouth shut. I know it's wrong, and I really am sorry. Especially for how I've been toward Nathan. He seems like a pretty cool guy."

"That doesn't excuse the way you treated him," I said slowly. "But I guess I understand why you did it. At least, better than I did before." I paused, trying to figure out how to word the next thing I wanted to ask him. "But, if you've been trying so hard to fit in with the team, why did you decide to join the Agape Club? I mean, it won't exactly earn you any popularity points at school. In case you haven't noticed, we're not exactly at the top of the food chain."

He sighed as if debating whether he should say what he wanted to say next. "Two months ago, my grandpa was diagnosed with Leukemia. Growing up, he was my hero and the only person who's ever believed in me. He's also a Christian. I guess now, more than ever, I want to know why his faith matters so much to him.

And why God would allow someone like him, someone who never did anything bad to anybody, to get sick."

"I'm sorry. I can't imagine how hard that must be." I paused, searching for the right words. "But I do know that God loves your grandpa. And whatever happens, He's with him."

"That's what he keeps telling me," he said, pain clear in his voice.

"Why don't we make a deal? If you promise to keep coming to the Agape Club and try to be nicer to people, I'll tutor you in reading. I understand if you still want to try for the football scholarship. But I think you need to know that you can make it into college without it."

"You'd do that for me? Even after all I've done?"

"Yeah." I nodded. "I would. Because that's what Jesus would do. And I try—as imperfectly as it may be, to follow His example."

"And no one would have to know about this? The tutoring, I mean."

"Well, I'd have to tell my parents, because I don't think they'd let me meet up with some guy every week if they didn't know why I was doing it. But I wouldn't tell anyone from school. Not even Jackson. So do we have a deal?"

He smiled, sticking out his hand for me to shake. "Deal."

"Cool." I smiled as his aunt came back into the kitchen.

"Sorry that took so long. It was my boss. So, what was it you wanted to show me?"

"This book," I said, remembering that I took a picture of the diary a while back. "I found it under one of the floorboards in my bedroom, and the librarian, Mr. Larson, said it might be yours.

"Mr. Larson." She chuckled. "I remember him. I was at that library almost every day during college."

I showed her a picture of the diary and let her read a couple of pages on my phone.

"I'm sorry, Katie, but this isn't mine," she said after a few minutes of reading. "I never kept a diary that looked like this. And her writing style is very different than mine. I'm sorry," she said again, shaking her head, "but I didn't write this."

"You didn't?" I asked, trying not to let my disappointment show.

"No. I'm sorry, Katie."

"It's OK. Thanks for checking."

"You're welcome. Good luck finding the real owner of the diary."

"Thank you." I smiled. "I'd better get going. My parents should be expecting me home soon. But it was nice meeting you."

"It was nice meeting you too, Katie. Would you like some cookies to go?"

"No, thank you. My parents are going to be making dinner soon, and I don't want to ruin my appetite."

"Okay. Well, have a good rest of your night. And be safe walking home."

"I will, thank you."

"You're welcome. Bye, Katie."

"Bye, Ms. Halle. Bye, Ian," I said as I headed out, suddenly hit with two big realizations. One, Halle wasn't the owner of the diary. And two, I had just agreed to tutor Ian Fairview.

Chapter Twenty-Two

If the world hates you, keep in mind that it hated me first.
- John 15:18

The following week, I felt a knot in the pit of my stomach as I went to school on Monday. After school today, I had my first tutoring session with Ian. And even though I'd done a lot of research over the weekend on how to help someone with dyslexia, I still had no idea how this meeting was going to go. Especially considering Ian and I weren't exactly friends.

"Hello!" I heard Tanisha say at lunch, snapping me back to reality. "Earth to Katie. Are you there?"

"Huh?" I asked, looking up from my soup, suddenly realizing that I had been dazing out for the last couple of minutes.

"I was just asking if you wanted one of my fries."

"Oh, no. I'm good. Thanks."

"No problem," she said, studying me curiously. "Are you alright? You've barely said a word since we sat down."

"Yeah, I'm fine. I just have a lot on my mind, that's all."

"The Agape Club?" Jenny asked.

I shook my head. "No, just . . . life."

"Hey, what are we studying this week in the Agape Club anyway?" Kyle asked, taking a bite out of his cheeseburger. "You mentioned that we were starting a new series."

"Yeah, we are." Atticus nodded. "We've been talking about doing it on the parables of Jesus. Speaking of which, we should probably get started on that pretty soon." He turned toward me. "Do you want to come over after school today, so we can start working on that?"

"Uh, I can't." I shifted in my seat. "I already have plans."

"What are you doing?" Jenny asked, with her usual level of pep in her voice. "Anything fun?"

"Um, I'm just meeting up with someone after school. That's all." *Please don't ask me who . . . Please don't ask me who . . . Please don't ask me who . . .*

"That's cool," Maya said. "Who are you meeting with?"

Dang it.

"Um, Ian Fairview," I replied, my voice muffled—praying they wouldn't hear me and that they'd drop it. But of course, I had no such luck.

"*Ian Fairview?*" Tanisha exclaimed. "*The* Ian Fairview? The one who's been a thorn in our side for almost two years now?"

"Uh, yeah. That's the one."

"Are you guys dating?" Amber asked, her jaw practically hitting the ground.

"No!" I exclaimed as a shadow crossed Atticus' face. "We're just friends—that's all!"

"Since when are you and Ian even friends?" Jenny asked, wrinkling up her nose in disgust. *God, help me.*

"I ran into him last week, and uh—he wanted to know if I'd be up for meeting him at the library sometime." That wasn't a total lie. We were meeting up at the library today.

And I did run into him last week.

"And you're sure all he wants is to be friends?" Atticus asked. "Because Ian doesn't exactly have a reputation for having a lot of girl friends." He finished his sentence by stressing the word *friends* as if to make it clear exactly what he was talking about.

"Yeah. Are you sure this is a good idea, Katie?" Tanisha asked, sounding concerned.

"I'm positive. I promise—I have no interest in Ian. We're just going to hang out and study together. Trust me, that's all he has in mind."

To my relief, Amber changed the subject and started talking about the new dog that her family picked up from the pound. But the whole time, I could tell everyone was thinking the same thing—that I was going out with Ian. The same Ian who has spent the last couple of months tormenting Nathan with his friends.

Everything in me wanted to scream the truth. To tell them that I was just tutoring Ian. But if I did that, I would be betraying his trust, and I knew that wouldn't be the right thing to do. *Breathe, Katie.*

Deep down, I felt something similar to the feeling I had at the karaoke place fighting to resurface. But I fought against it as hard as I could. I was not going to fall apart. Not here, in front of the whole school and all my friends.

"That's the bell," Tanisha said. "I'd better get going."

"Me too," Kyle agreed, picking up his lunch tray. "Later, guys."

"Later," I said as Atticus and I headed to our next class, silent most of the way there.

"Hey, you don't really think Ian and I are dating. Do you?" I asked as we got closer to our classroom, unable to take the silence anymore.

"Honestly?" he said, stopping in his tracks. "I don't think you have any interest in him, but I don't know if he feels the same way." He paused as if waiting for a reaction. "I just think you need to be careful, that's all. He's hurt a lot of girls, and I don't want to see you be one of them."

"You really think I'd let that happen?" I asked, feeling hurt by Atticus' words. "I thought you knew me better than that."

"I thought I did too. But I never thought I'd see you hang out with Ian either."

"Atticus," I said, but before I could say anything else, he had already walked into the classroom and taken a seat. Feeling my chest tightening by the second, I made my way to the girl's bathroom to try to pull myself together, even though I knew I was going to be late.

I hurried into the closest bathroom stall and locked the door—sitting on top of the toilet seat like I had seen so many people do in the movies when they didn't know what else to do. Because that's how I felt right now.

Like I had no idea what to do.

"God," I silently prayed, "are you sure I'm supposed to be helping Ian? Because right now, it seems to be ruining everything."

Before I even finished praying, a verse from Scripture came to mind. A verse that my parents had taught me a while back, from the book of Isaiah. "Do not fear, for I am with you; do not be dismayed, for I am your God. I will strengthen you and help you; I will uphold you with my righteous right hand."

"Okay God, if this is your will, I'll do it. And I'll trust that you'll help me handle whatever happens next."

With that, I flushed the toilet—as to not look totally weird for hanging out in a bathroom stall—and opened the door to wash my hands. *I could do this.*

"Hey," I heard a familiar female voice say as my head snapped around to see Sydney washing her hands beside me. "I overheard your conversation with your little friend out in the hallway about meeting up with Ian. I guess you missed the memo that *I'm* going out with him. We've been boyfriend and girlfriend for months."

"Actually, I didn't know that. But I promise you don't have anything to worry about. It's not a date it's just—"

"Well, I really don't care what it is. If you know what's good for you, you'll cancel it. In case you didn't know, I don't like sharing."

"I'm not going to cancel it," I said, with a courage that could've only come from God. "I promised him that I'd meet up with him today, and I'm not going to break that promise."

Sydney looked shocked. But to my surprise, she seemed to back down. "Well fine. Someone like Ian is never going to go for a girl like you anyway—some ex-homeschooled Jesus freak. *Besides,*" she added, "he's already got the perfect catch."

With that, she flitted off, leaving me alone as I made my way back to my classroom and took a seat. Somehow, managing to forget the insanity of the day, along with Atticus' comments and

Sydney's threats—focusing on one thing and one thing only. AP History. At least, for a little while.

»→ ←«

"Okay, so what are we doing first?" Ian asked later that day as he took a seat across from me at the library. The same one that Atticus had taken me to as we tried to uncover the mysterious identity of H.D.

"Well," I began, taking out my English textbook—along with one of my favorite books and a couple of pens and pieces of paper. "I did some research on helping people with dyslexia with their reading, and I found some pretty helpful information. And the first thing we're going to try is a method called decoding."

"De-*what*?"

"Decoding," I explained. "It's the process of sounding out printed words out loud. It helps to associate the words with their sounds. So, we're going to try this sentence right here." I pointed to the place where I wanted him to read as he squinted.

"Cami was known for her hospitality. The way that she treated others. She was very am-ama-ammma . . ."

"Amiable. It means someone who's pleasant and easy to get along with."

"I can't do this." He groaned.

"Yes, you can. Let's try something. You see the first part of the word—ami?"

"Yeah?"

"It means friendly. The last part of the word just explains the meaning of the first part. It describes someone who is something."

"Like, *tolerable?*"

"Exactly!" I said, excited that he was finally starting to get this. "Now try reading the whole sentence together."

"Cami was known for her hospitality," he read, this time a little faster. "The way that she treated others. She was very amiable, yet only had a small group of close friends. People who knew her. People who understood her."

"Excellent!" I nodded. "See? You're getting this!"

"Yeah, thanks to you."

"I'm just helping. You're the one who's doing the work. Now, let's try something else. You see this word right here?"

"Yeah?"

"Do you know what it means?"

"No clue." He shook his head.

"I want you to try to figure out the meaning by the words surrounding it."

"The cake that she made was pretty grody. In fact, it was worse than anything she had ever tasted before." As he read the sentence aloud, something seemed to click. "Does that mean it's really bad?"

"Exactly!" I exclaimed. "Now, let's try another one."

We continued on that way for another hour until finally, we were finished—walking through the large glass doors to head home.

"I think today went pretty well for our first session," Ian said, holding the door for me. "I feel like I learned a lot. My brain's a little sore, but nothing a chocolate milkshake won't fix." He grinned.

"Well, you did a good job with the reading exercises. In a couple of weeks, you'll be reading like a pro."

"Thanks." He chuckled. "And thanks for agreeing to help me. I really do appreciate it."

"It's no problem. I'm glad I could help." I paused, remembering something he told me last week when I saw him at his aunt's house. "How's your grandpa doing? Is he feeling any better?"

"Kind of the same as before," he confessed, leaning against the brick wall. "He hasn't really made any progress, but he hasn't gotten worse either."

"How are you doing with everything?"

"Okay, I guess. I mean, as good as I know how to. I just hope he gets better. I know everyone has their time to go. I just really don't want his time to be now."

"Yeah, I get that. I'll keep him in my prayers for sure."

"You really think that works?" He sounded doubtful.

"Prayer?"

"Yeah."

"Yeah, I really do."

"Why?"

"Well, because I've seen it work before." I paused. "Back when I was living in Africa, there was this lady in our church who got sick. She had Rift Valley Fever, which can be pretty deadly. By all natural medical expertise, it looked like she wouldn't have more than a couple of days to live. But we all prayed for her, and three days later, the virus was gone, and she was back to her normal self again. And I can think of countless other situations just like that.

The way I see it, there's no other way to explain those kinds of things outside of prayer."

"Wow," Ian said, intrigued. "That's pretty incredible." He was silent once again, as if thinking. "But do you think God could ever listen to, you know, someone like me?"

"Yeah, of course." I studied him. "Why wouldn't he?"

"Well, because I'm not like you. I haven't lived this perfect Christian life. I've made mistakes . . . I've done things I regret."

"So have I—and so has everyone else in the world. God doesn't listen to us because we're perfect. If He did, he wouldn't listen any of us."

"Then why does He listen to us? I mean, why would a God that's as big and as powerful as you say care about people like us?"

"Because He loves us unconditionally. No matter how many sins we commit or how royally we screw up, he still loves us. There's nothing we can do to change that."

"But why? I mean, why does He love us? Why would He have a reason to love us?"

"That's all part of the mystery of God." I smiled. "It's who He is. Love just comes with His character. I can't say I understand it, but I'm thankful for it." I paused. "Have you ever read Romans 5:8?"

"No." He grinned. "In case you forgot, I'm not much of a reader."

"Well, when you get home tonight, look it up. And if you have any questions, shoot me a text. I'd be more than happy to explain it."

"Thanks, I will."

"Promise?"

"Promise." He smiled. "I'd better get going, but I'll see you tomorrow? At school?"

"Absolutely. Later, Ian."

"Later, Katie."

With that, he headed off, and I headed to my car to drive home—the whole way there, convinced that I was doing the right thing. Even if no one else thought I was.

Chapter Twenty-Three

I have officially reached insomniac status. Ever since my horrendous conversations with Sydney and my friends, I've barely gotten any sleep. Every time my head hits the pillow, all I can think about is the look on Atticus' face when I told him I was meeting with Ian—and Sydney's words when she thought I was trying to steal her boyfriend. Even yesterday, when Atticus came over to my house to work on our lesson for the Agape Club, he seemed different than usual. *Distant.* And every time that I see Sydney in the hallway, I can almost feel the weight of her glare. Ever since the day that everything came out in the open, nothing has felt normal. And considering that a lot of my friends from school went to Ignite, I could only pray that things would be better tonight.

"All ready to go?" my brother asked, grabbing the keys out of the kitchen closet.

"Yeah, I'm ready." I nodded as we said goodbye to our parents and got into the car—a million thoughts fighting for a space in my mind as we drove. About Ian. About Atticus. About this whole mess that I had somehow created.

"Are you okay?" Jackson asked, after a long moment.

"Yeah. Why?"

"Well, because you've seemed kind of quiet lately."

"I'm fine," I insisted. "I just have a lot on my mind, that's all." Even though my parents and my friends knew about the situation with Ian, I've been careful to keep it hidden from my brother. After Sydney dumped him last year and finding out that she was now dating Ian, I knew that he was the last person on my brother's list of favorite people.

Not to mention that I knew he wouldn't love the idea of his sister hanging out with a guy who was a known player. Any way you looked at it, I was between a rock and a hard place. And I figured it was better to keep my mouth shut than risk another situation like the one I had on Monday in the school cafeteria.

Thankfully, he didn't ask any more questions, and once we arrived, I began to feel a sense of peace wash over me. No matter how horrendous this past week was, church has always been my safe place. And right now, I wanted nothing more than to put everything out of my mind and focus on tonight.

"Hey, Katie," Sammy greeted me as I walked through the door, "and Jackson. How's it going?"

"Good." I forced a smile—hating how this whole Ian situation was making a total *liar* out of me. "How about you?"

"I've been good. School's been crazy, but I'm hanging in there."

"I can understand that," I said, even though she had no idea how accurate that statement really was. A few minutes later, it was time for service to start. And after our usual rhythms, Pastor Sean went up to give the message.

"What's up, Ignite!" he shouted as he walked up onto the small wooden stage. "Is everyone having a good week?"

A couple of students shouted 'yeah' and 'uh-huh', while the rest of us nodded. "Great! I hope you're all as excited for tonight as I am because we are starting a brand-new series called—wait for it . . . until the tech team puts it on the screen . . . Alien Youth! As a culture, many of us are very familiar with the concept of aliens. We've seen movies like *Star Wars* and *E.T.*, and we all have our own perception of the word *alien* when we hear it. But the kind of aliens that we're going to be talking about tonight are not the green, wrinkled-up characters from outer space.

"Instead, we're going to be talking about a different kind of alien. Someone who is living in one place, but a citizen of another. Who is in the culture, but not of it. And we're going to be starting with a passage from Scripture that elaborates on this concept. So, if you have your Bible or your phone with you tonight, please turn with me to 1 Peter 2:11-12."

Quickly, I pulled out my phone and went to the passage he was referring to. One that I was familiar with—and that I had memorized years ago, as a kid.

" 'Beloved,'" Pastor Sean began, reading out of his Bible, "I urge you as aliens and exiles to abstain from the desires of the flesh that wage war against the soul. Conduct yourselves honorably among the Gentiles, so that, though they malign you as evildoers, they may see your honorable deeds and glorify God when he comes to judge.'

"As Christians, it can be easy to feel like an alien and a misfit in this world. To feel like an outsider, when we choose to walk in purity, instead of giving in to the temptations of the flesh. When we choose to use our words differently or listen to different kinds of music than our non-Christian friends. When we make decisions that seem crazy and outlandish to the rest of our friends. Sometimes, we can even feel like aliens among other Christians when we choose to love and embrace people that they choose, wrongly, to shut out.

"In this world, we have beliefs and customs about what is normal and acceptable. But so often, the words of Jesus turn our cultural ideals on their head. He challenges the ideas and beliefs that we have chosen to blindly accept. And He loves people that we, in our pride, have called irredeemable.

"But if you're feeling this way, like an outcast, or an outsider for your faith, you're in good company, because even Jesus was rejected by the very people who should have accepted him. By the very people that He created and breathed life into. He says to his disciples in John 15:18-20, 'If the world hates you, keep in mind that it hated me first. If you belonged to the world, it would love you as its own. As it is, you do not belong to the world, but I have chosen you out of the world. That is why the world hates you. Remember what I told you: 'A servant is not greater than his master.' If they persecuted me, they will persecute you also. If they obeyed my teaching, they will obey yours also.'

"You see, so many of us here tonight have looked for the type of approval from people that we can only truly receive from God. Don't get me wrong—God created us for relationships with other people. He wants us to have friends; friends who will encourage us in our faith and help us make good decisions. But that coveted stamp of approval—the one that says you are worthy and special and loved—cannot come from people. Only the Creator can breathe that kind of life into His creation. When you look for the approval of man, you will come up short every time. But when you live your life seeking only the approval of God, it will overflow in a way that touches every life around you—even without you realizing it. We will be looking at one more verse tonight, so please turn with me to Galatians 1:10."

Quickly, I typed in the verse in my Bible App as Pastor Sean read it out loud.

" 'Am I now trying to win the approval of human beings, or of God? Or am I trying to please people? If I were still trying to please people, I would not be a servant of Christ.'

"As Christians, we cannot serve two masters. We cannot live for both the approval of God and the approval of man. We will always place one above the other. So tonight, you have a choice. Will you live for the approval of your peers or the approval of God?"

Pastor Sean continued talking about living for the approval of God rather than the approval of man as I sat on the edge of my seat, taking in every word. Growing up in church, it wasn't anything that I hadn't heard before, but somehow, it seemed to breathe fresh insight into my situation with Ian.

If God wanted me to follow through on my commitment to help Ian, then it shouldn't matter if people didn't understand my intentions. All that mattered was that I was faithful in doing the right thing.

"Dear God," Pastor Sean began as he closed in prayer, "we pray that you would lead us and guide us as we go home tonight, to school tomorrow, and as we interact with our friends the rest of this week. We pray that you would help us to live for your approval rather than the approval of others. Help us make choices that honor you and bring glory to your name. We pray these things in the name of your son, Jesus. Amen, and amen.

"Before we dismiss, I have a couple of announcements, so please stay seated a little while longer. This summer we have a lot of fun activities coming up, including camp and a mission trip to Honduras. If you have any questions about either of these events, please come and talk with me or one of the leaders after service. We are also going bowling this Saturday at Superstar Bowling. If this is something that you would be interested in, please sign up at one of the side tables. That being said, I hope you all have a great week."

"That sounds like fun," Tanisha said as we walked over to the table together. "I used to bowl all the time as a kid, and if I remember correctly, I had a pretty sweet game back in the day."

"I'd be down for it," I said, readjusting my bookbag. "I've never bowled before, but I'd be willing to give it a try."

"You've never bowled before?" Tanisha asked in amazement as I shook my head. "Girl, we've got to get you some bowling shoes! I'll teach you. Trust me—with me as your teacher, you'll catch on fast!"

"Cool, I can't wait." I glanced over toward Atticus, who still seemed quiet, but I did my best to shrug it off. He would come around. Sooner or later, he'd realize that nothing is going on between me and Ian. Or at least, I hoped he would.

One by one, everyone started heading home, and before long, it was time for me to head home, too. And as soon as I got up to my room, I felt my phone vibrate, signaling that someone was texting me. To my surprise, it was Ian.

Can I call u?

It was soon followed by another text.

I know it's late, but there's something I want to tell you. It's important.

I closed my door and tapped back a reply.

Sure.

Within a couple of seconds, I saw a FaceTime call come through on my phone and pressed *accept* as I plopped down on my bed and leaned up against a pillow.

"Hey, what's up?"

"I have some good news." He grinned, holding up a piece of paper. "I got a B+. The highest grade I've ever gotten on an English test!"

"Ian! That's awesome! See? I knew you could do it!"

"Thanks, Katie. I didn't. But I'm really glad I did."

"For sure. Is that what you wanted to call me about?"

He shook his head. "Part of it. But not all of it. I visited my grandpa at the hospital the other day."

"And?"

"The doctors told me that he's better than he's been in months. They checked the tumor, Katie. And it's shrinking. The treatments are working. He's starting to move in the right direction!"

"That's awesome, Ian!" I smiled. "I'm really happy for you."

"Thanks. And thanks for your prayers. If I was doubting before, I'm definitely starting to believe now. I've even been reading out of the Bible that my grandpa gave me a couple of years ago. It's kind of old and beat up—" he held it up for emphasis, "but it was his back when he was in high school. He wanted me to have it, and I've been highlighting some stuff in it. I don't understand all of it . . . But the parts that I have been able to understand have been really helpful. I even found an audio version online, which has helped me with some of the passages that have been more challenging."

"That's great. It sounds like God's really moving in your life."

"Yeah, I guess He is, isn't He?" Ian shook his head. "It's crazy. My family has always gone to church on holidays . . . Easter, Christmas . . . You know the drill. But lately, it's been different. It's like, for the first time in my life, God feels real to me. Like a friend—someone I can talk to. It's really been changing the way I see things." He paused, a shadow crossing his face. "I just wish I could go back and change some of the things that I did. And the way that I acted—especially toward your friend." He shook his head again. "He didn't deserve that."

"Well, it's never too late to turn over a new leaf. And I'm sure Nathan would love to hear what you just said."

"I don't know. I just . . . don't know what I would say."

"Tell you what," I said, biting my lower lip—knowing that what I was about to say was what God wanted me to say, even though everything in me fought against it. "I'm going bowling with some of my friends on Saturday. Why don't you meet us there? It would give you the chance to apologize and make things right."

"Are you sure? I mean, I wouldn't want to intrude."

"I insist. I think it would be a good thing to do."

"OK, then I guess I'll see you Saturday."

"Yeah, I'll see you then."

"Night, Katie."

"Night, Ian," I said as I hung up and put my phone down. What did I just do?

Chapter Twenty-Four

*I*t was Saturday night, and I was trying my best not to freak out. I still couldn't believe that I had invited Ian to go bowling with me and my friends. The same friends he had tormented so many times before. Was I doing the right thing? It had seemed like the right thing, after hearing Pastor Sean preach about living for the approval of God, rather than man, but now, I wasn't so sure. And as I headed to the kitchen to leave for the bowling alley, I felt sure that my stomach was about to climb out of my throat.

"Hey, Katie—are you ready to go?" my brother asked, with the keys to our car jingling in his hand.

"Yeah," I said, taking a hard gulp and praying tonight wasn't the disaster that I feared it would be. "All ready."

"Great," he said as the two of us piled into the car, with some song by Twenty-One Pilots blaring from the speakers as I sat in my seat, lost in my thoughts. I know that God wanted me to invite Ian to give him the chance to apologize to Nathan and hang out with a better group of people.

But the whole way there, I couldn't help but overanalyze the situation a hundred times over. How would Nathan feel about having Ian hang out with us after having him bully him so many times before? And how much more would it look like Ian and I were dating, with me inviting him to a bowling outing with the church? *Breathe, Katie. It's all going to be okay. It's all going to be okay. It's all going to be okay . . .*

"Okay!" Jackson said as I felt the car come to a stop, snapping me out of my mini panic attack. "We're here!"

"Great." I forced a smile and tried to look calmer than I felt as the two of us climbed out of the car and headed inside.

Even though I was stressed about tonight, it was easy to distract myself with the details of the bowling alley. I had never been inside a bowling alley before, and from what I could tell, it was just like the bowling alleys that I had seen in all those teen movies so many times before.

On the radio, they played some pop/rock song with a heavy guitar riff. And throughout the alley, I could hear people talking amongst themselves as balls crashed into pins. I could also see crowds of friends huddled together and smell the faint scent of pizza wafting throughout the bowling alley air.

Making me more than a little bit hungry.

"Hey, Jackson, do you want to get some pizza before we meet up with the group?" Even though I was stressed about the whole Ian-Nathan-Atticus situation, it apparently hadn't affected my appetite.

"Sure." He shrugged. "Do you want pepperoni on yours?"

"Is that a trick question?"

"Right. Two pepperoni pizzas, coming right up."

With that, Jackson headed over to the concessions stand to get us pizza and two bottled waters. And as he did, I felt my phone start to vibrate. Quickly, I reached inside my pocket to retrieve it, and as it turned out, it was Ian.

R u here?

I swallowed hard and texted him back.

Yes. I'm by the concessions stand.

Cool. See u soon.

See you soon.

I put my phone back in my pocket and looked around, to try to find Ian amongst the sea of faces. But instead, I caught two familiar faces walking into the bowling alley together—waving as they made their way toward me.

"Atticus, Tanisha!" I exclaimed, waving back at my friends.

"Hey, Katie!" Tanisha said, running up to hug me. "Ready to do some bowling?"

"I think so." I smiled. "My brother is just ordering pizza, and then we'll get our bowling shoes and meet up with the rest of the group."

"Great, sounds good!"

"Yeah. Hey, by the way—is Nathan still planning on coming tonight?"

Atticus nodded as if to answer the question for his sister. "He's running a little late because of traffic, but he should be here soon."

"Cool." I smiled, relieved that Atticus seemed a little more like his old self. Maybe things were getting better.

A girl could hope, right?

"Hey, Katie," Jackson said, walking up to me and my friends with two warm boxes of pizza. "And Atticus and Tanisha. Ready get started?"

"You bet!" Tanisha exclaimed. "Let's do this!"

With that, the four of us took off to rent our bowling shoes. And by the time that we had them sized and ready to go, I heard a familiar male voice across the way.

"Hey, Katie!" the voice shouted as Atticus shot me a look.

"Hey, Ian." I forced a smile, fighting a growing awkward feeling and shooting Atticus a glance that I hoped said, 'I'll explain later.' "You know my friends, right? And my brother?"

"Yeah, hey," he said, shifting in place—looking noticeably awkward and uncomfortable. "Good to see you."

"Hello, Ian," Tanisha replied with a slight edge in her voice.

"I invited Ian to come with us tonight," I explained, trying to ease the tension of the moment, even though I was sure I was failing miserably. "I thought maybe he could bowl with us."

"If you guys are cool with it," he added quickly. "If not, I could uh, I could go now. I have plenty of stuff I could be doing like homework or . . ."

"No, Ian. We want you to stay. Right, guys?"

"Yeah, sure," Atticus said, his arms crossed and his brows furrowed together—more guarded than before. "I mean, it is a public place."

"Great." Ian looked toward me and then back toward them. "I'll get my bowling shoes and I'll meet you guys there!"

"Great." I forced a smile as he headed off.

"Okay, girl. Start talking," Tanisha said once she was sure he was out of earshot. "What's *football brains* doing here?"

"I invited him to come today. He's starting to seek God, and I thought it would be good for him to hang out with different kinds of people. Besides," I added, "he wants to apologize to Nathan for how he's treated him."

"Oh, so now he wants to apologize?" Atticus said, with a hint of something in his voice that I'd never heard before. "What . . . did he beat him up enough times to fill his quota for the year? Or is he just tired of trying to steal his lunch money?"

"I'm serious, guys. He's trying to change. And if God's given us a second chance, shouldn't we do the same for him?"

To my surprise, that must've convicted them. Because after that, they had no further argument about Ian's surprise appearance tonight. And as soon as he came back, they made an effort to be nice to him. Or at least, be cordial.

"Nice shot, bro!" Ian said after Atticus bowled a strike. "You've really got an arm on you!"

"Thanks," he said as he waited for the ball to come back. "I used to come here every summer as a kid. I guess you could say bowling is kind of my sport."

"Well, it's definitely not mine," Ian said, with a lopsided grin. "Football is really the only sport I'm good at. I pretty much suck at all the rest."

"No kidding?" Tanisha asked, a little too intrigued.

"Yeah, just wait. I'm probably going to end up in the gutter or something. One pin is pretty much my average."

"Well, I guess we'll find out soon." I smiled after Atticus used his next turn. "Because you're next."

"Wish me luck," he teased as I heard footsteps walking up from behind me. And as I turned around, I felt my stomach climb up to my throat. *Nathan was here.*

"Nathan!" I smiled and waved in his direction. "Good to see you!"

"You too," he said as he came over to hug me, a shadow crossing his face as he spotted Ian. "Ian . . . What are you doing here?"

"Katie invited me," he said, looking more nervous than I'd ever seen him before. "Um, mostly because I was hoping to see you."

"Really?" Nathan asked, looking over toward me and then back toward Ian.

"Yeah, um . . . this is hard for me to say. But I haven't been very nice to you. I mean, it's been Kent who's been the worst, but . . . I haven't done anything to stop him. Which, at the end of the day, makes me just as guilty. And I just wanted to say that I'm sorry for the way I've treated you. You haven't done anything to deserve it, and even though I don't know you that well, you seem like a pretty cool guy. I hope that someday you can forgive me."

"Wow," Nathan said, his face changing from shocked to relieved, back to shocked again. "That was pretty big of you to own up to that . . . And you don't have to wait until someday."

"Really? So, we're cool?"

"Yeah." Nathan grinned, sticking out his hand for him to shake. "We're cool."

"Thanks, Nate. You know to be honest, if I were you, I don't think I'd be able to forgive me."

"A couple of months ago I probably wouldn't have either. In fact, I'm sure I wouldn't have. But a lot has happened in the past year. And if God can forgive me for the things I've done, I can forgive you for what you've done."

Ian smiled, at that moment, totally speechless.

"You know, by the looks of the screen, it's your turn to bowl," Nathan said. "Are we going to find out once and for all whether you're as good on the alley as you are on the field?"

"I'll spoil it for you right now." Ian laughed as Nathan handed him the ball. "Not even close."

We continued bowling, soon finding that Ian wasn't kidding when he said he was bad at it. And after about an hour of bowling, talking, and listening to the radio, Atticus won the game.

"Nice job, man!" Ian congratulated him, giving him a high five and shaking his hand.

"Thanks, Ian." He grinned. "Hey, I'm going to get some more pizza. Does anyone else want some?"

"I do!" Tanisha said.

"Me too!" Nathan added.

"Great—hey, Katie, do you want to, um, do you want to come with me?"

"Yeah—that would be great," I said, noticing that his tone was warmer than it had been in the last two weeks.

"Cool," he said as we headed off toward the pizza stand, both of us silent for a good minute until Atticus finally spoke up.

"So, tell me, Katie. What's the story with Ian?"

"Atticus . . ." I hesitated. "I still can't tell you—I gave him my word. But I can promise you that there's nothing going on between us. And I really hope you believe me."

"I do."

"You do?" I asked, half shocked and half amazed.

"Yeah, I saw that tonight when he was hanging out with us. Katie, I'm really sorry for the way I've been acting. It was wrong and stupid and just plain pigheaded. I just lost my head when I heard you were hanging out with him because well . . ." He laughed, suddenly looking shy and nervous, more like a ten-year-old boy than the teenager that he was, standing there before me. "Well, there's something I've been wanting to tell you ever since you came here. And it's never been the right time, or something's come up, or . . ."

Suddenly, in probably the worst possible timing, my phone started to ring—playing, of all things, "Breakfast" by the News-boys. A ringtone that my dad set it to the other night when he was in one of his corny 90s throwback moods.

I pulled it out and checked the caller ID—Pastor Kip. My old pastor, back in Kenya. "I'm so sorry," I said as I pressed *accept* and held the phone up to my ear. "Hello?"

"Hello, Katie," Pastor Kip said, his African accent as thick as ever. "I tried calling your dad earlier, but he couldn't come to the phone, so could you please take a message?"

"Yes, of course." I nodded, even though he couldn't see me.

"I am planning to retire soon. And our associate pastor, Pastor Abebe, had a family emergency that he had to take care of. Everything is okay, but he will not be able to assume the pastorate position, after all. So, I am currently looking for someone else to replace me. Your family was with us for so many years, and your father was always such a faithful member of our congregation. I wanted to ask him if he would consider coming back to Africa and stepping up as the pastor of Christ's Fellowship Church."

"Wow," I said, willing my brain to register what he was saying, as a billion thoughts raced through my mind all at once. "I'm uh, honored that you'd think of us. I'll give him your message and let him get back to you."

"Thank you, Katie. Have a good rest of your night."

"Thanks, Pastor Kip. You too," I said as Atticus shot me a funny look.

"Who was that?" he asked once I was off the phone.

"Pastor Kip . . ." I paused, my voice trailing off, suddenly feeling a lump in my throat bigger than any bowling ball. "My old pastor."

"Why was he calling?"

"Because he's retiring soon. And he wants my dad to take over as the pastor of our old church."

"But your dad is the pastor at Hope Life," he said, his voice slower, more calculated. "I mean, he can't be the pastor there if he's already the pastor here."

"The *interim* pastor," I corrected him as he gave me a blank look. "It means he doesn't know if he's the permanent pastor here or not."

"So, do you really think he'd move again?" he asked, this time, with something in his voice that wasn't there a couple of minutes ago. *Fear.*

"I don't know." I hesitated with a shrug that came almost robotically.

"Do you want to move?"

"The truth?" I asked as he searched my eyes. "No. I mean, a couple of months ago, I wouldn't have thought twice about it. When I first got here, I missed everything about the way things were back home. But now, with my new church . . . The Agape Club . . . All my friends . . ." I paused. "It feels like *this* is home."

"I don't want you to leave."

"I don't want to leave either," I said as the two of us stood there, silent for a long moment, at a total loss for words.

"Hey—Katie, Atticus, is everything okay?" I heard my brother say from behind me as I turned around to see him, Tanisha, Nathan, and Ian standing a few feet behind us. "You guys have been gone a long time. We wanted to make sure you didn't get lost or something."

"Yeah, we're fine." I hesitated. "We just got sidetracked, that's all. We'll meet you back in a couple of minutes."

"OK, sounds good," Nathan called back as he walked off with the rest of them.

"Please, don't say anything to anyone about this. Not until I find out more."

"They're going to find out sooner or later."

"I know. But I'd rather be the one who tells them."

Atticus sighed. "Okay, but while you wait, I'm going to be praying."

"About?"

"That your dad says no."

I forced a smile. "I'm going to be praying for the same thing."

Chapter Twenty-Five

*L*ater that night, as I did my best to sort through a billion emotions that fought for a space in my heart, I did something I hadn't done in a while. I read H.D.'s diary.

Dear Diary,

It's funny how life can change in an instant. How one moment, you can be surrounded by the familiar sights and sounds of campus life, and the next, you can be on an airplane, flying halfway around the world. How one moment, you can be going about life as usual, and the next, you can meet someone who you don't even realize will someday be the love of your life. And how a simple stolen glance can one day turn into a first kiss, a marriage, and the birth of your first child.

Tolkien once said in his famous allegory, The Lord of the Rings, that we all have to decide what to do with the time that we have been given. The older I get, the more I realize why he said this. Time is a limited resource. You only get so much of it, and nothing except God and our souls will last forever.

Sooner or later, everything must change. We cannot hold onto a moment. We can only cherish it while it's here.

Until next time,

H.D.

"Reading something?" I heard a voice ask from behind me as I slammed the book shut, forcing myself back into the real world.

"Uh, yeah . . . Sort of." I forced a weak smile as I spotted my mom in the doorway. Even though I wasn't doing anything wrong, H.D.'s diary has been my personal secret for almost a year now. And though I usually tell her everything, this was one thing that I had, for whatever reason, kept to myself.

"What are you reading?"

"Um, just something that I found in my room a couple of months ago." I paused, still thinking about the entry I had just read. "I don't know who wrote it, but she always signs 'H.D.' at the end of each entry. I think those might be her initials. I've tried to figure out who she is, but I haven't had much luck."

"Are you sure you don't know who she is?"

"I don't think so . . ." I said, my voice trailing off. "Why don't you seem surprised by all of this?"

"Because." She grinned. "H.D. and I happen to be very good friends. Or, I should say, *Holly Danielle* and I happen to be very good friends."

"No way," I said, as suddenly all the pieces fit together perfectly. The college. The letter. The initials. "You're H.D.?" She nodded, a smile slowly making its way across her lips. "But how did it end up under the floorboard in my room?"

"Because I put it there. While you and your brother went on a walk around the neighborhood, I was looking for a good hiding place, and I saw that one of the floorboards was loose. And I thought that would be a good place to hide it. Not too easy. Not too hard."

"But, if it was you all along, why didn't you tell me about it? Or give it to me yourself?"

"Because I wanted you to have the same experience I had when I was your age." I must have had a blank look on my face because she went on to explain. "When I was fifteen, my grandma asked me to clean out her attic. She was older and couldn't do it herself anymore. And while I was up there, I found her diary. It didn't have her name anywhere in it or on it. Instead, she used the pseudonym, *Annette*. I guess to protect her privacy. As I started reading it, I realized this Annette girl and I had a lot in common. And when I asked my grandma about it later, she told me it was hers." She paused. "I always wanted to do something similar so that one day, when I had a daughter, she'd be able to see her mom the same way I saw my grandma. Not as someone *old*, but someone who, in a lot of ways, went through exactly what she's going through now."

"Wow, I had no idea," I said, my mind racing as I thought back on all the diary entries I had read so far. "But wait . . . If you're H.D., then what do those numbers in the front of the book mean? 596?"

She smiled as if remembering her reason for writing those numbers well. "May 5th, 1996. That was the day that I felt God calling me to the mission field. And that was also the day that I met your father. I wanted to remember that day, so I put it in the front of my diary."

"And the college that you describe at the beginning of the book . . ."

"Was West Lake University," she said, finishing my sentence for me. "I know I was a little older than you, but I hope that in some ways, it still felt relatable to you. I was going through a big change during that time, and I knew you were too with moving to the States . . . I thought it might resonate with you."

"It definitely did." I smiled, suddenly stopping as I thought back on my call with Pastor Kip. "And it just might all over again."

"The phone call?" she asked as I nodded. I had told my parents about the call from Pastor Kip at dinner, and though they didn't give me any definite answers, they told me they would be praying about it.

"It sounds crazy after how adamant I was about not moving here . . . but I don't want to move back to Kenya. I mean, now I have my friends, and my church, and my school . . ."

"And Atticus?" she asked, causing me to turn a couple shades of red.

"Yes." I nodded. "And Atticus." I paused. "Do you think we're going to move again?"

"The truth? I don't know. We talked about it, and a lot of it depends on whether Hope Life decides to bring your dad on as the permanent pastor. He needs a stable job. And if they let him go at the end of the school year, he's going to have to find something else—whether here or back in Kenya."

"Right." I hesitated. "That makes sense . . . I guess."

"But can I give you a word of advice?" she asked as I nodded. "Tomorrow isn't promised to anyone, and things are always going to change. That's just the nature of how life is. But don't let that stop you from living every bit of your life right now while you're here. And don't leave with any regrets."

"You mean, tell him how I feel?"

"Maybe, if that's something you want to do, but ultimately, just keep being the light that you are for as long as you're here. I have a feeling that there are a lot of people who you've impacted at your school. Don't stop showing up just because you don't know how much time you have left. The truth is, none of us know how much time we have left. But we can't let that stop us from living."

"Thanks, Mom. I won't."

"Good." She smiled, as she got up from my bed and made her way toward the door.

"Goodnight, Mom," I said before she left.

"Goodnight, Katie."

Chapter Twenty-Six

The following week, I walked through the halls of Winter Oaks High School with fresh resolve. If there was a possibility that I might be moving back to Kenya, then I wanted to enjoy every moment that I had here with my friends.

Even if I didn't have that much longer.

"Hey," I greeted Jenny by the lockers. "What's up?"

"Not much." She shrugged as I got out my books, notebooks, and three-ring binders. "You?"

"Not much," I echoed, forcing a smile. "Just the same old, same old. School . . . church . . . the drama club. Another day in life, right?" OK, so that wasn't as casual as I was hoping for, but it was the best I could do.

"Right," she said, shooting me a funny look, seeming to catch on to my less-than-casual tone. But she ignored it and changed the subject. "Hey, have you talked to Ian lately?"

"No, why?"

"Well, I know you guys hang out sometimes, and I saw him rush into the boy's bathroom as soon as he came in. Usually, he hangs out with Kent and the guys, and I haven't seen him with them at all this morning."

"That's not too weird. I mean, we all have to use the bathroom sometimes. Maybe he had stomach issues—ate a bad taco the night before, or something."

"Yeah, that's true. But it kind of seemed like something was bothering him, and I don't mean a bad taco."

"Hmm . . . that is weird. Maybe I should try to find him before class. See if everything is okay."

"That's probably a good idea," she said as I turned to head toward the boy's bathroom, hoping I'd be able to catch him on his way out. And as it turned out, I did.

He looked every bit like Jenny had described.

"Ian! Hey, Jenny said she saw you run into the bathroom this morning."

"Yeah, so? Guys use the bathroom all the time. Girls do too," he said, sounding surprisingly like his old self. The self that he was a couple of months ago, before he started following Christ. He kept walking, forcing me to walk faster to keep up.

"Yeah, I *know* that—but she said you looked upset. I wanted to see if everything was okay."

"If everything was okay," he echoed. "You wanted to see if everything was okay? Well, here's my answer for you. No. Everything is not okay. Everything is not okay at all."

"Alright, well, then talk to me about it!" I exclaimed, frustration ringing through my voice. "And maybe drop this whole macho I'm-too-cool-for-the-world attitude because I'll tell you this much. It's *not* a good look on you."

At that moment, he looked both surprised and convicted. And a little more like the Ian I had come to know recently. "I'm sorry. I had the worst night last night."

"Do you want to talk about it?"

"Don't you have to go to class?"

"Yeah . . ." I hesitated. "But I can miss just this once."

He sighed. "Alright, then let's go outside. I need some fresh air anyway." With that, I followed him outside to a nearby sycamore tree, as a cool breeze picked up in the distance.

"So," I began, taking a seat down beside him on the grass, which was still a little damp from the rain the night before, "what's up?"

For a moment, he didn't say anything, even though there was a visible pain in his eyes. "I got a call from the hospital last night. My grandpa passed away." He shook his head, looking like he was fighting back tears. "He started to get better, and then out of nowhere, he passed away. I didn't even get the chance to say goodbye."

"Oh, Ian . . ." I paused, at a loss for words. "I'm so sorry."

"Why would God do this, Katie? I thought God was supposed to heal people."

"God does heal people, Ian." I paused, searching desperately for the right words. "But there are times when He heals them on the other side, in Heaven. Each one of us has our time . . . For some people, it just comes sooner than we thought."

"But why does God heal some people here and not others?" he asked, something like anger flashing in his eyes. "And why not my grandfather?"

"The truth? I don't know. But my dad told me one time that God does what we would've done if we knew what He knew. I have to believe that God's decision to bring him home was born out of compassion . . . And that your grandfather is way happier there than he ever could've been here, even with perfect health."

"I know you're right. He used to tell me the same thing—before he died." Ian squeezed his eyes shut, taking a minute to compose himself before speaking. "It just *hurts*. I've never lost anyone like this before." As if out of habit, leftover from his old life before Christ, he cursed. "I don't know when this is going to stop hurting."

"I'm really sorry." I squeezed his hand, the way I would with Jackson if he were in this much pain. "You're going to get through this, though. And if you want to talk about it, I'm here."

"Thanks, Katie." He pulled me into a hug—also in a way that was more sibling-y than anything else. "You're awesome."

Suddenly, I heard footsteps walking up, causing us to turn around to see who was there. And once I looked, I felt my stomach twist into knots. This could *not* be happening right now.

"I knew it!" she gasped. "I just knew it!" To my horror, standing above us was Sydney, who looked as if she had just seen a ghost. "You've been cheating on me with Katie, haven't you?"

"What?" he exclaimed, standing up. "No, it's not like that! Let me explain—"

"Don't waste your breath. It's all making sense now. Why you guys have been hanging out together. Why you suddenly decided you didn't want to sleep with me anymore. Why you're into this *Jesus* stuff now out of nowhere—"

"Sydney, I promise you. Katie and I are just friends. None of that has anything to do with her."

"Right," she said. "That's why you two are out here putting your hands all over each other during school hours."

"We were not—"

"Save it." She put her hand up in a *stop* motion. "I just want to know why you would choose someone like *her* to hook up with."

"What's that supposed to mean?" he asked, furrowing his brows. Sydney laughed, but it was a laugh that lacked any humor.

"Look at her, Ian! The girl grew up in some third-world country. She's never even been in a real school until what? A couple of months ago? And on top of that, she dresses like it's still 2001. I don't think even her little friend—what's his name, Attamus? is really interested in her. He's just biding his time until a real woman comes along."

"Who are you?" he asked, disgust filling his voice.

"Someone you're never going to touch again. Goodbye, Ian."

"Well, if that's how you're going to be, then goodbye to you too. And for the record, I wasn't dating Katie, but right now I'm thinking she'd be a whole lot better a choice than you."

"Yeah." She turned around to face him. "In your *dreams*."

"I should get going . . ." I said, doing my best to hold back tears—Sydney's words cutting like a knife and making me feel sick as I thought about how fast this was going to spread around school.

"No—Katie, stay. What Sydney said was horrible, but it's not true. Not what she said about us . . . or what she said about you. The truth should be enough."

"I know, but everything's a mess and it's all my fault," I said, my arms crossed as I felt a familiar tight feeling in my chest. "If I hadn't been out here with you, none of this would have happened. She broke up with you because of me. I can't have that on my conscience."

"I don't want her back, Katie," he said, his voice quiet. "The only thing you did was help get me out of a relationship that I should have ended months ago. I don't want to be with someone who treats people that way. I want to be with someone more like . . . well . . . more like you." Suddenly, he looked vulnerable, as his eyes met mine.

"No." I shook my head after a long moment, as the gravity of what Ian was saying—or what he was *trying* to say hit me like a ton of bricks. "Not me."

"I'm a different person now, Katie. All my old relationship patterns—dating around, sleeping around . . . that's over now. Going forward things are going to be different. I know what she saw was nothing but . . . it could be. Couldn't it?"

I shook my head. "No, it couldn't. Look, Ian, I know you're a different person now. I've seen that over the last couple of months and when you apologized to Nathan. But that's not the point. The point is, I like someone else. And I couldn't see you while I still have feelings for some other guy."

"Atticus?" he asked as I nodded.

"I figured."

"Ian, could I tell you something? As a friend?"

"Yeah, of course."

I paused. "With your grandfather's death, and you, trying to process a billion emotions that you're just now starting to deal with, I don't think now is the time to make any big decisions like whether or not to be in a relationship with someone. I think right now, you just need to work on your relationship with Christ and finding yourself. Not finding a girl who will temporarily make you forget about what you're feeling."

"Yeah, you're right." He chuckled, looking embarrassed. "That would be more of an old Ian move, huh?"

"Kind of. But, whether or not you want to try things again with Sydney, I've got to find a way to explain what happened before this thing gets out of hand. I can't let her keep thinking what she's thinking right now."

"Because of Atticus?" he asked, an edge of jealousy in his voice.

"No." I shook my head. "Because I can't let Sydney think I'm the kind of girl who would try to steal her boyfriend. Sydney's never liked me, and that's fine . . . But I don't want to give her an actual legitimate reason not to like me."

"Right." He nodded. "I respect that."

"Cool." I smiled. "So, I'll see you around?"

"Yeah, I'll see you around."

⇥ ⇤

*L*ater that day, after school, I got into my car, put Sydney's address in my phone, and set off to her house. Even though I knew I would be the last person she'd want to see, I had to clear things up. And I couldn't think of a better way of doing it than talking to her directly.

Away from the drama of Winter Oaks High School.

I still couldn't believe all that had happened. That Ian's grandfather had passed away from cancer. That Sydney had gotten the wrong idea about me and Ian. That Ian had all but asked me out in the aftermath of it all. And on top of this whole mess, I might be moving back to Kenya. All these things combined caused my mind to race in a million different directions until finally, I arrived at her house. 234 Meadow Brook Pier. I put my car into *park* and got out, taking a deep breath and praying she'd be home. And that she'd have ears to hear what I had to say. I rang the doorbell and exhaled.

"Katie?" Sydney said as she opened the door, her face changing from shock to confusion to anger. "What are you doing here?"

"I came to explain what you saw today."

"There's nothing to explain."

"Actually, there is." I paused. "Can I come in?"

She hesitated, as if debating whether she should let me in or slam the door in my face. "Yeah, I guess for a few minutes. But make it quick."

"I will, I promise," I said as I walked into her house, which was bigger yet emptier than I imagined, and took a seat across from her on the couch.

"Okay," she said, looking eager for me to say what I had to say and leave. "Start talking."

"Sydney." I paused. "I know what you saw today looked bad, but I can assure you, there's nothing going on between Ian and me.

What you saw today was the most that's ever happened. We're just friends, that's all."

"Then why was he hugging you?"

"Because he's going through a lot right now, and he needed someone to talk to, but I have no interest in him beyond being his friend. And I would never try to steal someone else's boyfriend. I'm not perfect by any means, but I try to treat people the way I would want to be treated. I wouldn't want someone to do that to me, so I would never do that to someone else."

"You came all the way here just to tell me that?"

"Yeah, pretty much."

"I don't get it. Were you worried I was going to start telling people what I saw?"

"A little," I confessed. "But mostly, I just didn't want you to think I would do something like that to you."

"You'd have every right to if you did. I mean, I haven't been very nice to you since your brother and I broke up, and I cheated on him. Seems like if he did cheat on me with you, it'd pretty much serve me right."

"Yeah, well, I don't believe in an eye for an eye. And even though I hate what you did to my brother, I don't hate you."

"Why not? I mean, if I were you, I'd hate me."

"Because I guess I'm a big believer in second chances. God gave me a second chance and . . ." I smiled and gave a small shrug. "It'd only be right to extend that grace forward."

"Wow, you really are a missionary kid, aren't you?"

"Guilty as charged."

"Well, thanks, Katie. I mean, I know I don't deserve it—but thanks." She chuckled. "I guess it just messed me up seeing you two together like that after . . ." Sydney stopped, her voice trailing off. "Never mind. That's my issue to deal with."

"After what?" I asked, curiosity coloring my voice.

She sighed. "Can you keep a secret?" I nodded as she paused, with a heaviness in her eyes that wasn't there before. "I was late this month, and I took a pregnancy test last night." She shook her head, looking choked up as she sat there, alone on the couch. "I'm *pregnant*, Katie. With Ian's baby."

"Wow," I said, realizing that was probably a stupid response after I said it, but by then, it was too late to take it back. "Are you sure? That you're pregnant, I mean?"

"I'm sure." She nodded. "I took it twice."

"What are you going to do?" I asked. "Are you . . ." I swallowed, shifting in my seat. "Are you going to keep it?"

"You know, I never thought I'd say this . . . but I think I want to. I always thought that if this happened, I'd get an abortion. No question about it. But now that I'm actually in this situation, I don't want to do that. I want to keep it. The only problem is . . ." She bit her lower lip. "My parents will *not* be supportive of that at all. And there's no way I can afford to keep it without their help."

"You know, if you want, I'm sure my dad would be willing to help you," I began as she gave me a curious look. "Our church partners with the local Crisis Pregnancy Center, and they help new moms all the time who are in the same situation you're in right now. I'm sure they'd be more than happy to help if you asked them."

"You think your dad would be willing to help me? You know . . . after what happened between Jackson and me?"

"I have a feeling he would." I smiled. "In case you haven't figured it out already, my family's not too big on holding grudges."

"Thank you so much, Katie. I . . . I really appreciate it."

"Anytime." I paused. "Are you going to tell Ian?"

"Are you going to tell him if I don't? Since you guys are buddies now?"

I shook my head. "No. It's not my news to tell. But my advice? I think you should tell him soon. As the father, he has the right to know."

"I had a feeling you would say that." She hesitated. "I'll tell him. It just needs to be in my timing, that's all."

"Okay. I can respect that."

"Thanks, Katie." She smiled, to my absolute shock, walking over to hug me. "For everything."

"Anytime. See you at school tomorrow?"

"Yeah, I'll see you then. Bye, Katie."

"Bye, Sydney."

With that, I left—getting back in my car to drive home, struck with a million realities at once. Sydney, who once hated my guts, had *hugged* me. Ian was going to be a father. And I had just promised Sydney that I wouldn't tell him about the baby.

A knot formed in the pit of my stomach.

Was I doing the right thing? Keeping this from Ian after he had confided so much in me? Not telling him about his unborn son or daughter until Sydney was ready—whenever that may be? When he found out, how would he react? Ian was brand new in his walk with God. And on top of that, he was already struggling with the loss of his grandfather. How would he take the news of a baby? Especially when he was so set on getting into college?

Another thought hit me as I felt my chest start to tighten.

What if the baby wasn't even Ian's? Sure, Sydney and Ian were a couple, and they've been dating for the last couple of months, but I had seen during her time dating my brother how easy it was for her to move from one guy to the next. What if she just wanted it to be Ian's because of the changes she's seen in him recently?

No, Katie. Don't think like that. She said he's the father. She wouldn't say that unless she was sure, would she?

Where was I? Somehow, I had gotten so lost in my thoughts about Ian and Sydney that I had lost my bearings. I'm supposed to turn left here, right? Or maybe it was right. For the next ten minutes, I drove around the area, before I realized that I was totally and completely lost. *Don't panic, Katie. Now's not the time to freak out . . . You're going to be okay . . . You're going to be okay . . .*

I exhaled as I came to a stop, about ninety-seven percent sure I was supposed to take a left here. The only problem was cars were coming from both directions. My eyes darted from one car to the next until it seemed to be clear. *Or was it?*

Suddenly, as I pulled out, I saw a car speeding around the corner. *No . . . no . . . no . . .* Without thinking, I stepped on the gas, lunging my car straight ahead.

That was the last thing I saw before everything went black.

Chapter Twenty-Seven

In my distress I called to the Lord; I cried to my God for help. From his temple he heard my voice; my cry came before him, into his ears.

- Psalm 18:6

"Where am I?" I asked about an hour later as I woke up to a bright light shining in my face. At first, I thought that maybe I had died and gone to Heaven, but I figured out I was still alive after realizing that the light was coming from a lamp next to my bed. And I'm pretty sure they don't have lamps in Heaven.

"Thank God she's awake," my mom said, turning toward my dad, who sat on the other side of a very uncomfortable hospital bed with his hands folded, as if he had just been praying.

"Thank you, Jesus," he muttered under his breath before turning toward me. "You were in an accident, Katie. They found your car in a head-on collision with a tree. You were passed out in the front seat from the impact. Thankfully, you weren't injured other than a couple of bumps and bruises."

"An accident?" I asked groggily, sitting up the best that I could, even though every bone in my body felt sore. "Was anyone else hurt?" I asked, suddenly remembering the other car coming my way as a knot the size of California grew in the pit of my stomach.

He shook his head. "One of the witnesses said that you sped up to avoid an oncoming car and lost control of your vehicle."

"Katie, what happened?" my mom asked with more concern than judgment. "You're always such a careful driver."

"I know," I said, feeling choked up as I thought about everything that had happened. "I was coming home from Sydney's house, and I had a lot on my mind . . . like, *a lot*—and then before I knew it, I started panicking because I was lost, and the feeling came back, and before I knew it everything had already happened too fast to take it back." I swallowed hard, at this point, unable to stop the details of the story from spilling out. "I saw a car coming, and I sped up to avoid hitting him, but I guess by that point, it was going too fast for me to steer it back to the road in time."

"Katie—" my mom paused, as her eyes met mine, "you said that the feeling came back. What are you talking about?"

I looked down at the ground.

For the past year, I haven't said anything to my parents about my struggle with anxiety. But now, I realized I had no choice but to tell them. "I had a panic attack . . . I felt like I couldn't breathe and . . . like I couldn't even think straight."

"How long has this been going on?" my dad asked, exchanging glances with my mom, and then looking back toward me.

"Does it happen a lot when you're driving?" my mom added, sounding worried.

"They started last semester at that karaoke place—Burgers and Beats. And . . . I've had them a couple of times since then. Sometimes when I'm driving . . . and sometimes just in general.

Usually, I can get them under control, but this time, I guess I let it get out of hand."

"What do you usually feel when you're having one of these panic attacks?" my dad asked, with equal amounts of curiosity and concern.

"Like I can't breathe." I paused. "Like my heart's going to pound out of my chest. Like my hands are shaking uncontrollably—and I can't stop them."

They both exchanged glances once again until finally, my dad spoke up. "Katie, I think it would be a good idea for you to talk to someone about this. There's a lady at our church who's a licensed counselor—Ms. Elena. I think she could really help you."

"But Dad, I'm fine—really! I don't need a counselor."

"This isn't up for discussion, Katie. Not if you're getting into accidents because of this. I can't let you take that kind of risk."

"But I'm not crazy," I protested weakly.

"Katie—" my dad paused, "I've been in ministry for a long time. First as a missionary and then as a pastor, and I've seen a lot of people struggle with anxiety. Struggling with anxiety or depression doesn't make you crazy—it makes you human. But you don't have to suffer through this alone. There are people who can help you, and your mom and I are going to be here to help you too. Every step of the way."

"Speaking of which," my mom added, "there are some people here who want to see you." Slowly, she went to the door and knocked. And to my surprise, Atticus, Tanisha, Jenny, Nathan, and Ian all came in—followed by my brother, Jackson.

"What are you guys doing here?" I asked, amazed that all of my friends were here to support me. "How did you . . .?"

"Atticus and I found out when we saw your parents rush outside to go to the hospital," Tanisha explained. "And we called Jenny, Nathan, and Ian and asked them to meet us here."

"As soon as Atticus called, I rushed right over," Nathan said. "You scared us all pretty badly, but I'm glad you're okay."

"Me too," Jenny chimed in.

"Me three," Ian agreed.

"I can't believe you all came—just to see if I was okay."

"Of course, we did." Atticus smiled—clearly still shaken up from the accident but trying to be strong for me. "That's what friends are for."

"Yeah. We weren't going to let you go through this alone," Jenny added.

"You've been there for all of us. Now it's time for us to be there for you," Nathan said.

"You guys are the best." I smiled, feeling choked up as I thought about what great friends I had. "Thank you so much."

"Hey." Ian grinned. "You'd do it for any one of us."

"Alright, guys. Why don't we let her rest for a while?" my dad suggested. "She's had a long day and she could probably use it."

"Mr. Carter?" Atticus began. "Could I talk to her first? Alone? I'll only be a couple of minutes."

He hesitated before finally speaking up. "Yes, Atticus. But just for a couple of minutes, alright?"

"Yes, sir." He nodded, as the rest of my friends made their way out of my room, followed by my parents and my brother.

Both of us were silent for a long moment until finally, he spoke up. "What happened out there, Katie? What made you spin out of control like that?"

"I had a panic attack." I paused. "The same way I've been having panic attacks all year."

"Why didn't you ever tell me?"

"Because I didn't want you to think I was crazy." I looked down at my feet, embarrassed. "Or messed up."

"I could never have thought that. The truth is, I deal with anxiety sometimes too."

"You do?"

He nodded. "A lot of people do. It's not as uncommon as you think."

"My dad wants me to see a counselor." I cringed just thinking about it.

"The truth? I don't think that's a bad thing." He paused as if hesitating to say whatever it was that he wanted to say next. "I went to counseling a couple of years ago, right after my older cousin died, and it helped me a lot."

"How did he die?" I asked, amazed that Atticus had never told me this before. Once again, he was silent, a vulnerability in his eyes that wasn't there before.

"He died in a car accident. It was a head-on collision with a drunk driver. He died instantly."

Suddenly, the gravity of the situation hit me like a ton of bricks. "I'm so sorry, Atticus. I had no idea. I—"

"It's okay. He's . . . he's in a better place now." He paused. "Katie, as much as I'd like to, I can't be the knight in shining armor.

You're going to have to do the fighting, but I'm going to be here for you every step of the way. I promise. However I can, I'm going to help you get through this."

"Thanks, Atticus." I smiled. "Hey, by the way . . . earlier today, you may have heard a rumor about me. And I just wanted you to know that it's not—"

"I know." He put up his hand to stop me. "I knew the minute I heard."

"You did?"

He nodded. "Yeah. Because I know *you*—and I knew there was more to the story than what I was hearing." He paused, as if putting the pieces together for the first time. "Is that why you drove to Sydney's house today?"

This time, I was the one who nodded. "I didn't want her to think I would do something like that. Even though she was horrible toward me."

"That was pretty cool of you to do that. Not everyone would have."

"I know, but it was the right thing to do."

For a moment, we were both silent once again, until Atticus finally spoke up. "I'm going to let you rest, but if you need anything, please—call me."

"Thanks, Atticus. I will."

With that, Atticus left, leaving me to hang out with my family and watch old reruns on the small, boxy TV in the hospital room. And after a couple of hours, the doctor released me to go home. Even though I had a concussion and had to stay awake through the night, I was pretty much treated like royalty.

My parents let Jackson and I pig-out on junk food, and we all watched one of my old favorite Disney movies, *Freaky Friday* together—with surprisingly no complaint from my chick-flick averse brother. And on top of that, I got a call from Sammy later that night to check up on me and pray with me. All in all, it was a pretty good ending to a not-so-great day.

And as soon as my parents said that I could, I slept harder than I have in a long, long time.

Chapter Twenty-Eight

Cast all your anxiety on him because he cares for you.
- 1 Peter 5:7

The following week, my parents took me to my first appointment with Dr. Elena Kincaid. And as I walked into her office, I felt as though I had officially crossed the line from normal-anxious-teenager to certified-crazy-person. I exhaled.

Deep breaths, Katie. Take it one session at a time.

After all, the last thing I needed right now was more anxiety.

"Katie," Dr. Elena said as I walked into her office and shook her hand, her long brown hair falling over her shoulders. "Just the person that I wanted to see. Would you like to take a seat?"

I knew it was more an order than a question, so I just nodded. "Yes, thank you."

"Wonderful. How are you feeling today, Katie?"

"Okay," I said as she raised an eyebrow, suddenly realizing that if I were really okay, I probably wouldn't be in this situation right now. "I mean, I don't really know what to expect." I paused. "Are you going to give me pills or . . .?"

She laughed, as if that were the funniest thing that she's heard all day. But then again, it probably was. "I'm not that kind of counselor. I'm a psychologist. Only psychiatrists can prescribe medication. I just want to talk to you—see how you're doing. Just pretend I'm one of your girlfriends, okay?"

"Okay," I said, crossing my legs and trying to imagine her as Tanisha or Jenny. I also tried to ignore the degree on her wall that said Masters of Art in Counseling Psychology.

"Great. So, tell me, Katie—how do you like high school?"

"I like it." I paused, thinking over the past school year. "I mean, it can be a lot sometimes, with drama and homework, but it's good overall. And then there's the Agape Club—"

"What's the Agape Club? Tell me about it."

"It's a Christian club that I lead on campus with my friend, Atticus. We started it at the beginning of the school year."

"So, you have your normal classes, the Agape Club, and your youth group?" she asked, as if she were reading off a grocery list.

"Yes." I nodded. "And I help my friend Tanisha with props for the drama club."

"That sounds like a lot for a girl your age."

"It can be, but I enjoy everything that I do."

"Do you ever get anxiety when you feel overwhelmed with your schedule?"

"Sometimes, when I have a lot of exams, or a lot to do to prepare for my club."

"Now tell me, Katie. What do you do when you have these anxiety attacks?"

"What do I do?" I asked, confused—wondering if this was a trick question.

"Yes, do you have any ways of dealing with the stress? Journaling? Taking time for self-care—to watch a movie, or read a book? Doing something physical, like exercising?"

"Not really. Usually, I just try to push through it. To be honest, it usually scares me so much when it happens that I don't know what to do." I paused. "Is that weird?"

"Not at all," she assured me. "A lot of people feel scared when they have anxiety, but it's not something that you need to be afraid of. Anxiety happens to a lot of people, but it's not dangerous. In fact, one thing I've noticed is that usually, it's trying to help us."

"It's trying to help us?" I asked, suddenly totally confused—and, at that moment, wondering whether my parents picked the right psychologist. "But how . . .?"

"Katie, do you have an iPhone with you?"

"Yeah, I have one right here," I said, pulling it out of my pocket.

"When it's about to die, does it notify you that you have a low battery?"

"Yeah, why?"

"Well, the human body is, in that way, wired sort of like a cell phone. Your brain is wired so that when you're in a challenging situation, it will notify you that something is wrong. That's why one psychiatrist that I particularly like, Dr. Caroline Leaf, refers to anxiety as a *signal*. It's trying to tell you something that may not be in the forefront of your mind."

"So, when I have anxiety, it's actually a good thing?"

"It's not good in the sense of it being pleasant," she confessed with a smile. "But it's also not bad in the way that we would typically define bad. It's not a sign that you're defective or that something is wrong with you. It's a neutral stimulus, which means you have to learn how to manage it."

"How do you do that?" I asked, as once again, she smiled.

"That's exactly why you're here today. Together we're going to figure that out and play detective with your brain. Are you okay with that, Katie?"

"Yes," I said, relieved that this wasn't as scary as I initially thought and kind of liking the way that she worded it. *Playing detective with my brain.* "I think I am."

"Wonderful. Now tell me, Katie. What are some situations that cause you to feel anxious?"

"Well," I began, "I guess sometimes I get anxiety when I'm in a new environment. Or when a friend tells me about something they're going through that I can't help them with," I said, thinking back to the whole situation with Ian and Sydney. "Or, when I'm driving."

"I see," she said, jotting down a couple of quick notes. "And why do you think these things cause you to feel anxious?"

"Well, I guess with being in a new environment, it's the fear of the unknown. And with the friend thing, I guess sometimes I put a lot of pressure on myself to help the people around me. To solve their problems."

"And the driving thing?"

"Fear of crashing. Fear of getting lost . . . Fear of hurting someone."

"Those are all perfectly normal fears, Katie. Now, what do you think you could do to lessen your anxiety with those things?"

"Well, I guess with the new environment, I can try to keep an optimistic perspective about it. Not always assume the worst. And I guess with driving, I can use a GPS and only drive by myself where I'm comfortable driving. At least, for a while."

"There you go, Katie. Now, how about the friend thing? Why do you think it is that you put so much pressure on yourself to solve other people's problems?"

"I guess because I want to be a good friend and because I genuinely like helping people."

"You sound like an excellent friend, Katie. But tell me—do you think that you can solve everyone's problems in the world?"

"Well, no." I hesitated. "I guess not. But I just feel so helpless when I can't."

"Katie, you believe in God—right? I mean, I'd assume that you would, with your dad being a pastor, and you, running the Christian club at your school."

"Yeah, of course." I shrugged. "I have for as long as I can remember."

"And you believe that He's good, loving, and kind, right?"

"Absolutely." I nodded, thinking back to what I told Tanisha when we were making the posters that day. About the meaning of the word 'Agape.' "That's why I named my club the Agape Club. It means love. The kind of love that God has for us."

"You really are your father's daughter." She smiled. "And you also believe that He's powerful? More powerful than we are in our own human strength?"

"Yes, absolutely."

"So, do you really think that if a problem is too big for you, it's also too big for God?"

"I guess I never thought about it that way."

"Sometimes it's easy to take on the weight of the world for ourselves, but we're not big enough to fix everything on our own. Sometimes we just have to pray and leave the results in God's hands—trusting that He can handle it better than we ever could."

"I guess I probably should have been able to figure that out myself," I said sheepishly. "You know, with my dad being a pastor and all."

"Sometimes we need other people to point out the things that God has been trying to tell us all along. Remember what God said about Adam before He created Eve?"

"It's not good for man to be alone?" I asked as she nodded.

"Exactly. You see, Katie, He wasn't so much talking about marriage as He was talking about community. The people in our lives who know us and love us. Hands, reaching out and touching another hand. People, helping each other with the things that are too heavy to carry alone."

"I like what you said," I replied thoughtfully, her words painting a picture in my mind, "about hands touching hands."

"It was something my mother used to say all the time when I was younger. She went on to be with the Lord, but her legacy lives on in here." She pointed to her heart.

"I'm so sorry."

"It's okay. It happened when I was very young. It was around that time that I went to go speak with a counselor myself, which helped me a lot. It was what inspired me to go into this field. Much like you, I wanted to help people—to make a difference."

"That's cool that God was able to use that."

"God uses everything, Katie. That is, if you let Him."

"Thank you. I really appreciate it." I paused. "Is there anything else that we're going to talk about today?"

"Not today. Our session is actually over, but we can talk again next week if you'd like?"

I smiled. "I'd like that."

"Wonderful," she said. "Tell you what—why don't you do some journaling this week. Write an entry each day about your thoughts and your feelings and share with me what you wrote in our next session."

"That sounds great," I said, thinking back to the diary that Atticus got me for my birthday—and how I'd finally have an excuse to use it.

"Wonderful. Have a good day, Katie."

"Thank you. You too."

"And Katie?"

"Yes?"

"Let God be God."

"I will." I smiled. With that, I left her office and headed toward the waiting room, where surprisingly, I felt about a million times lighter than I did before.

And at least for right now, completely anxiety-free.

Chapter Twenty-Nine

Give praise to the Lord, proclaim his name; make known among the nations

what he has done.

- Psalm 105:1

For the next two months, I went to see Dr. Elena every week, and little by little, I felt my anxiety start to lessen. And when I did have anxiety, I tried to put what she said in our sessions into practice. Recently, much like the famous H.D., I've started journaling in the new diary that Atticus got me for my birthday. And as I read through my diary entries on Easter morning, it was amazing to see just how far I've come.

Dear Diary,

It's officially April. The month when spring has sprung. When plants that had once been dead start to grow once again. When birds fly freely through the warm, sunny air. When people trade the boots of winter for the sandals of summer. And just like the seasons, my life is changing too.

I had an anxiety attack the other day (typical, right?), but now I know how to handle them when they come my way. After forcing myself to 'play detective with my mind', I realized that the root of my anxiety was the possibility that my family might be moving back to Africa. So, I texted Atticus and asked if he could talk, and he helped bring me back down again. And of course, remind me that nothing is written in stone. Somehow, even though he wasn't able to fix my problem, that made me feel a lot better. Things have also been looking up for my friends lately.

Nathan's relationship with his dad has been better than ever, Liv is opening up more in the Agape Club, and Sydney finally told Ian about the baby. He seemed kind of freaked out at first, but he's doing better now, and he's determined to be there for Sydney and the baby however he can. He's still grieving over the loss of his grandfather, but I think that will get better for him too, in time.

Until Next Time,
K.C.

I smiled. Who knows? Maybe one day, I'll have a daughter, and she'll be able to read about my life. And maybe it will help her with what she's going through.

"Katie!" my dad called from downstairs. "It's time for church!"

"Coming!" I shouted, grabbing my purse and my Bible and heading downstairs to meet my family, in my new blue sundress that I bought at the mall the other day.

"You look nice," my mom noted as I walked into the family room, where my dad, my mom, and my brother were already standing and waiting.

"Thanks, Mom." I smiled. "So do you."

"Thanks, Katie."

"Alright, everyone. Are you ready to go?" my dad asked, looking nervous, the way he did right before the Christmas Eve service last year.

"All ready." I nodded. "You're going to be great, Dad."

He smiled. "Thanks, Katie."

With that, the four of us piled into his car and headed to church, with the sun shining and an old Jeremy Camp song blaring from the local Christian radio station. I sat in the back and stared out the window—caught up in the music and the scenery. And before I knew it, we were there.

There were about six more rows of chairs than usual. And in front of the stage stood a cross with a purple cloth draped across it, which, I learned from my dad, is symbolic of Jesus' kingship.

"Hey, Katie!" I suddenly heard a voice say from behind me.

I turned around to see Tanisha, Jenny, Atticus, and Nathan. I smiled. "Hey, guys—how are you?"

"Good!" Tanisha said, hurrying over to give me a hug. "Excited for the service today!"

"Me too," Nathan agreed. "My dad's coming today. It will be his first time here since my baptism."

"No way, that's awesome!" I said. "So, things have been better with you guys?"

He nodded. "Much better."

"Hey, guys!" Sammy said, as I saw out of the corner of my eye that the countdown for service had begun. "Are you excited for our Easter service today?"

"Definitely." I smiled.

"Awesome. It's going to be a lot of fun. And rumor has it that Micah is going to be a part of some Easter skit."

"No way, really?" Tanisha laughed.

"That should be pretty funny," I said.

"Definitely. Hey, by the way, there's something I've been meaning to ask you." She paused, looking over toward Nathan. "Well, actually, you and Nathan both."

"OK?" I asked, curiosity filling my voice.

"Well, in a couple of weeks, we're going to have a testimony night at Ignite, and I was wondering if you would be willing to share your stories. Not so much of coming to Christ, but of how God has moved in your lives this year. Pastor Sean and the rest of us leaders think it would be good for some of the teens to hear about how God has been moving from people close to their age, and we agreed that you both would be great people to ask."

"Yeah," I said quickly, before I could give it much thought. "That'd be great! I'd love to!"

"Yeah, me too," Nathan agreed. "It would be an honor."

"Awesome!" Sammy exclaimed as the band went up on stage. "Well, I'd better go sit down. But thank you so much for agreeing to do this! You guys are awesome!"

"Back at you, Sammy!" I replied as she walked off.

It wasn't until she walked away, and I started clapping along to an old Chris Tomlin song that it hit me. I was going to be speaking. On stage. In front of over fifty other teenagers.

What had I just done?

⇒ ⇐

*T*estimony night came quicker than I expected, and I was officially freaking out—praying I wouldn't freeze up the way that I did at

Burgers and Beats a couple of months ago. But I was also excited, because maybe, just maybe, my testimony would be able to help someone. The way it might've helped me if I had heard someone else say the same things.

"Are you ready, Katie?" Sammy asked as we stood off to the side, talking before service.

"I think so. I'm a little nervous, but I think I'm ready."

"You'll be great," she assured me, with a look that said she was way more confident about me speaking than I was. "Just think of how many people you're going to inspire tonight. A lot of teens here struggle with the same thing you do."

"Thanks." I smiled. "I hope you're right. I mean, about the message being inspirational. Not about people struggling."

"I know I am. Just remember, God is with you. You've got this."

"OK, guys. Are you ready to worship tonight?" Markus asked, wearing his usual attire of torn-up jeans and a beanie cap.

I took a deep breath, trying to calm myself down—using one of the techniques that Ms. Elena taught me. Talking back to my anxiety and countering the lies with God's truth.

"You ready?" Nathan whispered, just loud enough for me to hear over the music.

"I think so." I nodded. "Are you?"

This time, he nodded. "I think so. I prayed about it earlier, and I feel good about it."

"Me too." I smiled, excited for my friend who, just a couple of months ago, had no interest in God. Who now, after coming to

Christ, was about to share his testimony in front of a whole youth group. God really is so good.

"What's up, everybody!" Pastor Sean said as he made his way to the front of the stage. "Tonight, we have a few very special guests from Ignite who have agreed to share their testimonies. Some of them are new faces, and some of them have been with us for a while. But God has been moving in each one of them in such a powerful way that it only felt right to give them the mic tonight. So, please welcome Audrey, Leo, Nathan, and Katie!"

The group clapped and cheered as Nathan and I walked up onto the stage, along with the rest of the students who were speaking tonight. I took a deep breath as I felt the old familiar feeling fighting its way to my chest. The same feeling that I had at Burgers and Beats when I went up to sing.

No. Not tonight. Tonight's going to be different. I'm going to be okay.

Thankfully, the feeling started to fade as they began speaking. First, Audrey, about how God saved her from an addiction to prescription pills. And then, Leo, about how God helped him break free from pornography. And after they spoke, it was Nathan's turn.

"Hi everyone, my name is Nathan, and I'm pretty new here." He smiled, looking over toward me before turning back toward the crowd. "I started coming here a couple of months ago after a good friend invited me. But my story's not quite that simple. I don't think if we're honest, most of our stories are." He paused.

"Growing up, I had very little knowledge about God. My family went to church and prayed before meals, but if asked, I couldn't tell you anything about having a personal relationship with God. In fact, the few thoughts that I did have about God were mostly negative, because if God is a Father, and my own father didn't seem to want a relationship with me, how could God the Father want a relationship with me?" He paused again, giving the audience a chance to process what he was saying before continuing. "This was something that I struggled with for a long time. It was also something that I usually tried not to think about. That is, until I became friends with Katie, and she wouldn't let me leave it alone."

This got a few laughs from the audience.

"Time and time again, I watched Katie talk about Jesus in a way that was foreign to me. She would talk about Him like He was her friend. Someone who is kind and compassionate. Someone who is worth knowing. Though I didn't immediately start seeking Him, this sparked my interest—enough to come to church with her and start going to the Christian club that she started at Winter Oaks High School, along with another one of my good friends, Atticus. And I started to get to know this Jesus that they talked about for myself. I started reading my Bible, asking questions— even the hard ones, and talking to God in prayer. I was determined to find out what was at the end of this journey. And rather than finding the pain and rejection I had feared, I found something that I had been afraid to let in for far too long. *Love.* And on December 15th of last year, I accepted Christ for myself. One month later, I was baptized by Pastor Will." This got a round of applause as Nathan smiled, waiting for it to die down before continuing.

"But this still wasn't all. Because after I started walking with Christ, I felt Him nudging me to do the one thing that I thought was impossible. The one thing I thought could never be done— and that was to restore my relationship with my dad and forgive him for the mistakes that he made. At first, this was hard. Forgiveness usually isn't easy. But today, I can honestly say that my dad and I are closer than we've ever been, and while we're not where I'd like to be yet, we're making progress. I can honestly say that I've forgiven him.

"If forgiveness is something you're struggling with, I want to be the first to say that forgiveness—for yourself or someone else—isn't easy. But it is possible. Because once you know Love, you can't help but give it away."

"Thank you, Nathan," Pastor Sean said as the group started clapping. "The last person who's going to be sharing tonight is Katie, speaking about her struggle with anxiety and how she's been working to overcome it. Everyone, let's give it up for Katie!"

"Thank you," I whispered as Nathan handed me the mic. "You were great."

"Knock 'em dead, Katie," he whispered as he went to take a seat, and I looked out into the crowd. *I could do this.*

"Hi everyone, my name is Katie," I said, taking one more deep breath before I started. "For most of my life—like a lot of you here, I've wanted to make a difference. To help people. But until recently, I haven't been so good at helping myself.

"I moved here at the beginning of the school year, with my family. My mom, my dad—who most of you know as Pastor Will, and my brother, Jackson. We moved here after my dad had a dream about working with a church in California—after living our whole lives on the mission field of Kenya. It was a life that I loved and the only life that I've ever known. But after living here for a couple of months and making some really good friends, I began to love this life as well, and I hoped that maybe, God could use me as a missionary here, at my school. I figured, growing up on the mission field and being surrounded by God, faith, and church all my life, I had nothing left to learn. I soon found out that I couldn't have been more wrong." I smiled as a couple of teens in the audience laughed. "Because, over the last couple of months, God has taught me far more than I ever thought I could learn in one short year: about Him, about people, and about myself. And how to handle things that I've never had to deal with before.

"At the beginning of the school year, I started dealing with panic attacks. At the time, I didn't know what they were, and they kind of scared me. I just thought of them as the tight feeling in my chest that came whenever I felt nervous or afraid. At first, they didn't seem too threatening, but over time, they got worse and more frequent. Eventually, they got so bad that they caused me to get into a car accident." I paused, giving my words a chance to sink in. "No one was hurt, but it was a wake-up call for me and my family. After that, I started going to counseling with one very kind, very patient lady from our church, who some of you know as Dr. Elena, and little by little, the anxiety has gotten better; more manageable. I learned what it is, what causes it, and how to cope with it. I learned that a lot of people deal with it and that it doesn't make you weird or defective. I also learned that it's your body's way of telling you something.

"If you're struggling with mental health in any way, shape, or form, I want to tell you that there's hope. For so many people, there's still a stigma surrounding things like anxiety and depression, and some people think that if they struggle with one of these things, they must be crazy. That there must be something wrong with them. I'm here to tell you that you're not crazy, that there's nothing wrong with you, and that it is okay to talk about it. Because anxiety can't get better when you hide it away. It only gets bigger. It's only when it's let out in the open, with the help of other people, that it gets better, because that's where the light gets in. That's where we find hope. When we dare to be honest with God and each other."

"Alright, give it up for Katie!" Pastor Sean said as I gave him the microphone, and the crowd began clapping and cheering. "I am so proud of each one of these students for sharing. It's not easy to share from a stage like this, but each one of them wanted to give glory and praise to God for what He's doing in their lives. And remind all of us here tonight just how present God is in each of our lives. That being said, we're going to close in prayer and then dismiss. If you're able to stay a little longer, there are walking tacos in the lobby. If not, have a good night, and we'll see you back next week!"

With that, Pastor Sean prayed and dismissed the service. And as Nathan and I walked off the stage, Atticus, Tanisha, Jenny, Ian, and Sydney were there waiting to congratulate us.

"You guys!" Tanisha exclaimed, running up to hug us—practically tackling us in the process. "You were amazing up there! I am so proud of both of you. That couldn't have been easy!"

"It wasn't," I said as a slow grin made its way across my lips. "But I'm glad I did it. God definitely guided me through that."

"Agreed," Nathan added.

"Well, you were both great," Atticus said. "I think you inspired a lot of people tonight."

"Thanks. I really hope so," I said, caught off guard by a familiar jittery feeling as Atticus smiled back at me. Although this time, the feeling wasn't anxiety. It was something way better.

"Hi," a small, blond middle schooler who couldn't be more than about twelve said as she walked up to me. "Your name is Katie, right?"

"Yeah, that's me." I nodded as I looked curiously at my friends and then back toward the girl.

"My name is Izzy, and I just wanted to tell you that your message really helped me tonight. I struggle with anxiety too, and until tonight, I haven't met anyone else who does."

"Oh wow," I said, surprised that someone so much younger than me could be dealing with exactly what I've been dealing with. "Well, I'm glad I could help. And I'm here every week if you ever want to talk."

"Thanks, Katie." She smiled as she ran off to go hang out with her friends.

"Wow, Katie," Jenny said, impressed. "Looks like you've become an inspiration."

"Thanks, Jenny." I laughed. "I don't know about that, but I'm glad I could help her."

"Well, if you needed confirmation that your prayer was answered, I think that was your answer," Nathan pointed out.

"What prayer?" I asked, curiously.

"The one you mentioned up on stage. That you would make a difference." He grinned. "I think you just did."

"Yeah, I guess I did." I smiled, at that moment, beyond thankful for everything God has done over the last couple of months. For the ways that He's used me and worked in my life—and for the people that He's brought into my life. And I felt convinced that the best was yet to come.

No matter where God leads me next.

Chapter Thirty

*T*onight was the last play of the school year, and just like last semester, I came out with Jackson, Atticus, Nathan, and Jenny to support our friend.

"This place looks incredible," Jenny breathed as the five of us walked into the auditorium with our families—the lights dim, as slow violin music played from the loudspeakers. "Looks like all of our hard work paid off."

"For sure," I agreed, surveying the props that we had designed during rehearsals—including the tall, cardboard tower that Nathan had painted himself. "We spent hours working on the set for this play."

"To put it mildly," Nathan said. "You guys want to sit near the front?"

"Sounds good to me." I turned toward my brother and the rest of my friends. "You guys?"

"I'm down with it," Jackson said as I took a seat between Atticus and my brother. I did my best to keep my eyes focused on the stage—and fight the temptation to look over at Atticus. Even though I'd done my best to keep my feelings hidden, I still felt nervous and jumpy whenever he was around.

"Oh Romeo, Romeo, where art thou Romeo?" the young actress exclaimed, reciting her lines for the play. Of course the play was a love story. Just what I needed to get over a crush.

Especially when it may not have a chance to turn into anything, with the possibility of me moving back to Kenya, away from Atticus and everyone else. I squeezed my eyes shut.

Don't think about that right now, Katie.

What did Ms. Elena say? You control your thoughts . . . not the other way around. I just needed to take things one day at a time and trust God with the rest. That's all I could do.

Two hours later, the play was over, and each one of us rose to our feet for a standing ovation. I cheered extra loud as Tanisha came out, presented with a large bouquet of red roses for her hard work directing the play.

"Go, Tanisha!" I shouted, loudly enough to be heard over the crowd. As soon as the applause died down and Tanisha was off stage, I hurried over to congratulate her.

"Great job directing the play!" I said, proud of my friend.

"Thanks, girl. I had a lot of help."

"Yeah, but you were the genius behind the operation," Nathan reminded her. "There's no way this play could have been what it was without you."

"Well, thank you." She smiled. "You guys are the best."

Little by little, we began pouring out of the building. And as I expected, after congratulating Tanisha and some of the other actors and actresses, my parents wound up talking to my friends' parents, lingering long after the performance was over.

"So," Atticus began as the two of us took a seat on a nearby bench, the sky already starting to get dark, as evening set in, "have you heard anything? You know—" his eyes drifted away from mine, and then after a moment, met them again, "about the thing?"

By the tone of his voice, it was easy to tell what he meant by the *'thing'*—which was something he hadn't brought up in weeks. It was also clear that he had respected my wishes and hadn't told anyone that I might be moving.

I shook my head. "Not yet. I should be finding out soon, though."

"I know it's not up to you . . . But I really hope you stay."

"I know." I paused, emotion clear in my voice. "I hope so too."

"You know, life is funny sometimes. One minute, you're sitting on a bench outside of school talking to someone, and the next, they're gone."

"I'm not dying, Atticus," I reminded him, hoping to lighten the mood.

"No." He paused for a moment. "But it feels like we are."

"I'll write, I promise. And we can still text and talk on the phone."

"I know. But it won't be the same."

"I know," I said, staring down at my new black heels.

At that point, when it was clear that neither of us had anything left to say, I changed the subject.

"My parents are throwing Jackson and I an end-of-the-year party at my house on June 1st. They told us we could each invite ten friends and I wanted you to be one of the first people I asked. Well, you and Tanisha." I smiled. "It's going to be a cookout, and they're supposed to be making hot dogs and hamburgers and everything. All of our close friends are invited."

"Man, I wish I could." Atticus groaned, cupping his hands around his face. "But I volunteered to be a camp counselor at Lakewood Christian Camp that week. I signed up months ago, and I can't get out of it now."

"It's okay." I forced a smile, trying my best to hide my disappointment. "I understand."

"I'm so sorry, Katie." I could tell by the look in his eyes that he meant it. "I really wish I could come."

"It's really okay. Do the camp counselor thing, and we'll hang out when you get back. I promise."

"Katie!" I suddenly heard my dad call from across the way. "It's time to go!"

"Okay, Dad." I nodded before turning back to Atticus, searching for the right words to say. "So . . . I'll see you later?"

"Yeah," he said, his blue eyes catching mine as I stood up. "See you later."

Chapter Thirty-One

If God is for us, who can be against us?
- Romans 8:31

The day of the party came quicker than I expected, and I was impressed with the way we had pulled together to fix up the backyard for our guests. My parents strung various pastel-colored paper lanterns from the branches of the trees and, off to the side, stood an old wooden table with food and refreshments strategically laid out upon it. And two small speakers blared some of our favorite songs, which was a strange, eclectic mix of Taylor Swift and Aerosmith. But somehow, it was perfect, just like everything else about the party.

Except for the fact that Atticus wasn't here.

"Wow, this place looks incredible!" Tanisha said, gazing at the lanterns and the decorations in my backyard. "I love what your parents have done with the place!"

"Thanks." I forced a smile, trying my best to get Atticus out of my mind. "They worked hard putting everything together."

"I can tell!" Jenny said. "I love the little lanterns. *Very* retro."

"Thanks. The lanterns were my idea. Jackson fought me on them."

"Well, I'm glad you won." Tanisha grinned as the next guest arrived—one who I never would have expected to see at a party like this at the beginning of the school year.

"Hey—Ian!" I said, waving in his direction.

"Hey, Katie." He smiled, walking over to give me a hug. "Hey, Tanisha. Jenny."

"Hello, Ian," Tanisha said, as this time, I smiled.

After that day at the bowling alley, things were much better between Ian and the rest of my friends. Especially Nathan, who now considers him a friend.

"This place looks nice. Did you decorate it yourself?"

"No. My parents did. But I picked out the lanterns."

"They look nice." He gave a slight nod. "A little girly for my taste, but nice."

"Thanks," I said, stifling a laugh, since we were literally just talking about the lanterns. We filled our plates with snacks as more people streamed in, one by one.

The only one missing was Nathan.

"Where is he?" I asked, starting to get worried as I checked my phone. "He told me he was planning on coming today."

"He just texted me," Tanisha said, looking down at her own phone. "He's still coming. He's just running a little late. Traffic is bad where he's at."

"Well, hopefully he gets here soon. We're supposed to start in a couple of minutes."

As if on cue, Nathan's car pulled up about a minute later. And as soon as he parked, he came running out.

"Hey, Katie," he said, clearly out of breath. "I'm so sorry I'm late. Traffic was horrible. It was backed up all down the Pacific Coast."

"It's okay." I smiled, leaning in to hug him. "I'm just glad you're here."

"Me too." He smiled. "Hey, by the way, even though he couldn't come today, Atticus gave me a letter that he wanted me to give you." He paused as if he knew something I didn't. "You might want to wait until later to read it."

"Okay . . . thanks. But why? Is everything okay?"

"Yeah. Just trust me on this one."

Even though everything in me fought against it, I took his advice and shoved the letter inside the pocket of my lightweight, cream-colored cardigan. After all, it would still be there later tonight once everyone was gone.

"Alright, everyone," my dad said, banging a plastic spoon against one of the cups that he set out for the party. "Now that everyone's here, we can get started. But before we do, Nathan requested that he have a few minutes to speak. So, everyone—give it up for Nathan!"

"Woo-hoo! Go, Nathan!" Ian shouted as everyone began clapping. I stared at my friend as he made his way to the front of the yard. What was he doing?

Nathan cleared his throat. "Hello everyone, my name is Nathan, as most of you already know, and the rest of you figured out by Pastor Will's introduction. I'm standing up here in front of all of you today because a couple of weeks ago at Ignite, Katie shared that she's always wanted to make a difference.

"So, I thought it would only be right for her to see just some of the difference that she's made. That is why Tanisha, Jenny, Ian, and I will be sharing how Katie has impacted our lives. Since I'm already up here, I'll go first.

"Katie, I know I already sort of said this at Ignite when I shared my testimony, but your faith and the way that you care about people has had a huge impact on my life. I wasn't an easy person to get to know and I had a lot of pent-up bitterness about my family situation. But you broke through those walls that I had built and helped me start to get real with myself. You also showed me that God wasn't who I thought He was—through your example, your club, and inviting me to Hope Life Church.

"So, thank you for that and for being my friend." He smiled. "And thank you for being the awesome person that you are." As he finished, a couple of people started clapping. I stood there in shock, as Tanisha jumped up.

"I'm going next!" she said, hurrying to take her turn. "Katie, over the last couple of months, you've become one of my best friends. A lot of people are scared to get close to me because I have a bit of an uh, *strong* personality." She grinned. "But you weren't. And even with all your commitments at school and at church, you always managed to come through for me and be there for me whenever I needed you. So, thank you, Katie," she said, wiping a tear that I spotted in the corner of her eye. "You're the best, girl!"

"Thank you," I mouthed, feeling teary-eyed myself as Jenny rolled up.

"Katie has had a huge impact on my life too. Before I met her, I was a new student with zero friends at school, but immediately, when Katie met me on the bus, she befriended me. And little by little, I became friends with all of you guys too." She paused. "I also didn't really know God before I met her, but after coming to her club and asking about a half a billion questions, I came to know God for myself. And I don't think that would have happened if Katie hadn't been so bold and so willing to share her faith. So, thank you, Katie."

I smiled and mouthed, 'You're welcome,' as she rolled back toward the rest of us, feeling myself getting choked up.

"I'll go next," Ian said, walking up to the front. "I haven't always been the nicest person—in fact, I've been pretty mean to a lot of you here. But Katie saw good in me even when no one else did. Even when I didn't see it in myself. She welcomed me into her club when I came for the first time. And about a month later, when she found out I was struggling in school, she agreed to tutor me—after coming to my house looking for some lady named H.D." My mom glanced over at me with a surprised look that said, 'we'll talk later.' "And from there, she and the rest of her family have walked with me through some pretty hard things—the death of my grandpa . . . and an unplanned pregnancy. Her, her brother, and her mom and dad have been there through it all. And it's because of them that I've decided to start following Jesus. So, thank you. To all of you." He smiled, raising his plastic cup in a *cheers* motion before heading back toward the crowd.

"Can I go next?" Jackson asked as my dad nodded. "Even though I didn't plan anything, I'd like to say a few words. Katie, even though you're my sister, and you drive me crazy sometimes, you've impacted me too. At the beginning of the year, I was on a pretty bad path—not walking with God and rebelling against everything I had always believed in. But even during that time, you still treated me the same way you always have and never judged me. Even at the times when I probably deserved it. But seeing your faith made me want to start walking with God again. And if you weren't my sister, I don't know if I would be where I am today. So, thank you, Katie. Even though you can be a total pest sometimes, I love you, and I'm thankful for you too."

"Back at you, bro." I grinned, fist-bumping him as he headed on back.

"Well, Katie," my dad said, "I think you should feel pretty loved right about now. That being said, we're about to get back to the party. But before we do, I have some good news that I'd like to share. Some of you standing here today go to Hope Life Church, and if you do, this news affects you too. I've been talking with the staff and the elders, and they've changed my title from interim pastor to permanent pastor. So, I am now the new official pastor of Hope Life Church."

"What?" I mouthed as he nodded.

"A couple of months ago, my wife and I were talking about moving back to Kenya, which I know Katie and Jackson were trying to keep a secret until they knew more. But now we know— and we're here to stay!"

"Oh, I'm so glad!" Tanisha said, running over to hug me. "My bestie is staying!"

"Me too!" Jenny agreed, getting in on the hug. "I couldn't imagine you leaving!"

"Me neither." I smiled, looking toward both of my friends, and feeling blessed beyond measure. "This is home."

"Alright, now how does everyone feel about getting back to the party?" my dad exclaimed, turning up the music as my friends clapped and cheered—all starting to mingle amongst themselves. I couldn't believe it. I was staying in California! With my friends. With the Agape Club. With . . .

Suddenly, I remembered the letter Nathan had given me.

Even though it was earlier than I had promised, I walked off to a corner by myself to open the letter.

And I nearly gasped when I saw what it said.

Dear Katie,

I know you think I'm good with words, but I'm not. Not really. That's why I needed to write this. Because I can't let you leave without letting you know how I feel. When I met you last fall, you changed my life. You understood me in a way that few people ever have, and you challenged me to be better. You changed the way that I approach my faith and the way that I approach life. Before I met you, I thought that truly great adventures only happen in books.

You showed me otherwise.

You showed me what it looks like to be courageous. I don't know if you always feel courageous or if you see yourself that way, but you are. You're also the funniest, prettiest, most interesting, most special girl I've ever met, and I was an idiot. I was an idiot not to tell you that sooner, back when I still had the chance.

I know I'm going to miss you terribly if you move because I already miss you, and you haven't even left yet. But I also know that God is going to use you as such a light wherever you go and that you're going to change so many lives along the way.

After all, you've already changed mine.

Your friend,

Atticus

So that was it. That was how Atticus felt about me. And any questions that I may have had about his feelings were answered in this simple piece of paper. Atticus Bentley had feelings for me.

The same way I had feelings for him.

>→ ←<

*T*wo weeks later, Atticus came back from Lakewood Christian Camp, and as soon as I found out he was home, I walked over to his house and rang the doorbell. Thankfully, he was the one who answered the door.

"Hey, Katie. You're here," he said, sounding surprised.

"What, did you think I would've flown back to Kenya without saying goodbye?"

"No, I guess I'm just surprised to see you, that's all." He paused, hesitating for a moment. "Did, uh, did Nathan give you the letter?"

I nodded. "Two weeks ago, at the party."

"I guess I should have told you in person. I mean, it was dumb to put it in a letter, but every time I tried, well . . ."

"We got interrupted?" I grinned.

"Yeah, kind of." This time, he grinned. "I hope you didn't find it too corny."

"No, it was really sweet. And I'm glad you wrote it. There are uh, two things I wanted to tell you. Do you have a minute?"

"Yeah, sure. Do you want to sit down?" he asked, motioning to the bench by his house.

"Yeah, that would be great," I said as we took a seat.

"So," he asked, his eyes searching mine, "what did you want to tell me?"

"Well, the first thing is . . . I'm not moving back to Kenya. I'm staying right here, in California!"

"What?" he asked. "You're really staying?"

I nodded. "My dad is now the permanent pastor of Hope Life Church. He already called our old pastor and told him the news."

"Katie, that's awesome! I'm so happy to hear," he said, stopping himself, as suddenly, something clicked. "But what's the second thing you wanted to tell me?"

"The second thing that I wanted to tell you . . . ." my voice trailed off as I pulled a piece of paper out of my pocket, "is all right here," I said, handing him a letter of my own. "I'm not the writer that you are, but I think you might like what I have to say."

Slowly, he read the letter, and when he was finished, he looked back up at me. "Really? You have feelings for me?"

I nodded. "Since the beginning of the school year."

"So, what do we do now?" he asked, as his eyes looked deep into mine, and this time, stayed there.

"Well . . . we could go get pizza next Saturday," I suggested. "And maybe see a movie?"

He smiled. "I'd like that."

"I would too," I said, my heart racing as he leaned in to kiss me—with a year's worth of feelings in one kiss.

"Wow," he said, pulling away after a moment. "Well . . . that was definitely better than in the books."

"Way better." I grinned.

Way better. Those words could pretty much sum up my whole year. And I had a feeling that God wasn't finished yet.

Epilogue

"Katie! Are you almost ready? we're going to be late!" my brother called from downstairs.

"All ready!" I shouted back from my room, where I stood in front of the mirror in my new dress. A special one that I picked out with my mom for Jackson's graduation—bright yellow.

Just like my mood.

"Is that really what you're wearing today?"

"Yeah, why?"

"Because it sort of makes you look like a giant banana."

"Better than looking like a giant beanpole." I grinned, taking note of his height as he rolled his eyes.

"I still can't believe that my oldest baby is graduating!" my mom said, not hearing a word that either of us had just said. "Can I get a picture of you two before we leave?"

"Mom!" Jackson groaned.

"Please? It's a big day. And it only comes around once."

"Oh, alright." He sighed, realizing that she wasn't going to take no for an answer. "Cheese," he said, pulling me into an awkward side-hug.

"Perfect!" She smiled as she snapped the picture with her camera—an old one that looked like it was from 1990-something. "I'm going to have to add this one to the scrapbook!"

With that, the four of us headed to the car. I sat down in the backseat, watching the neighborhood pass me by as we drove to Winter Oaks High School. Who would have thought nine months ago that this neighborhood, which once felt so foreign, would one day feel like home? That over the course of one year, I would start a Christian club, meet so many new friends, start driving, and get a boyfriend?

It was all so much that I couldn't help but smile. I thought back to a Bible verse that I had learned when I was young, one that I still remembered to this day. "When you pass through the waters, I will be with you; and when you pass through the rivers, they will not sweep over you. When you walk through the fire, you will not be burned; the flames will not set you ablaze . . ."

When I moved here, it felt like I was going through deep waters. But God was with me. Every step of the way.

Even when it felt like everything was falling apart.

"All ready to graduate?" Dad asked as we pulled into the parking lot.

"You bet I am," Jackson said, adjusting his cap and gown as we got out of the car. Suddenly, I noticed Jenny, Atticus, and Tanisha out of the corner of my eye.

"Hey, guys! Over here!" I waved to my friends.

"Jackson!" Atticus exclaimed, fist-bumping my brother. "Today's the big day. How do you feel?"

"Good." He smiled. "Really good."

"I'm proud of you, Jackson," Jenny said as she wheeled over to give him a hug. "You earned it!"

"Thanks, Jenny," Jackson said as I smiled.

Jackson and Jenny may not be dating, but they have become pretty good friends—especially since Jackson rededicated his life to Christ and Jenny got baptized last week.

"You guys, we should probably head over," Tanisha said as people began flooding toward the football field. "They're about to start in a few minutes, and I do *not* want to miss seeing Mario graduate!"

Within the next few minutes, we were seated, and before I knew it, it was time for Jackson's graduation to start.

As usual with graduations, the principal came up first to give a few words about the graduating class, followed by the valedictorian, and ending with the ceremony—where each student was called up to receive their diploma.

"I bet you're glad your last name is Carter," Atticus whispered as I laughed.

"Very." I grinned.

"Ethan Conway. Janessa Carpenter. Jackson Carter . . ." the principal said robotically, reading off a list of names as students made their way to the stage, and my brother walked up to accept his diploma.

"Woo-hoo!" I cheered loudly. "Go, Jackson!"

"Go, Jackson!" Atticus echoed, standing up beside me as our friends and my parents followed our lead.

This year may have gotten off to a rocky start with moving and trying to adjust to something resembling normal, whatever normal even is, but with my brother graduating and all of my friends surrounding me, life couldn't have felt more perfect. I couldn't wait to see what happened next.

And just how many adventures lie ahead.

Acknowledgments

Thank you so much to all the incredible people who have made this book possible. Writing a book truly is a collaborative effort, and I'm thankful for all of the amazing people who helped *Faith Under Pressure* come to be.

Thank you to my parents, who have been so supportive of my writing career. When I was just a kid with a love for stories, you both encouraged my love of the written word—through reading to me, typing up my story ideas, and teaching me to read when I said at just three years old, "Mommy, I want to learn how to weeeed!" Also, huge thanks to my mom for helping me edit this manuscript. It would not be nearly as neat and tidy without your mad cool English teacher skills.

Thank you to my friends, who have been my own personal cheerleaders throughout the writing process. For years you have heard me talk about "the book in progress" and continued to believe that it would one day be a reality. You guys are the realest, and I'm thankful for each one of you.

Thank you to Marta at Breogan Book Covers. I couldn't have asked for a cooler cover design. I am truly thankful for designers like you who save the authors of the world from scary photoshopped covers. Seriously, without people who make book covers, this book cover would have looked beyond cringey.

Acknowledgments

Thank you, Marta, for saving me from my artistic skills, or lack thereof.

Thank you to Derek Murphey at Creative Indie, who provided an amazing template for the interior layout of this book. When I first started formatting, I realized that I don't have a clue what I'm doing. Thank you for saving me from myself.

Thank you also to Grammarly. I know you are not a person, but you have caught more grammar and spelling errors than I can count. You are one of the best AI robots around.

Thank you to all of the incredible people who I've been blessed to have on my launch team. Jenn, Julia, Alex, Leslie, Disneyana, Caprice, Sophia, Sunita, Darianna, Maggie, Emily, Marysol, Kiley, Tiara, Mrs. Owen, Mrs. Carson, Mrs. Bonczyk, Mrs. Wald, and of course, my Grandma, you guys are truly the best. I am eternally grateful for your help and your feedback!

I am also eternally grateful to my cat Precious who is now jumping up on ottomans in Heaven. I have had the absolute joy of reading and writing beside her for seventeen years, and I look forward to the day when we are united once again.

Ultimately, thank you to Jesus for your grace, salvation, and love! Those things have sparked the inspiration for this book. Just like Katie, Jesus has gotten me through some of the hardest seasons of my life—including my own personal struggles with anxiety! Thank you, Jesus, for who you are and all you are doing, seen and unseen!

Dear Reader,

A book is never written in a vacuum. Every book is a product of the people and experiences that have shaped it, including the book that you hold in your hands today.

Over two years ago, God gave me the idea for this book through a conversation that I had with a high school student. We were talking about school and faith at a Wednesday night gathering and she brought it up in conversation that she wanted to launch a Christian club at her high school. After that conversation, the idea hit me like a ton of bricks. What if I wrote a book about a teenage girl who wants to do the same thing?

From there, this book, the main character, and our eclectic cast of fictional human beings slowly started to take form in the crevices of my mind.

Although Katie, the Agape Club, and Hope Life Church are fictional, the truths found in this book are taken straight from God's Word and are as real as the paper (or smart device) that you hold in your hands. We are all called to be a light and bring hope to those around us, and we are all also called to a real relationship with a Savior who loves us with an otherworldly, unconditional love.

If you have never heard the message of the Gospel, it's as simple as that. There's no works, no hoops to jump through, and no gimmicks. When Jesus died on the cross, He said, 'It is finished', bridging the gap between us and God and making a way for us to spend all eternity with Him in a place where there are no tears and there is no more suffering.

That's how great His love for us is.

If you already know Christ, I want to challenge you to step out in faith like Katie. There is so much brokenness in the world and your courage could change the lives of the people around you forever.

If you decide to take that step out in faith and share Jesus with a friend, invite someone to your church, or start your own version of an Agape Club, please feel free to shoot me an email at authorcourtney1@gmail.com. I would absolutely love to hear about it and pray for you! I wish you the best and pray that God used this humble little book to touch you in some way.

Your friend and sister in Christ,

Courtney M. Whitaker

Reading Group Guide

1. In this book, Katie experiences a huge change in her life when she moves to California. Have you ever navigated a change like this? If so, what helped you through it?

2. Throughout this book, Katie meets variety of characters who are all at different places in their faith. Which one did you most relate to and why?

3. In this book, Katie impacts Atticus' life tremendously through her example and her strong faith. Is there anyone in your life who has impacted you in this way?

4. One of the themes in this book is standing strong in your faith even when you're surrounded by pressure from the world to conform. Have you ever struggled with this in your own life?

5. In this book, Katie learns about her mom's life through her diary entries and discovers that they have more in common than she previously thought. Have you ever learned something about your parents that shed new light on their lives and yours?

6. Family relationships are brought to light in this story as we see the contrast between Katie and Nathan's families. Have you ever had a conflict with someone in your family? Explain.

7. In this story, Jackson struggles with questions about his faith. Have you ever gone through a period like this in your faith journey? What did it look like?

8. In this book, purity is an issue that is discussed. First, when Jackson makes the courageous choice to stay true to his convictions and later, when we see the consequences of sex outside of marriage. Do you believe that purity is important? Explain.

9. In this story, Katie meets a girl with a disability. Have you ever met someone with a handicap? If not, what did you learn through the character of Jenny?

Sneak Preview of my next book:
Soul on Fire

"I can't believe we won't be going to school together this year!" Madison exclaimed as the last bit of the summer beat down on the warm cement pavement at the local swimming pool.

"I know!" Shelby chimed in, pushing strands of brown hair out of her face. "I'm going to miss you guys so much!"

"We need to find a way to keep in touch," I said. "We've been friends for too long to stop talking now!"

"Natalie's right. We need to stick together no matter what!" Shelby said, slapping her hand down on her knee in resolve.

I looked out over the pool, watching people soak in the last bit of summer. There were kids splashing in the shallow end, adults relaxing in lounge chairs, and teenagers jumping off the diving board, talking with friends, or swimming laps.

I pulled my cover-up tightly around myself as a slight breeze picked up against the summer heat. Chlorine and suntan lotion mixed together, filling my senses with the smells of the season. My friends and I swam in the pool for a little while, but after a long day in the sun, we finally decided to sit out on the side and talk about school and life.

"Have you started shopping for school supplies yet?" Madison asked curiously.

"A little," I said. "I'm not quite finished yet, though. I'm probably going to finish next week."

"Same," Shelby said. "Although I don't have much to buy this year. Being homeschooled and all."

"What do you think that will be like?" Madison asked.

"I don't know." She squinted. "I just hope my parents can't deduct points for chores." We all laughed.

"Yeah, that'd be pretty bad," I agreed.

"How about public school?" Shelby asked. "How do you feel about that?"

"I don't know. I've never gone, so I can't say."

"I went for a little while in elementary school," I said. "But I've gone to Trinity ever since the second grade, so I don't remember it that well."

"I hear public school is a lot bigger," Shelby noted.

"Madison should be fine with that," I said.

"What do you mean by that?" she asked.

"You know, you don't get nervous in a large group. You're totally comfortable talking to new people."

"Not all the time. It depends on the situation." She shrugged. "I'm sure you'll get better with that, Natalie. You're going to have to if you're going to become the next big singing sensation."

"Yeah, that's *not* going to happen."

"But you're so good! You could easily be the next Taylor Swift!" Shelby jumped in.

I laughed. "Yeah, I don't think that will ever happen."

"I'm sure she didn't think she would be the next Taylor Swift either!" Madison argued as Shelby and I both raised an eyebrow in her direction.

"You know what I mean."

"Thanks, guys, but I'm way too shy to ever sing in front of a crowd."

"You'll never know unless you try!"

"I don't know. I think I'll stick to singing into my hairbrush at home in my room."

"Suit yourself." Madison shrugged. "Hey, do you want to head back? It's really hot outside!"

"Sure," I said, gathering my things, throwing a T-shirt and shorts on over my swimsuit, and walking with my friends.

I checked my phone. It was only 2:37, so we still had time before my family had to leave for the airport to pick up Eva.

"Hey, what's this?" Madison asked, taking note of a flyer on the fence.

"It looks like a local band is playing here at 2:45. That's only a couple of minutes from now!"

"We should stay and watch!" Madison exclaimed. "We don't have to be back at your house until 3:30. We have plenty of time!"

"I don't know." I hesitated. "What if it runs longer than we think?"

"I'm sure it won't be that long! Besides, we could always leave in the middle if we have to. It's free admission!"

"Come on," Shelby pleaded. "It will be fun! Besides, how often will we be able to do things like this once school starts?"

"Oh . . . alright!" I finally said as we walked into the park and took a seat on our towels.

Before the band came on, they played radio hits from a loudspeaker, which was currently blaring a new song by Maroon 5. I leaned back and looked around the park to see people crowding in like sardines. Finally, the music faded out, and four guys walked up to the stage—and the lead singer walked up to the mic to introduce his band.

"Hey, my name is Roger, and these are my bandmates, Aaron, our guitarist, Jerry, our bassist, and Samuel, our drummer. Ladies and gentlemen, give it up for Force Four!"

The crowd responded with a round of applause, and some of the teenage girls let out a shrill squeal. Immediately following the applause, Force Four launched into their first song, which was a cover of a popular song by OneRepublic.

They continued on with various other covers. Most of them were current radio hits, but a couple of them were from the 80s, 90s, and early 2000s. I recognized one old Backstreet Boys song and another that I'm pretty sure was Bon Jovi. I clapped along with the rest of the crowd, feeling the adrenaline that comes from watching a live performance.

Finally, after about ten songs, the band thanked us for coming and exited the stage. The sound guys adjusted the speakers back to radio music, and the crowd began talking amongst themselves.

"I'm going to see if I can find a bathroom," I told my friends. I realized I had to go during the fifth song, but I didn't want to miss the performance. "I'll meet you back here after I'm done."

"Alright. I have to go to the water fountain anyway to refill my water bottle. We can all meet back here by that old tree," Shelby said, pointing to it and setting up a landmark for us to identify.

"OK. I'll be back in a couple of minutes," I promised, taking off to find a restroom.

I picked up speed as I glanced at my cell phone. 3:09.

That meant that I only had twenty-one minutes to get home. I scoped out the park, searching for a path to the nearest bathroom. Unfortunately, as it turned out, I wasn't watching where I was going because suddenly, I crashed into something solid and fell into the grass. I looked up and found that, to my horror, it was one of the guys from the band.

"I'm so sorry!" I exclaimed, my face hot with embarrassment. "I didn't see you there!"

"It's okay." He smiled, reaching out his hand to help me up. "I should've been watching where I was going."

"Thanks," I said, looking down at the spilled contents of my bag to avoid making eye contact.

Just my luck. I crash into a guy who will probably end up becoming some big celebrity.

Could this situation get any more awkward?

"My name is Aaron," he said calmly, with kind blue eyes, as if I hadn't just crashed into him. "Yours?"

"Mine?" I asked, trying to collect my thoughts in the moments following the incident. "Oh, my name. Um, Natalie." I laughed, trying to make this situation somewhat less humiliating.

I was pretty much failing miserably.

"Nice to meet you. Do you need help picking up your stuff?"

"Oh, it's okay. I got it."

"I don't mind," he said, beginning to gather my things and put them back in my bag.

"Thanks," I said, kneeling down to help and praying that there weren't any *'personal'* items that he could stumble across.

How embarrassing would that be?

Thankfully, there were no feminine items in sight.

"You guys were really good," I said, breaking the silence that was growing more awkward by the second.

"Thanks. We've been doing gigs here all summer, trying to get our name out there."

"Well, I think you guys have a good chance of making it."

"Thanks, I hope so," he said, placing the last of my items— my songbook, back in my bag. "It's been a dream of mine ever since I was a kid." He dusted his hands off. "There, I think that's everything!"

"Thanks again for helping. And sorry again for running into you."

"Don't worry about it. It's cool," Aaron said with a smile that could *easily* appear on the cover of any teen magazine in the country. Suddenly, a group of girls ran up, all trying to get a word in at once. Though they were trying to get close to Aaron, not me, I felt trapped in the giant circle of girls. My heart started to race, and I looked for a way to escape the madness.

Finally, I caught an empty space between two of the teenagers and made my way through the crowd. As my feet pounded against the sidewalk, I felt something fall out of my bag, but I was too focused on trying to get away to pay much attention to it. Once I was far enough away, I kneeled over to catch my breath. I made it!

"There you are!" Madison exclaimed, as her and Shelby ran up to meet me. "We were starting to get worried!"

"Where were you?" Shelby asked. "We checked the girl's bathroom, but you weren't in there!"

"It's a long story." I hesitated, trying to figure out how to explain everything that just happened. "I kind of ran into one of the band members. *Literally.*"

"Ooh." Madison grimaced. "Well, I'm sure it couldn't have been that bad."

"I fell flat on my butt, and the stuff in my bag kind of went everywhere . . ."

"I'm sorry, Natalie," Shelby sympathized. "But you're okay now, right? I mean, nothing's hurt or anything?"

"Just my pride." I sighed, cringing as I replayed the situation over and over again in my mind.

"Which band member did you run into?"

"I think his name was Aaron. He was the guitar player."

"*Whoa*, really?" Madison exclaimed. "He's cute!"

"And that only makes my situation more humiliating," I muttered.

"How did he react?" Shelby pressed.

"He was really nice about it. He helped me pick everything up and he didn't seem mad or anything."

"I knew it! He seems like a nice guy—you can just tell!" Madison squealed.

"You, my friend, are boy-crazy," Shelby said, patting our friend on the back.

"Anyway, we'd better get going. We have ten minutes to get back to the house. My family needs to be at the airport when Eva's plane lands."

"Alright," Shelby said as we headed back home.

Shelby and Madison's parents were both there to pick them up, so we said goodbye. I used the bathroom—finally—and I went up to my room to change into some clean clothes. Once I was there, I looked through my bag, remembering that I had felt something fall out.

Frantically, I rummaged through my stuff in search of my songbook, but to my horror, it was nowhere to be found.

"It's got to be in here," I muttered as I felt my heart rate speed up. What were the odds that I could lose my songbook, of all things? I got it as a gift from my grandmother, and it contained some of my deepest thoughts and feelings.

It couldn't possibly be gone, could it?

"No, no, no, come on!" I exclaimed under my breath as I dumped out the contents of my bag.

Little by little, the reality of the situation began to sink in. My songbook, which contained some of my most personal thoughts and feelings, was gone.

And it was lying in the grass where anyone could read it.

About the Author

Courtney M. Whitaker is an author of Christian fiction and a recent graduate from Liberty University. She has served as a youth leader and Director of Youth and Young Adult Ministries, and currently works as a substitute teacher. In her spare time, she enjoys reading, spending time with her family and friends, and binge watching her favorite shows while enjoying Häagen-Dazs vanilla ice cream. You can connect with her through social media or email—she would love to hear from you!

Instagram: @authorcourtney1
Email: authorcourtney1@gmail.com
Website: www.courtneymariewrites.wordpress.com

www.ingramcontent.com/pod-product-compliance
Lightning Source LLC
Chambersburg PA
CBHW021233310726
48971CB00006B/1804